FACES IN THE LIGHT

13 Intriguing Short Stories
and
THE KING'S WINEMAKER

STEVEN HAGY

WingSpan Press

Printed in the United States of America

Published by WingSpan Press, Livermore, CA
www.wingspanpress.com

The WingSpan name, logo and colophon are the trademarks of WingSpan Publishing.

ISBN 978-1-59594-391-0

First edition 2010

Library of Congress Control Number 2010932174

Cover Model and Photograph: Kamille Freske
Story Consultant: Craig Barnett
Doce Robles Winery (Paso Robles, Ca.): Wonderful friends, great wines, heavenly vineyard, and an inspiring place to write.

Contents

Light is a stark floodlight and a glowing candle; it is violent lightning and a vivid rainbow; it shimmers on a pond, sparkles in a diamond, and flashes for a photo; it blinds yet gives sight; it burns yet soothes; it is sunlight, moonlight, and starlight; it is hope for now and for hereafter; it is emotional, physical, and spiritual; it reflects in a mirror and there I am.

To My Sons,
Gary, Kevin, And Jeffrey

Be a shining star; create your own light,
pursue your own path, and fear not the darkness,
for that is when you will shine brightest.

HAVE A QUIET SOUL

Sirena Bellows sat in the peculiar waiting room of Dr. Yelsa. She had arrived thirty minutes earlier, had filled out a new patient questionnaire, and now waited to see the unconventional psychiatrist. She had heard of the doctor's odd method of treatment and every so often, her apprehension broke out in a slight tremble. She sat in the first of five blue chairs that lined the wall, while a pudgy, middle-aged man in a suit, who had only just arrived, fidgeted four chairs away. She clutched her purse in her lap as her eyes scanned the bizarre room. Fluorescent lights glowed overhead. The stark, baby-blue walls were devoid of pictures and windows and only an empty magazine rack hung on the wall. A sign above the rack read, *Please leave all reading materials at home.* Among the sky-blue acoustic panels of the ceiling were four shiny round speakers, however, no sedating songs seeped out of them. Navy-blue carpet covered the floor. Across from Sirena, a receptionist sat at a blue desk. The lovely, young woman, wearing a cornflower-blue dress, had short, blonde hair with a teensy flippy-do out to each cheek. She wore no make-up, so her blonde eyebrows and eyelashes nearly disappeared amidst her subtle skin and she practically whispered when she spoke. Next to the receptionist was a closed, blue door with the name, *Arthur J. Yelsa Ph.D.* and next to it, was another blue door that read, *Restroom.* Although all was quiet in the strange waiting room—except for the squirming businessman with his heavy sighs and the natural looking receptionist shuffling papers—in Sirena's head, she heard a scream and the longer she sat in the blazing blueness, the louder it screamed.

Fearful that the scream percolating inside her head might spill out of her mouth, she abruptly stood, gripped her purse, and while ignoring the staring eyes of the man and the receptionist, she hastened across the small waiting room to the restroom. She stepped inside, flipped on the light, shut the door, and hugged her purse to her chest as she blinked against the harsh brightness. A curly, energy saving bulb brightened the restroom's blue walls bluer than the blue walls of the waiting room. The room had a porcelain sink and toilet, both blue, and a small trashcan, of course blue, but unlike every other restroom, it did not have a mirror. The only non-blue anything, were the paper towels stacked on the lid of the toilet tank and the discarded ones in the trashcan. She placed her purse on the sink, sat down on the toilet, closed her eyes, drew in a few calming breaths, and while wondering if the businessman and the receptionist just outside the door could hear her, she tinkled. She washed her hands, dried them with a white paper towel, opened the door, flipped off the light, and again, disregarding the ogling eyes of the man and the receptionist, made a beeline back to her chair.

Blue, all blue, taunting blue, unnerving blue, and after waiting another antsy five minutes in the blue, a hysterical impulse gripped her to run screaming out of the waiting room, to her car, and all the way home. However, just as she shifted forward in her chair, drew in a deep breath, and opened her mouth to do so, the doctor's door swung open and out stepped a short, stocky, elderly man sporting his silver-gray hair in a buzz-cut. He was followed by an ordinary, yet professional looking young man, wearing a light-blue shirt, a blue paisley tie, denim-blue jeans, dark-blue sneakers, and a midnight-blue sport coat. The two men talked as they strolled across the waiting room toward the exit. Sirena closed her mouth, quelled her scream, and listened.

"Thank you, Dr. Yelsa. Thank you so much," exclaimed the old-timer, thrusting out his leathery hand. "I feel much better now."

"Truly, it was all you, Sergeant Peal," replied the youthful doctor as he shook the veteran's hand. "You went deep, found it, and yanked it out like a dried up weed. Outstanding!"

The weathered, timeworn man slid into a *stand at ease* position with his feet exactly ten inches apart, his legs straight, and his hands interlocked at the small of his back. He stared into the doctor's eyes and spoke in a low, somber voice, sounding like an idling army jeep, "I'll admit, back in '51, Korea, the *Chongchun River*, as my buddies in the Eighth were blown to smithereens all around me, I wanted to let it out—I wanted to real bad, but at the time, I was too busy dodgin' bullets, duckin' shrapnel, and swimmin' in the blood of my pals. I never thought that the horror of those days would haunt me all of these years. In that crazy blue booth of yours, it seemed as real today as it did back then. It sure was a tough one, Doc."

"It *was* a tough one," Dr. Yelsa replied nimbly with a calm confidence, "but you were tougher. You stormed that heavily fortified hill, captured it, and planted your flag of victory. For you soldier—the war is over."

The combat-hardened soldier breathed deeply, exhaled slowly, and grinned as if he had earned a permanent furlough to peace and happiness. He glanced around the room and said gruffly, "My war has got to be over Doc, 'cause this confoundin' blue doesn't rile me any more. I don't hear nothin' in my head."

"That's a very good sign, Sergeant Peal. Now remember, if you feel like there is still another old one in there or a new one crops up, then, please call us and set up an appointment."

"I will, and Doc—have a good day."

"I will, and Sergeant Peal—have a quiet soul."

The retired soldier beamed gratefully, snapped to attention, briskly saluted Dr. Yelsa, and marched out the door.

Dr. Yelsa smiled, respectfully saluted back, and turned to his receptionist who handed him Sirena's completed questionnaire on a clipboard.

"Thank you, Aura," he said in a hushed tone as if in a library.

"You're welcome, Doctor," she replied softly just like a librarian.

Dr. Yelsa glanced at Sirena, a petite, middle-aged brunette, sitting on the edge of her chair and clutching her purse. She looked like the subject of a Van Gogh painting, wearing her lemon-yellow dress in contrast with the backdrop of the blue wall. He smiled.

Sirena sheepishly smiled back and as the doctor perused her questionnaire, she sized him up. Contrary to what she had envisioned during her aggravating wait, Dr. Yelsa's appearance was not that of an old and wrinkled shrink with a Freudian beard or Einsteinian hair; nor did he wear round, Windsor-style spectacles. He was around thirty, clean-shaven, and wore his shiny, black hair in a short, conventional haircut with a left-side part and a lofty, comb-up in the front. Rather than tall and intimidating or short and intimidated, he stood average in height and appeared to be more of a jogger than a weightlifter. He paced back and forth in front of his door with his brow furrowed in concentration as he skimmed over Sirena's personal information. After a couple of minutes, he stopped reading, engaged his hypnotic, blue eyes with Sirena's anxious, brown eyes, and said, "Please, Ms. Bellows, step into my office."

His tranquil voice, friendly face, and composed mannerisms communicated a sense of trust and security. Sirena, still clutching her purse, jumped to her feet, and hurried past the doctor and into his office.

He acknowledged the businessman in the corner chair and said, "Sir, I'll be with you very soon."

"Okay," the businessman replied, commenting, "it sure is blue in here."

The doctor nonchalantly glanced around the room, stated, "It sure is," turned, followed Sirena into his office, and gently closed the door behind him.

Sirena's eyes darted about the inner room and found the same stark, blue walls as the waiting room with no pictures or windows, the same navy-blue carpet, and the same sky-blue ceiling. In the middle of the small room sat two velour armchairs, both Persian-blue, about three-feet apart and somewhat facing each other. Off to the side of one chair sat a small blue table with a pen, a notepad, a microphone on a gooseneck stand, a bulky set of headphones, and a monitor with a control panel of dials. In front of both chairs, about five-feet away, stood a blue booth. The rest of the room was empty.

Again, as in the waiting room, the brazen blueness coaxed her subconscious scream to the tip of her tongue. So again, she clinched her teeth and clamped shut her lips to restrain the riotous urge.

"Hello, Ms. Bellows, I'm Dr. Yelsa," said the psychiatrist, extending his hand.

The scream in Sirena's head momentarily quieted as she held out her hand and he gently shook it.

"So nice to meet you, Doctor," she replied timidly.

"Nice to meet you too, Ms. Bellows. May I call you Sirena?"

"Yes, please do."

"Okay then, Sirena," he said, walking her a few steps and motioning with his hand toward the first velour chair, "please, have a seat in this chair."

She stepped over, sat in the chair, placed her purse alongside her hip, and pulled her ruffled dress out from under her. He sat in the chair next to her.

They peered at each other in stone silence as Dr. Yelsa gathered his thoughts. In the blueness, his blue eyes gleamed bluer and in the silence, her secret scream screamed louder.

"Let me explain," he finally blurted out, "how I'm going to help *you* help yourself."

Sirena, desperately trying to suppress her scream, quivered.

The doctor noticed her tremble and said, "Before I explain my therapy, let me ask you, are you nervous?"

"Yes, uh, to be honest, kind of."

"Most of my new patients are, but I assure you, you are safe. No matter what is bothering you, as we progress with my treatment, you will someday feel a sense of peace and happiness again."

"I sure hope so, but Doctor, why all the blue?"

Dr. Yelsa chuckled with professional reserve and answered, "All of my new clients wonder, *why all the blue?* and there is a great significance to it all, of which I will gladly explain in just a minute, but first, from your answers on my questionnaire: you have recently turned forty, you divorced last year after twenty-two years of marriage, you have a sixteen-year-old daughter of whom you have full custody, and you have a son, nineteen, serving in Afghanistan. You work in a pharmacy and one of your co-workers, a Ms. Jennifer Howell, recommended you to me. I remember, Ms. Howell. How is she doing?"

"She seems very well. One day, during our lunch break, she shared with me about how her husband is a mean alcoholic, how her mother is battling breast cancer, and how her fifteen-year-old son was expelled from school for smoking pot. I asked her how she stayed so calm through it all and she told me that you had helped her. I told her about my screwed-up life and she gave me your business card. She said that '*you* saved her sanity'."

"When you see her again, please thank her for her kind words and for recommending me to you, but remind her for me, that *she* saved her sanity and I was very happy to help."

"I'll be sure to pass that on to her, Doctor."

"Okay now, Sirena, please tell me in your own words why *you* are here." He laid the clipboard on the table, leaned forward in his chair, propped his arms on his legs, rested his chin in his hands, and gazed compassionately into Sirena's eyes.

Sirena fidgeted in her chair for a few seconds and stuttered, "I'm here—well—because—I hear a—a—oh, I know it will sound crazy."

"I promise you Sirena, to me—nothing sounds crazy."

"Okay. Well—in my head—" she started rubbing her forehead as though she had a migraine, "I hear—well, I'll just say it. I hear a scream."

"Sirena, you have come to the right place," said the doctor, sitting upright. "Screams are my specialty. The fact that you are hearing a scream in your head sounds extremely *sane* to me. Believe me, most people have a scream in their head. We all experience disappointments, hardships, broken promises, shattered dreams, and all sorts of trauma. When people experience a physical pain, let us say, they stub a toe or bump their head, they usually express their discomfort immediately. They yell, cuss, or cry, or at least say 'ouch!' but unfortunately, people hold their emotional pain inside, where it churns in their soul and eventually clumps into a scream. So inside all suffering souls, there is a muted scream on the verge of a piercing shriek. You were wise to come here and deal with your scream. Please continue." He leaned back, getting comfortable in his chair.

"Well, sometimes," she spoke with greater confidence, "the scream is so unruly that I fear that it will burst out at an inappropriate place and time: in front of my daughter or my ex-husband, at work, at the bank or even at the grocery store."

"You are not alone. Nearly all of my patients have that same fear. How about when you were sitting in my waiting room? How did you feel?"

"Oh my," she shook her head re-imagining the struggle she had endured trying to repress her scream, "I had a very difficult time. I almost yelled at the top of my lungs."

"It's the blue," he stated matter-of-factly. "Through a multitude of tests and countless evaluations, I have discovered that screams are agitated by the color blue, all shades of blue. Blue lures the scream up from the depths of your soul to the tip of your tongue, where all you have to do is open your mouth and let it out. The longer you wait and the more blue you visually absorb, the easier it will be for you to shriek. It's all part of your therapy."

"Also, Doctor, why no magazines, no windows, no pictures, no mirror, and no music, and why does your receptionist whisper and wear no make-up?"

"Magazines, windows, pictures, mirrors, music, loud voices, and the pretty face of my receptionist are all sensory stimuli. Stimuli tends to distract you, which in turn suppresses screams, but ahhh, though it seems absurd, we keep the sensory stuff to a bare minimum. So by the time you step into my office, you are positively ready to scream and I provide for you a confidential place and time to express all of your screams."

"All of my *screams*? There's more than one?"

"Most definitely. What you hear inside your head as one, loud, annoying scream is really a thick strand of many screams. This compilation of screams has accumulated over your lifetime and goes all the way back to your childhood or maybe your birth. So as I help you to unravel this blaring rope of screams, you will release each strand as a shriek."

"A shriek?"

"While still in your head, a scream is a scream. Once out of your mouth, a scream is a shriek. To begin, you will enter the blue booth, which we fondly call *Edvard*."

"Edvard?"

"Yes, Edvard, after Edvard Munch, a 19th century expressionist, famous for his painting of a figure screaming." The doctor stood, walked a few steps to the booth, opened its door, and said, "Please, step over here and I'll introduce you to Edvard."

Sirena stood, left her purse in her chair, and took a few steps over to the booth.

"As you can see," continued Dr. Yelsa as Sirena leaned forward and peered inside, "Edvard is the size of a small elevator, and for the sake of many of my patients who suffer from claustrophobia, there is quite a large window in the door and the door shuts but does not lock." He demonstrated this feature by pointing at the lockless doorknob and by closing and opening the door. "The window is made of soundproof acrylic and the inside of the booth is padded with foam, cut in this sound deadening, diamond-shaped pattern. The high back, metal stool, of course blue, is not very comfortable. Remember—no sensory stimuli. In the ceiling is an air conditioner vent, blowing cool fresh air. Next to the vent is a speaker from which you will hear me and mounted next to the speaker and dangling down to your mouth is a microphone from which I will hear you. Now, this retractable wire with the finger socket that's hanging on the wall is a heart rate monitor." The doctor reached out and grabbed hold of it. "It will be placed on your index finger. So Sirena, please, step inside Edvard and we shall begin."

Sirena hesitated, shuddered, and said, "Ohhh, I don't know Dr. Yelsa, it all seems so weird."

"I agree, it's weird. Nevertheless, it works. Please trust me and please, step inside."

Sirena stepped into Edvard, rubbed her hand over the bumpy, diamond panels, and sat on the hard stool. She studied the booth from floor to ceiling. It had the same curly, fluorescent light bulb as the restroom and generated the brightest blue of all the blues yet.

Dr. Yelsa attached the heart rate monitor to her finger, closed Edvard's door, sat down in the velour chair, and slipped on the headphones. While he switched on the heart rate monitor and adjusted the dials on his decibel meter, he glanced at Sirena in her lemon-yellow dress sitting inside the bright-blue booth. She looked like a canary in a fish tank. He grinned, adjusted the microphone to his mouth, and said, "Sirena, how are you doing?"

"I guess, I'm okay,"

"Good. You can be quite confident that only you and I will hear your scream. In addition, I'm listening to it to evaluate it—not to judge you."

Sirena pulled the dangling microphone toward her lips and said, "I understand," and asked, "how long do I have to stay in Edvard?"

"You do not *have* to do anything and that includes staying in Edvard. You are free to enter and exit but most importantly—when you are ready—you are free to shriek. Are you comfortable?"

"Not really."

"Good. No cushy stimuli. Okay, I'm ready and you are certainly ready too, so …."

Sirena drew in a deep breath, opened her mouth, and cutting Dr. Yelsa off mid-sentence, ripped a red-faced, eyes shut, bloodcurdling shriek.

"Sirena! Sirena!" shouted Dr. Yelsa, interrupting her.

Sirena stopped shrieking and breathed heavily, catching her breath.

"Sirena, that was quite a remarkable shriek, but please wait."

"I thought you said, we were 'ready.'"

"I did, but what I was about to say, was that, we were ready for the next step. You see, we must first attach to each scream an emotional pain or what I call the *why*. Once we establish the *why* of your scream and you re-live and express the emotions of the original traumatic *why,* then, at that moment, to release the repressed pain of the *why* and to resolve the imprinted trauma of the *why*, you must shriek at the top of your lungs."

"I think I understand about the *why* and I'm sorry that I shrieked before we were ready Doctor. It's just all this blue and I feel nervous and the scream was right there."

"I completely understand and I appreciate your eagerness. It's obvious to me that you will be very successful with my therapy. Okay, there is no way of going deep without first going shallow, so we'll start with your most current episode of distress and work our way back through your childhood. So Sirena, think for a minute—what is bothering you?"

"Well—I just recently turned forty."

"And why does turning forty distress you?"

"I feel old. I've increased my dress size from eight to frumpy and no matter how hard I try with diets and exercise, I can't lose weight. Every day, new wrinkles appear while the older ones grow deeper, and every three weeks, I have to dye my hair to hide the gray. I now have to use reading glasses and my body aches. I was thinking, if I live to be eighty, my life is half over. I thought life would be different at forty."

"Different how?"

"Just happier, that's all."

"Do you have control over the fact that you are aging and that your body is changing?"

"No."

"How does knowing that make you feel?"

"I'm very angry and I just feel like—like screaming."

"Sirena, now is the time," decreed Dr. Yelsa. "Please shriek."

For a few seconds, Sirena stewed about turning forty, then,

scrunched up her face, growled with anger, sucked in a deep breath, popped open her mouth, and shrieked like she was plummeting from a forty story building.

The doctor checked her heart rate, noted the decibels, nodded his head, and smiled with satisfaction.

Sirena exhausted the air in her lungs, stopped shrieking, cupped her face in her hands, and sobbed.

Dr Yelsa opened the door, helped her out of the booth, offered her tissues, and exclaimed, "Very good, Sirena! Nice shriek! Heart rate up and great decibels." He helped her over to her chair and she plopped down into it. He gave her a few minutes to compose herself and asked, "So, Sirena, how do you feel now?"

"I feel much better," she admitted between sniffs while dabbing a tissue under her nose, "however, I still feel like I need to scream."

"You did wonderfully on our first session. You released one strand of your rope of screams. Each week you will release another until you no longer hear a scream. On your way out, Aura will schedule you appointment for next week."

Sirena stood up, picked up her purse, walked across the blue room, opened his office door, turned, and said, "Thank you so much, Doctor."

She extended her hand and as Dr. Yelsa shook it lightly, he said, "Sirena, you're very welcome."

She turned to leave, spun back around, and said, "Oh and Doctor, have a nice day."

"Thank you Sirena, and Sirena, have a quiet soul."

Sirena and the doctor both stepped into the lobby. Aura handed Dr. Yelsa the clipboard with the next patient's questionnaire and scheduled Sirena for her next week's appointment. Sirena left while the psychiatrist studied the new questionnaire.

After a long moment, the doctor looked at the businessman who was now sitting on the edge of his chair and holding in his scream with a twisted look on his face. Dr. Yelsa grinned, knowing that the blue had again worked as expected, and said, "Mr. Shoutman, please step into my office."

The businessman sprung from his chair and hurried past the doctor into the inner office. Dr. Yelsa turned and faced an ancient-looking lady with her thin hair dyed a bright-red and said, "So nice to see you again, Mrs. Fortissimo. I'll be with you shortly."

"I sure hope so," she grumbled in a haggard voice, "because I'm ready to scream now."

The next week, Sirena returned to see Dr. Yelsa. She waited in the compelling blueness and felt a scream ballooning inside her head. Although, this time, she trembled from eagerness rather than apprehension. After she had waited for thirty-five minutes, Dr. Yelsa opened his office door and escorted what looked to be a college-age, young lady over to the exit. Just before the co-ed left, she wrapped her arms around the doctor, hugged him with the exuberance of a cheerleader and cheered, "Have a wonderful day, Dr. Yelsa!"

"Okay, Blair, I sure will," he said, blushing. "Now remember, your future prosperity is more important than present popularity. I'll see you next week, until then, have a quiet soul." Blair fluttered out the door as he turned to Sirena and said, "Hello, Sirena, are you ready?"

"Yes," she replied with a smile, "very much so."

They entered his office. She bypassed the armchair, stepped directly into Edvard, closed the door behind her, sat on the stool, and slipped the heartbeat monitor on her finger.

"I see that you are ready to shriek," said Dr. Yelsa.

"Yes, Doctor, I am!"

"Good." He relaxed in his chair, checked his equipment, and spoke into his microphone, "So how did it go this last week?"

"I felt really good for a few days, but the scream returned to haunt me."

"Well, let's let another one out then. Tell me about your divorce."

She winced, but began, "Well, I always thought that marriage was forever and that two people in love should grow old together. But, not with Jake, he'll grow old and ugly while his new wife still looks young and pretty. It all caught me by surprise—his affair, the separation, and the divorce. He turned my entire world upside down. I felt worthless. It was horrible. It was absolute Hell. We had to sell our house and leave the neighborhood where our children grew up. Jake and I divided our belongings and parted with families and friends. He got our dog and I got our cat. I feel hurt, alone, and afraid. My kids need their dad, though he's seldom there for them. I need a man to help me when the car breaks down, the washing machine leaks, or when I need a hug. You know, I have a lot of love to give a man. The worst of it all—I hate waking up in the middle of the night and feeling so alone."

"I understand. That does sound rough. Did you have control over your husband's choices?"

"No," she snapped.

"Do you really think that if you had done anything different you could have saved your marriage?"

"No," she spat.

"How do you feel?"

"Angry. Very, very angry," she hissed through clenched teeth.

"What do you feel like doing?"

Sirena didn't answer the doctor. She simply drew in a voluminous breath and shrieked as if she just drove her car off a cliff. Once she exhausted her breath, she wept for the remaining minutes of her session.

At the exit in the waiting room, while dabbing her eyes

and her nose with a handful of *Kleenex*, she told the doctor, "Although, I've been crying, I do feel much better. Thanks again, Dr. Yelsa. Have a good day."

"Again, you're welcome, Sirena. See you next week and in the meantime, have a quiet soul."

Week after week, she came. Week after week, she shrieked. On one visit, she talked about her daughter Michelle.

"What is Michelle doing that's upsetting you?" inquired Dr. Yelsa.

"It's not only what she's doing," Sirena answered from inside Edvard, "it's what she's *not* doing. She's hanging around with older boys who I don't approve of one bit. She stays up all hours of the night texting, emailing, and playing video games—sometimes all three at once. She hates her dad and won't speak to him. She despises me and gives me back-talk. She blames us both for ruining her life. She dresses like a hooker. She had her ears pierced and got a small tattoo above her behind. Both without my consent. She acts weird and I suspect she's taking drugs of some sort. She wants birth control pills, which I've decided to sign for. She's flunking her classes, because she won't do her homework. She won't eat right, she won't clean her room, she won't get out of bed, and she won't help around the house. She's totally out of control and I get no help from her jerk father."

"How does that make you feel?"

"I'm frustrated and fuming mad!"

"Do you hear that distinct scream in your head?"

"Yes and it's very, very loud!"

"Sirena, you know what to do!"

Sirena shrieked as if she had abruptly woke up in the dead of night to see a strange man with a butcher knife, hovering over her bed. She cried, composed herself, felt better, and on leaving, wished the doctor a good day.

As usual, he replied, "Have a quiet soul."

On another occasion, the moment she sat in Edvard, Dr. Yelsa asked, "How do you feel about your son in Afghanistan?"

Sirena squirmed on the blue stool. She closed her eyes as the scream in her head swelled. She tried to repress it until she could wrap her feelings around it. "Well," she began slowly, "I worry every waking moment, which prompts me to pray every waking moment. During the divorce, my son ran as far away from us as he could. He enlisted in the Marines, they shipped him off to Afghanistan, and now he's in the worst of it. I fear that one morning, I will wake up with a knock at my door and open it to find a Marine Corp chaplain. I don't know if the war is right or wrong—I just want my son home."

"Do you have control over a war in the Middle East or the safety of your soldier son?"

"No, I just want my boy home."

"Do you hear that specific scream inside your ...?"

She began shrieking before he finished his sentence. She shrieked like a woman lying over the flag draped coffin of her military son. Again, she wept, composed herself, and left bidding the doctor to, "Have a good day."

Just like every day with every patient, he replied, "Have a quiet soul."

Over the months of visits with Dr. Yelsa, Sirena shrieked about the frustrations with her job, with her apartment neighbors, and with her unreliable car. She shrieked about dates with losers, about being a single mom, about too many bills with not enough money. She shrieked about the price of oil, natural disasters, and world chaos. Finally, her shrieks shifted from the present to her past. She shrieked about mistakes, regrets, wrong paths, hard times, harsh words, and lost loves. She shrieked and shrieked and with each shriek, the cordage of screams in her head quieted.

On what Sirena thought might be her last visit to Dr. Yelsa, she sat in Edvard.

"Sirena, do you still hear a scream?" the doctor asked.

"Yes, I do."

"Well, you've shrieked from turning forty all the way back through your life to when you were coming home from your first day in kindergarten and you got off the school bus at the wrong bus stop. What is still causing a scream inside your soul?"

"Well, I didn't think it bothered me, but as a newborn baby, I was adopted."

"Adopted. Interesting."

"When I was a few days old, my birth mother didn't want me, so she gave me away. It still bothers me that she would give me up. How could a mother give up her child?"

"I suppose, that maybe she did it out of love, so you would live a better life than she could offer."

"Yes, yes, that could be true, but I still feel angry about it. She could have wondered how I was doing and searched for me instead of disappearing. We could have at least been friends."

"How does that make you feel that you had no control over your birth mother's choices?"

"I feel like I want to scream."

"I have a feeling this will be your last shriek, so make it a good one."

Sirena drew in a huge breath and shrieked. It had volume, but not longevity. It quickly lost steam and faded into silence."

"Sirena, what's the matter?"

She bowed her head and didn't answer.

"Sirena, what is it?"

She raised her head and gazed at the doctor through the acrylic window and said, "Doctor, I thought I was on my last shriek, but as I shrieked, I heard a faint shriek upon the shriek that I shrieked—and it frightened me."

"A shriek upon a shriek. I'm astounded. Usually the screams unravel one at a time."

"I had hoped to cry with joy at having a quiet soul, but I still hear another scream in here," she said, pointing at her head, "and though it's faint, it's shrill."

"My goodness! A shriek with a shrill. A shrill is a very immature shriek that originates at birth."

"At birth?"

"Yes, at birth, therefore it would be very difficult for you to remember. Birth is an emotional and physical trauma, but nearly all babies shriek at the time of birth, neutralizing that trauma. Therefore, it must be something other than your actual birth. I recommend that you find your biological mother and ask her what happened."

"Find my mother? Really? I mean—it's been so many years and she has her own life—a life without me."

"I know it may be unpleasant for you and awkward for her, nevertheless, I feel that there is a good chance that you will discover the *why* of that shrill and finally find the peace of mind you're striving for. I think that out of all of our sessions and out of all of your screams, that this shrill, quite possibly, is at the core."

Sirena became quiet as the shrill in her head became louder. She knew she needed to deal with the *why* of this shrill and said, "Okay, Doctor, I'll search for my birth mother and if I find her, I'll ask her about the circumstances surrounding my birth and if I find out anything, I'll be back to see you." Consumed with thoughts of finding her mother, she charged out of the booth, scooped up her purse, and raced out of the room without saying a word.

Dr. Yelsa bounded out of his chair and hollered after her, "Good luck, Sirena, and have a quiet soul!"

Months passed and Sirena booked another appointment with Dr. Yelsa. A few days later she sat in his blue waiting room. Another woman wringing her hands sat three chairs down from her. As Sirena waited, the blue conjured up the shrill to the tip of her tongue. Just as she was about to burst into a high pitch shriek, the doctor's door opened and he escorted a boy of about twelve years old across the room to the waiting woman.

The worried mother sprung to her feet and asked, "How is my boy?"

"Don't ask me, ask Matt here," said Dr. Yelsa

She turned to her son and asked, "How are you doing, honey?"

"Much better," Matt said with a smile.

"Yes, bullies at school can wreak a lot of havoc on nice kids," said Dr. Yelsa, "and while he couldn't express his horror at school in front of his peers, he did so today. He should be over the trauma, however, I recommend that you enroll him in karate lessons."

"Thank you, Doctor, I will," said the boy's mother and as they stepped out the door to leave, she turned and said, "Oh, and Doctor, have a nice day."

"Mrs. Caterwaul and my main man, Matt, please—have a quiet soul." He waved goodbye, turned to Sirena, and exclaimed, "Welcome back Sirena! I'm so happy to see you again. I trust you found your birth mother and you were able to gain some information that will help you with what is surely your final shriek."

"I did, Doctor!"

"In that case, please, step into my office and let's get down to business!"

They entered his office and he closed the door. She bolted straight for Edvard, jumped inside, slammed the door, jammed on the heart rate monitor and immediately started talking as Dr. Yelsa slid into his chair and crammed on his headphones.

"Over the last few months," she began, "I searched and searched to locate my birth mother, Harmony Jones, but I couldn't find her, until I enlisted the help of an Internet company called *Find My Family*. Although she had been married three times and was currently divorced, they found her rather quickly. Remarkably, she still lived in town. The service provided me with an address and a phone number. I was so nervous, I waited a few days, but eventually called her."

"How did she react to hearing from you?"

"She was shocked, but happy. She never stopped wondering about me over all these years. She invited me over to her house and when we first met, we cried and hugged for a long time."

"Wonderful. Crying and hugging—very therapeutic."

"We ate lunch, sipped tea, and talked all afternoon. We even looked alike. You would have thought we were sisters. She explained to me that at fifteen, she had met an older boy at a party and one thing led to the next; she was pregnant and he was gone. I realized that as she talked, the shrill inside my head grew louder and louder. When she went to the kitchen to make us another pot of tea, I listened very intently to the shrill in my head and I heard a loud heartbeat and a soft heartbeat, however, as I continued to listen, I heard another yet softer heartbeat."

"Ahhh," said Dr. Yelsa, "of course, you've regressed all the way back to when you were still in your mother's womb. The loud heartbeat—your mother's; the first soft heartbeat—yours; and the second, softer heartbeat was—no—you tell me. What happened?"

"As I listened, I realized that the third heartbeat just didn't sound right. It was weak and erratic. Then, my mother returned with the tea and I told her about you, Doctor, and your therapy. I explained to her that I had one last scream and how you suggested it might have something to do with my birth. When

I told her about the heartbeats, she gasped, set her cup of tea down on the coffee table, reached out, held my hand, and shared something tragic." Sirena became quiet as tears welled up in her eyes and she sniffed.

"Sirena, what did she tell you?" the doctor whispered.

She gazed out at the doctor, their eyes locked, and she continued, "I was not alone in my mother's womb. I had an identical-twin sister who my mother named Corina. Corina was born first, but she had heart trouble and died. I was born healthy. My mother never had any more children after me. It's all so sad." Sirena buried her face in her hands and cried.

"So you shared the womb with a twin sister," Dr. Yelsa repeated softly. "You were curled up next to her and for nine months you could hear not only your heartbeat and your mother's, but Corina's too; however, at birth, the erratic heartbeat vanished and so did Corina, your womb-mate, your sister, and your twin. You screamed over the trauma of birth, but not over the grief of losing your sister."

"I can still hear her little heartbeat even as I sit here," sobbed Sirena. "I miss her and I feel like I've longed for her my entire life. It just doesn't seem fair that I would live and my sister would die."

"Sirena, I'm sorry for your loss," he said with sympathy, "but you had no control over the death of your sister. Let's let that last scream out. Are you ready?"

"Yes," she murmured.

Sirena drew in a deep breath and exhaled slowly. She drew in another deep breath and exhaled slowly. She drew in a third deep breath deeper than the first two, opened her mouth, closed her eyes, scrunched up her face, and shrieked shrill and piercing like an infant stuck with a diaper pin.

Dr. Yelsa checked his monitor with satisfaction. Heart rate up. Decibels through the roof.

Sirena shrieked longer than she had ever shrieked and afterwards, sobbed harder than she had ever sobbed.

"Sirena," whispered Dr. Yelsa into his microphone, "are you okay?"

"Yes, I'm okay Doctor; better than I've ever been." She opened the door, stepped out of Edvard, and scanned the blue room. She sniffed, grabbed a few tissues, and said, "Doctor."

"Yes, Sirena."

"I'm staring at all this blue and I don't hear a scream anymore."

"No scream?"

"No scream."

"No shrill?"

"No shrill. It's quiet inside my head. I finally feel at peace."

"Good. Very good. Well done. We are finished. Now remember if any old one creeps up or a new one surfaces, then, please come back and see me."

"I will Dr. Yelsa," said Sirena, picking up her purse and walking over to his office door. Before she opened it to step out into the lobby, she turned and said, "Thank you, Doctor. I feel much better, indeed, I actually feel happy. For the rest of my life, I'll do the best I can with my ex, my daughter, and my son, and I know if I again hear a scream inside my head, I'll be back sitting in that crazy booth."

"Edvard and I are here whenever you need us."

"Thanks again and Doctor—"

"Yes, Sirena."

"Have a good day."

Dr. Yelsa smiled broadly and with a soothing confidence, said, "Sirena—"

"Yes, Doctor."

"Have a quiet soul."

LOTTA'S FOUNTAIN

The fire in the fireplace popped and crackled as Carol and Nancy, both twenty-eight and best friends since junior high, sat together on a sofa in the warm glow of the flames. Each sipped a glass of red wine as they chatted softly about Nancy's pending divorce. They were at the home of Carol's parents in Pleasanton, California, a charming, little city, twenty miles east of San Francisco Bay. They had just finished cleaning up after Thanksgiving dinner, the TV was off, and Carol's parents had gone to bed. The house was quiet, except for the crackling fire and the soft voices of the two women. Outside, the cold, night fog crept in from the bay.

Carol, petite and pretty with brown hair and brown eyes, stood up, tossed a small log onto the fire and stoked the embers with a poker. She poured more wine in each glass and nestled back on the couch. Nancy, shapely and stunning with blonde hair and green eyes, continued moaning about her conniving ex-husband, the ugly legal battles, the unfair settlement, and the court arranged custody of their dog. Carol listened sympathetically.

"Another thing," said Nancy, wrapping up her lamentations, "I'm so glad that we didn't have any kids or we'd be at war over them too."

Carol didn't respond, but stared at the hypnotic flames of the fire.

Nancy reached over and held Carol's hand and said, "My

divorce is absolutely horrible. I've lost my husband, I get my dog every other week, and we have to sell our house and divide everything in it, but that's nothing compared to the nightmare that you're going through."

Carol remained silent, staring into the fire; lost in her thoughts; her eyes moist.

"What are you thinking?" whispered Nancy.

"I think," replied Carol in an almost inaudible whisper, "that I can't bear it all. When the earthquake hit—" she began to quietly sob.

"I'm so sorry, Carol," said Nancy. She reached over, pulled a couple of tissues out of a box on a nearby table, gave them to Carol and squeezing Carol's hand, said softly, "Anything you need, I'm here for you."

"I know you are," said Carol. She took a deep breath, sniffed, and stopped crying. She transferred her tear-filled gaze from the fire over to Nancy's worrisome eyes and said, "You're a wonderful friend and I'm sorry for all that you're going through with your divorce. I'm really happy you're here." She paused for a second, gathered her thoughts, and said, "For awhile now, I wanted to tell you something—but I couldn't. But now that some time has passed, I'm ready to talk about it."

"Since seventh grade, we've always told each other everything," said Nancy, "so please, tell me."

"Well," said Carol, "when the house collapsed and I was trapped under the rubble—I experienced something very—well—very strange."

On October 17th, during the third game warm-up of the 1989 World Series—between the San Francisco Giants and the Oakland Athletics—the ABC network's live broadcast began to break-up as the sportscaster exclaimed, "I'll tell you what—we're having an earth ...." At that moment, the video feed from Candlestick Park was lost.

On that autumn day, the customary cool weather was warm, the familiar winds were calm, and the normally whitecapped bay was eerily placid. Indeed, it was a pleasant afternoon for a baseball game, but at 5:04 p.m., the earth groaned as the San Andreas fault, near Loma Prieta peak in the Santa Cruz mountains, shifted seven feet, launching a 6.9, fifteen second, shock wave across the heavily populated peninsula.

In the stadium, during the first five seconds of the quake, the fans, mostly locals accustomed to tremors, joked, "Earthquake." Over the next five seconds, as the quake rumbled louder and shook harder, the crowd gasped, "Earthquake!" During the final five seconds, as the violent shaking intensified, the spectators, their faces contorted with fear, clutched each other, as each cried out, "Earthquake!" As the shock waves hit, the stadium's light stanchions, upper deck windscreen, and packed seats swayed several feet. The baseball diamond rolled like waves on the sea. The *Goodyear Blimp*, airborne above the stadium, bounced as the aftershock passed beneath it. As soon as the shaking in the stadium stopped, there were a few seconds of silence and then, the fans, unaware of the tragic destruction to their city, roared, "Let's play ball! Let's play ball!" The stadium was evacuated and the World Series postponed. Across the city of San Francisco, homes toppled and high-rises rained debris on the streets. Cars were crushed, power lines fell, traffic snarled, fires burned, and water mains gushed. A section of the San Francisco-Oakland Bay Bridge collapsed and the top level of the Nimitz Freeway fell. Telephone, radio, and television signals ceased. Military, civil, and volunteer rescue workers scrambled to help the shaken city.

When the earthquake struck, Carol wasn't at Candlestick Park, she was at her home—a seventy-year-old, Victorian style house perched above its carport on a steep hill in San Francisco. Carol, an account manager for a wine distributor and her husband Daniel, a thirty-year-old loan officer, had been married five years. They had a three-year-old daughter, Christina, who looked like a miniature Carol, petite, with long brown hair and big brown eyes instead of the dark hair and blue eyes of her father. On the afternoon of the quake, Carol had picked up Christina from day-care and had arrived home at 4:45 p.m. She parked in the carport and holding her little girl's hand, they walked up the steps and entered their house. She set her daughter, wearing a sun-yellow play dress, in the middle of the family room, gave her a few toys, and turned the World Series on TV. Stepping into the kitchen, she clipped her hair on top of her head, kicked off her high heels, put on her house slippers, and without changing out of her olive-green business suit and skirt, she began preparing an early dinner. While listening to the pregame rhetoric, she tossed a handful of spaghetti in boiling water, placed a pound of hamburger in a skillet, and slid a loaf of French bread into the oven. She uncorked a bottle of red wine, poured herself a glass, and took a sip. Every few minutes, she checked on Christina playing joyfully with her toys.

At a few minutes past five-o-clock, Daniel walked through the front door, set his briefcase down, and hollered, "Hun, I'm home!"

Christina ran to her daddy. He scooped her up and kissed her on her rosy cheeks. She gave him a big sloppy kiss on his cheek. Tickling her tummy, he said, "I sure missed my cutie-pie today and I'm so happy to see her."

"Me happy too!" Christina giggled.

"Now, Daddy wants to go kiss Mommy," he said, placing her back on the floor with her toys. He removed his suit jacket and loosened his tie, glanced at the baseball game, stepped into the kitchen, and said, "Hi, babe. Smells good. My day was totally crazy. How 'bout yours?"

"Hectic, but productive. I nailed another big account."

"Congratulations, you gorgeous sales-machine."

They gave each other a hello peck on the lips and Daniel

said, "I'm so ready for dinner and a cold beer, and just plopping down on the couch to watch the game."

"Grab yourself a beer, honey. Dinner will be ready in a few minutes."

The digital oven clock blinked from 5:03 to 5:04. Daniel reached into the refrigerator and grabbed a frosty bottle of beer. Carol dumped a jar of spaghetti sauce into the sizzling meat. Christina played with toys. The baseball players at Candlestick Park warmed up. The fans roared with anticipation. Across the city, people pursued their day-end routines. Commuters exited the city. In the hills near Loma Prieta peak, a wispy cloud drifted in front of the late afternoon sun, the breeze lulled, bird songs stopped, crickets ceased, and in the remote stillness, the earth violently shifted.

As Daniel twisted off the bottle cap and as Carol stirred the meat sauce, they felt the first tremor. The shock wave began as a buzz in their feet that rapidly climbed up their legs to shake their entire bodies. Since small tremors were a common occurrence, Carol and Daniel just stared at each other, waiting for it to pass. Seconds ticked. Instead of diminishing, the trembler magnified, rising from the sound of stampeding cattle to that of rolling thunder. Plates and glasses in the cupboards rattled. Windows shook. The hanging lamp above the kitchen table swayed. Daniel slammed his beer down on the counter and raced into the family room for Christina. The TV was static. Christina cried out, "Daddy! Daddy!" Carol turned off the oven and stove and took a step for the family room, but the floor rolled, lifted her up, and slammed her down.

She screamed, "Daniel! Daniel!"

In the family room, Daniel tumbled to the floor next to Christina. He clutched her into his arms, jumped up, and yelled, "Carol! I've got Christina! Get out of the house!"

Christina started wailing. The house groaned. Carol struggled to get up, but the merciless earthquake knocked her down again. She peered into the family room. Her terrified eyes met Daniel's fearful eyes and then darted to the horrified eyes of her sobbing little girl. Just as her husband took a step to help Carol and as Carol crawled toward him, the most forceful shock wave hit. The house moaned in distress and buckled, careening off its foundation. Daniel and Christina were catapulted back into the family room. The entertainment center with the TV, the video player, and the stereo crashed down on them. Electrical wires sparked, water lines burst, windows shattered, and in a deafening, grinding slide, the entire house collapsed, toppling into the carport, crushing their two cars, while pitching into the street in a heap of wood, plaster, glass, and shingles. Dust filled the air and a fire broke out near the gas water-heater. Daniel, Carol, and Christina lay trapped under the rubble.

Six weeks had passed since the earthquake. Carol recovered at her parent's house. Her best-friend Nancy had traveled up from Fresno to join Carol and her parents for Thanksgiving. Carol and Nancy sat on the sofa next to the fire. Both sipped wine. Nancy shared about her pending divorce until Carol stared trance-like into the flickering flames of the fire. She transferred her gaze from the flames to Nancy's eyes and told her, "When the house collapsed and I was trapped under the rubble—I experienced something very—well—very strange."

"Strange?" replied Nancy. "What happened?"

"When the house toppled, the sound was deafening. All became dark. I was terrified, but all I could think about were Daniel and Christina."

Recalling the horror, Carol buried her face in her hands and wept. Nancy wept too. After a few minutes, Carol drew in a deep breath, dabbed her teary eyes and runny nose with a tissue, and began again, "I called out their names over and over, but there was no answer. I felt like I was suffocating. Dust filled my lungs and there was a crushing weight on top of me. I couldn't move. I panicked and screamed for help. I heard nothing, except my own labored breathing. What happened next, is what's so strange. One second, I'm buried under the rubble and then—I'm standing in the street."

"You weren't trapped anymore?" Nancy asked. "How'd you get out?"

"I don't know, but it was unearthly quiet and I was alone. Water from broken water mains flowed down the gutter. From where I stood high on the hill, I gazed out across the city and saw fires burning everywhere. The entire city was cloaked in smoke and the approaching nightfall. I turned away from the damaged city and searched for Daniel and Christina in the ruins of my house. I saw flames in the debris. I scrambled on top of the wreckage and shouted their names. I heard Daniel's voice call out my name. Then, I heard Christina cry out, 'Mommy!' and I frantically searched the rubble, but didn't see a sign of them. When their voices called out again, I turned and saw Daniel holding Christina. I couldn't believe it, but they were at the corner of our street."

Nancy gasped, "They were alive! They weren't trapped in the rubble?"

"Alive and no longer trapped, so I ran to them."

"You ran, even though you were injured?"

"I didn't feel any pain at all. Even our clothes were like new. I raced up to them, hugging and kissing them both. They kissed and hugged me too. Daniel turned to walk toward downtown and said, 'This way! We need to go this way.' I asked him, 'Why that way?' He stopped and said with a smile, 'It's the way to Lotta's Fountain.'"

"Lotta's Fountain?" interrupted Nancy. "What's Lotta's Fountain?"

"Since the earthquake," said Carol, "I've searched the Internet about it and I've also visited it. It's a historical monument in downtown San Francisco, at the intersection of

Market and Kearney Streets. During the Gold Rush, a young barroom dancer named Lotta Crabtree entertained the gold miners who tipped her with gold nuggets. She invested her gold in real estate and became very wealthy. In her gratitude, she donated the iron monument to the city. It's weird looking: very ornate and shaped like a square church steeple. On each side is a drinking fountain and on each corner is a lion's head with scrolled gables above them. Perched on top of the pillar is a very odd looking globe. Strange thing is—after the 1906 earthquake, survivors met at Lotta's Fountain to search for their missing loved ones."

"Survivors of the 1906 earthquake met at Lotta's Fountain," said Nancy. "How bizarre."

"It is bizarre and people still meet there on the anniversary of the 1906 earthquake. Anyway, Daniel, Christina, and I walked for just a short while. Broken glass, masonry, and whole sections of collapsed buildings littered the streets. The streets and sidewalks had huge cracks. The entire city was without power. We passed by a lot of crushed cars and a stranded cable car. It was eerie. We didn't see a single soul until we reached Lotta's Fountain."

"Where was everybody?" asked Nancy.

"I don't know, I was just happy that Daniel, Christina, and me were together. When we arrived at the fountain, a few others had already gathered around it and more were coming from different parts of the city. Everyone, including Daniel and Christina, just stared at the fountain with a tranquil look on their face and waited."

"Waited for what?" asked Nancy.

"Again, I didn't know, but a man walked up to us and said his name was Tom. He worked in a downtown clothing store. I asked him why he was at Lotta's Fountain. He told me that he had been heading home driving east on the lower level of the San Francisco-Oakland Bay Bridge, when he felt a vibration in his steering wheel as though he was sliding on ice. He heard a loud metallic groaning as the bridge violently swayed and twisted. Traffic stopped and there was an explosion of disintegrating bolts. He watched the upper level of metal plates unhinge like a trapdoor and collapse in front of him."

"How terrifying!" exclaimed Nancy.

"He said that the fierce shaking on the bridge stopped almost as soon as it had started. Not long afterwards, the cars behind him turned around and he followed them off the bridge to Yerba Buena Island. The police mistakenly sent him east onto the upper level toward the perilous gap in the bridge."

"They sent him back onto the damaged bridge?" asked Nancy.

"Yes, it's hard to believe, but the poor man was sent back into harm's way. He told me that all of a sudden there was no bridge in front of him. He stomped on the brakes, but his car soared into the gap and crashed to the deck below; the very deck he had left only minutes before. He was gravely injured. A helicopter airlifted him to Letterman Army Medical Center. They landed on the hospital's helipad on the roof and set him down. As the helicopter lifted off to help someone else, he faded in and out of consciousness. A paramedic told him to 'hang on' as another held his hand. Tom said he closed his eyes and took a deep painful breath and when he opened them again, he was alone on the helipad. He stood up, gazed out over the city, and counted twenty-seven fires blazing. He felt no pain and his only thought was to go to Lotta's Fountain. So he rode down the empty elevator, walked out onto the lonely street, and made his way to the monument."

Both Carol and Nancy took a sip of their wine and Nancy commented, "What a really weird experience with that Tom guy. That they would just leave him on the helipad."

"It sure was, but as soon as Tom finished telling us his story, an aftershock hit. It wasn't as destructive as the first one, but it still shook hard. The funny thing is that no one, including me, were frightened. Just as the aftershock subsided, a group of about forty or fifty people strolled into the intersection. They had all come from the Nimitz freeway across the bay. I noticed a woman, a few years younger than us, holding the hand of a small boy. I asked her what had happened. She told me her name was Brianna and her boy's name was Brian. She had just picked him up from kindergarten and they were driving home on the lower level of the 880. As she drove on the Cypress Street Viaduct, she heard a rumbling sound and felt a horrible shaking in her car like four flat tires. Traffic stopped and she rolled down her window. A booming sound drew closer, becoming louder. Her car shook as she peered out her windshield and saw huge cracks forming in the cement freeway overhead. Massive chunks of cement fell and flattened the vehicles in front of her. She frantically unfastened her seatbelt and her son's, grabbed him, flung open the car door, and dove out, just as the upper level freeway crushed down on them."

"Oh, Carol, I can barely listen," said Nancy. "How terrible, but somehow she survived—to tell you what had happened."

"It was a miracle that they had survived, just like Daniel, Christina, and myself had survived. Brianna said that one second, she was diving out of her car with Brian and the next second, they were standing with the rest of the commuters alongside the destroyed freeway. Everyone, all at once, just turned and headed for Lotta's Fountain."

"Again, Lotta's Fountain. How strange," said Nancy.

"So as Brianna finished telling me her story, I saw a flash of bright light reflect off of her face and I heard a whooshing sound. I spun and peered at Lotta's Fountain. Everyone watched it. A streaming, ghostly wind revolved around the monument as a tall narrow door facing Market Street slowly opened inward. A radiant light emerged out of the ever-widening door. The globe at the top of the monument flashed into a blinding light and shot a dazzling beam up into the night sky. People gathered near the fountain's door and stepped calmly and willingly into the light. I saw Tom enter and vanish. I watched Brianna and Brian enter and vanish followed by all the others. Daniel held Christina with one arm and wrapped his other arm around me. We approached the light together—together as a family."

"Were you afraid?" asked Nancy.

"Yes, very much so, but Christina reached out her little hand, brushed my hair, and whispered, 'Don't be afraid Mommy. It's okay.' I smiled at her and she smiled back. We stepped through the door and stood inside Lotta's Fountain. We were completely bathed in bright light. I felt no pain or suffering; no anger or sadness; no regret, only a welling sense of joy and peace. I gazed above me into the divine globe and its rushing, spiraling stream of brilliancy. I felt an upward pull, but I also felt a strong tug away from Daniel and Christina. Suddenly, I felt a sharp pain in my chest."

"Oh, no," exclaimed Nancy, her hand over her mouth.

"I reached out to hold onto my husband and daughter as they both reached out to grasp me, but I was torn away from them. They remained in the light as I stood just outside the fountain's door. Daniel said, 'I love you Carol,' and smiled. Christina said, 'I love you Mommy' and waved bye-bye. Before I could tell them how much I loved them too, they vanished up into the light, while I, within a blink of an eye, was whisked away from Lotta's Fountain, through the silent night, down the empty streets, and back—back under the rubble."

"Back under the rubble. How dreadful," gasped Nancy.

"I felt pain and moaned. I heard a man's voice cry out, 'Someone's alive. Over here! Have hope down there! Help is on the way!' I felt thirsty and weak. I could barely breathe. I prayed as though I was speaking my last words. I heard debris shifting above me. I groaned and someone shouted, 'Hang on, we've almost got you.' I felt near death. I just wanted to be with my husband and daughter. Four men hoisted the refrigerator up off my legs. Another man said, 'We've got you now!' and I felt him grab my arms. A different man said, 'You're going to be all right! Hang on, hang on!' and he lifted my legs. They carefully lifted me out of the ruins, laid me on a stretcher, and carried me across the rubble. A fire burned where the family room used to be. Smoke filled the air. Lights flashed from an ambulance and a firetruck. A fireman asked me if there were others buried under the house. I told him that my husband and daughter used to be, but now they're gone. He shook his head confused, turned, and yelled, 'Keep searching, her husband and daughter are still buried.' They slid me into the ambulance. I raised my head, peering out at the debris that used to be my home and said, 'I love you Daniel and oh, how I love you Christina,' and I whispered, 'Goodbye.'"

Carol wept. So did Nancy. The fire crackled.

Every time Carol peered into a mirror and saw the scar across her forehead, every time she felt the pain of her broken ribs, and every time she took a step and limped, she would remember. Furthermore, every time she glanced at a baseball game on TV, every time she smelled spaghetti cooking, and every time she saw a three-year-old little girl with brown hair and brown eyes, she would remember that horrifying day.

On October 17th, at 5:04 p.m., on that still and sultry day of the 1989 World Series, the earth quaked as the San Andreas fault, near Loma Prieta peak in the Santa Cruz mountains, shifted seven feet, launching a 6.9 shock wave. Candlestick Park was evacuated and the game postponed, a section of the San Francisco-Oakland Bay Bridge collapsed, and a stretch of the Nimitz Freeway fell. In a mere 15 seconds the Loma Prieta Earthquake stole 57 lives, injured over 3,700, and caused $5.9 billion in damages, yet in the aftermath, still standing on the corner of Market and Kearney is Lotta's Fountain.

RYAN'S BIRTHDAY

Ryan said to his wife, "See you in a little while." He glanced down and punched the cell phone's end key with his thumb and as he did, out of the corner of his eye, for a split second, he noticed something shiny, child-like dart out of the dark cornfield and into the foggy beams of his headlights. His *Ford Taurus* slammed into the short, scurrying thing with a loud thud accompanied by an unearthly scream. He reacted at once, dropping his cell phone, gripping the steering wheel, stomping on the brakes, and stopping his vehicle. Trembling, while muttering in horror, "Oh, my God. Oh, my God," he shifted the green sedan into park. With the engine running and the headlights battling the blinding night fog, he unfastened his seat belt, thrust open his door, and leapt out of his car. The key in the ignition chimed ding-ding-ding into the fog-smothered silence. The strange something that he had hit looked a lot like a kid; a kid in an alien costume; a kid from a Halloween party at a nearby farm house; a kid, lost in the fog, now dying or dead; for God's sake, a kid; he killed a kid.

A few minutes earlier, Ryan had called his wife, who along with their son, were waiting for him to come home from work. With her long, blonde hair tied in a ponytail and wearing her pink kitchen apron with printed cupcakes over her baby-blue sweater and jeans, his wife, twenty-eight-year-old, Summer stood at the kitchen sink washing cake pans, beaters, and a mixing bowl. Her cell phone rang on the counter next to her.

She dried her hands with a kitchen towel, glanced at the caller ID, answered the phone, and with fun twinkling in her bright-blue eyes, burst out, "Hello, birthday boy!"

"Hi babe, how ya doing?" asked her husband Ryan, wearing his *Bluetooth* as he zoomed south on the 99.

"I'm fine, just waiting for my sexy man to get home."

"If you think a short, paunchy, balding guy is sexy, well, I'm a very lucky man."

"Yes I do, so count yourself lucky, mister. How far away are you?"

"I'm coming up on the Betty exit, so I'll be there soon."

After a long week of working at a Fresno distributor, selling pipes and pipefittings, Friday finally arrived; Friday, October 30th, Ryan's thirtieth birthday. He couldn't wait to get home, relax, and celebrate.

"Good, perfect timing," said Summer. "Dinner is almost ready and just like you wanted, 'no big party for your birthday; just a quiet night at home with Justy and me.'" She kept an eye on their son, five-year-old, Justin, standing on a chair at the kitchen counter as he slapped a spatula heaped with chocolate frosting on top of a two-layer chocolate cake.

"How's Justy?" Ryan asked, wondering what his energetic boy was up to.

"He's been so excited over celebrating your birthday that he's been a bit of a pill since I picked him up from kindergarten."

"Well, put that little rascal on the phone."

"Okay, hold on. Justy, Daddy wants to talk to you."

Ryan turned onto the Betty exit at Goshen just north of Visalia and headed east down a backcountry road toward his home in Woodlake. He switched on the headlights as the dimming twilight of the short autumn day turned to night.

Justin, a tow-headed little guy, set down the spatula, clutched his mother's cell phone, smearing it with frosting, and said with a happy smile on his freckled face, "Hi daddy. When you coming home?"

"I'll be there shortly, son. I won't be long."

"I have a surprise for you! Me and mommy made it," said Justin, his big blue eyes flashing with excitement as he licked the frosting off his fingers, "so hurry home!"

"A surprise for me! Wow, I'd better hurry then. But for now, put mommy back on the phone, please."

"Okay. Here mommy," said Justin, handing the phone to Summer. She wiped it off with a paper towel as her son snatched up the spatula, licked it, and joyfully smeared more frosting on the cake.

Ryan peered out his windshield into the night. Cornfields crowded both sides of the two-lane road creating a canyon of cornstalks. Cold, tule fog, infamous in the San Joaquin Valley had crept in after two previous days of rain, so he slowed, concentrating on the road barely visible in the rebounding glow of his headlights.

"Wow, this fog is thick tonight," stated Ryan, staring straight ahead into the ghostlike layer of moisture.

"Ryan, be careful," cautioned Summer. "Just slow down."

"Don't worry, I'm taking it slow."

"Mommy," interrupted Justin.

"Ryan, just a minute, Justy wants to ask me something." She covered the phone with her hand and asked Justin, "What is it, sweetie?"

Justin whispered so that his daddy on the phone couldn't hear him, "Can I wear my Halloween costume and can we light the candles on the cake to surprise Daddy?"

"That sounds like a great idea," she whispered and then said in her normal voice, "Ryan, I'm back. We have a surprise waiting for you, so see you soon. Bye-bye."

"Okay, oh and honey," Ryan said before she ended the

call, "don't forget to turn on the porch light. See you in a little while."

Ryan glanced down at his cell phone and tapped the end key. Something short and shiny darted out of the cornstalks and into the beam of the headlights. He slammed into it and it screamed. He stopped the car, leapt out, raced to the front, and saw in the glare of the beaming headlights, dents in the grill and bumper, but no writhing or lifeless body. The victim, he surmised, was under the car. The cold, wet fog, and the shock of the accident seized him and he shivered. He peered up and down the deserted road; no blurry headlights; only oppressing fog. In an urgency to call 9-1-1, he dashed back to his open door, all the while, the disturbing ding-ding-ding rang out. Reaching in for his cell phone, he looked down, reeled back two steps, and gasped, "Oh, my God!"

Directly below his open door, on the damp asphalt, and illuminated by the car's interior lights, lay the lifeless hand and arm of the hapless victim extending out from underneath the car. Ryan stepped closer, curious, fearful, cautious, and peered down at the creature and saw that it was not an earthly hand and arm of some star-crossed trick-or-treater in a space costume, but a small, shiny hand with spindly fingers attached to a long, wiry arm of gleaming, metallic skin. In the fog-strangled silence, a rustling sound emanated from the cornfield on the other side of his vehicle. He raised up on his toes, peered over the damp roof of his sedan, and saw the tassels of the cornstalks shudder. He took a step around the car's trunk to investigate, but hearing movement under his vehicle, he stopped and peered down to see the hand sliding, skidding, vanishing as though someone or something on the other side had grabbed the victim's legs and yanked it out from under the car. Startled, he shuffled back a step, stooped, and peered under his car just in time to see two, iridescent feet dart into the cornfield. He dove into his car, reached across the front seats, opened the glove box, grabbed a small flashlight, and switched it on. No light shined, so he smacked the flashlight in the palm of his hand until it beamed. He searched for his cell phone, but couldn't find it hidden under his brake pedal, so he rushed off without it, racing into the cornfield. As he ran, brushing up against long, wet leaves and plump ears of corn, he could hear crackling footsteps twenty yards ahead of him, yet couldn't see who or what he chased. His flashlight only shined ten yards out in the fog. He encountered paths of flattened cornstalks; some stalks squashed, facing one way; others smashed, facing the other way. Strange. Dressed in jeans, work boots, and only a cotton, long sleeve shirt, he shivered from the cold. Out of shape and unaccustomed to jogging, not to mention in a cornfield on a foggy night, he tired quickly. He decided to stop, turn around, and return to his car, but couldn't, drawn deeper into the corn by a compelling force. A short distance ahead of him, a fuzzy, blue light blinked in the fog. He shut off his flashlight, crept up ten yards from the light, and crouched, listening, watching, quietly huffing and puffing behind a thicket of cornstalks. Moisture dripped off the plants; one drop landing on the balding spot in the middle of his thinning, dark hair; another running down the back of his neck. He shuddered from an icy chill and trembled from fright, peering out from behind his hiding place. As his eyes adjusted to the darkness, the fog momentarily lifted, and in the moonlight, he saw flattened cornstalks swirled and overlapped in circular patterns and above them glints of a shiny, hovering craft; an unfamiliar craft, whirring softly; mirroring its surroundings, camouflaged as misty gray fog until the patch of fog wafted past and the craft reflected the cornfield and the starry night. Although the craft would be difficult to discern from a distance, up close, he could see it. The body of the ship, the size of a H2 Hummer pointing up at the stars, looked like a metal toy-top without the hand pump at the top or the point at the bottom. Where the top and the bottom cones met in the center, they sandwiched a thin, metallic saucer. The saucer, a bit larger diameter than the girth of the cones, silently revolved with a fast-orbiting, blue light, which appeared to blink in the fog.

Ryan's eyes scanned the area. His eyes grew wide and his breath quickened as his mind convinced him that he indeed saw what he saw. On the ground amongst the toppled cornstalks and next to the spaceship, were two beings. One being knelt on its knees, shaking, sobbing, while cradling the other lifeless being in its arms. The two shiny visitors, human-like except with smooth, elongated heads and pear-shaped bodies, possessed two arms, two hands, two legs and two feet; however, the diminutive, earless strangers, the height of an eight-year-old child, were rangy with an extended neck, stretched out arms and legs, and small hands with long weedy fingers. From head to toe, they wore gleaming, form-fitting spacesuits, which at first glance had seemed like luminous skin. The dead alien looked more muscular with wider shoulders and bigger arms while the kneeling, crying extraterrestrial seemed more petite with a curvaceous figure. A clear shield wrapped around their faces and a thin square panel of blinking lights protruded out from their chests, both integrating flawlessly with their suits. The visitor on its knees raised its face toward the stars, hugged the lifeless being to its chest, and cried out in an unnerving, mournful shriek. Ryan winced. Dogs barked. The grieving alien raised a glittery hand into the air, clenched it into a fist and the dogs stopped barking. Ryan, feeling afraid, should have fled, but overcome with awe and again coaxed by a compelling force, he watched as the being laid its deceased comrade flat on the ground. A large cold drop of water hit Ryan in the face, he flinched, and a cornstalk crackled under his foot. The alien shot a glance toward where Ryan hid, stared for a few seconds, and again focused on the departed being. With one gleaming, gangly finger, it pressed a series of buttons on the dead being's control pack, then stood and stepped back a few paces. The lifeless creature on the ground glowed fluorescent green, surged into an opalescent blue, and with a burst of bright light more blinding than a camera's flash, it vanished, discharging a wave of warmth that brushed across Ryan's face. The alien stared over at the cornstalks where Ryan hid. Ryan, ready to run for his life, stood, but blinded by the flash memory on his retinas, couldn't see to take a step.

Within seconds, Ryan could see again, but within seconds, the iridescent humanoid stood a foot away, glaring up at him. Ryan, startled, jumped back a step, fumbled with the flashlight, and switched it on, shining it into the alien's face. The being stood its ground, staring up into Ryan's horrified face and fearful, brown eyes. Ryan peered into its face shield and saw a pale, bluish face, a bump of a nose with two small nostrils, a lipless slit for a mouth, and green cat-like eyes full of rage. Ryan gulped, thinking, *I'm so totally screwed.*

Though the alien was shorter and skinnier than him, and most likely the female of their strange species, Ryan feared for his life and took another step back. The she-being stepped forward. Ryan spun, tried to run, but froze. His mind screamed, *Run man, run*, however, he also heard in his mind an eerie, unnatural voice: a high pitched voice; albeit, a woman's voice, commanding, *Stop!*

Ryan stopped, turned back around, and peered again into the alien's furious face. The she-being ordered, *Come with me,* without moving her mouth slit. Ryan dropped the beaming flashlight and as his brain wrestled to disobey the command, his body willfully followed the small, shiny alien with the enlarged cranium over to the hovering spacecraft.

The girlish creature pressed buttons of varied-color lights on the control panel on her chest: a remote control for everything from alien cremation to the handling of the flying top. The ship floated down closer to the ground, a concealed door opened, a ramp slid out, and Ryan heard telepathically, *Enter* and he marched like a robot into the craft followed by the angry alien. The door closed. Ryan wanted to scream; he wanted to run back to his car; he wanted to embrace his sweet wife; he wanted to hug his rowdy, little boy; he wanted his birthday party with his favorite dinner; he wanted a slice of his birthday cake.

The interior of the ship felt cramped as Ryan ducked under instruments, gages, and containers of earth specimens: soil, seeds, plants, and live insects. The she-being mentally communicated, *Sit* and Ryan sat, sliding into a contraption resembling an alloy kayak. A clear dome lid stored in the ceiling, slid over him, locking him in. He panicked, but could do nothing but attempt to remain calm by visualizing a happy thought: his birthday cake with thirty flaming candles.

Next to Ryan's space seat, the space being slid into her alloy kayak. She removed her face shield, glared at Ryan, and out of her gash of a mouth screamed in English, her voice shrill and harsh sounding like an upset school girl, "Because of your negligence, you murdered a star pilot; my space partner since the exploration of the planet Zath. Our world praises him as the greatest explorer of the universe."

Ryan, feeling regretful, yet trying to defend himself, said, "I'm truly sorry. I only looked down for a second. Honestly, it was an acci...."

The she-being held up a gleaming hand and clenched it into a fist, forcing Ryan to shut up in mid sentence. She continued, calmer but with strict resolve, "Now, Earth-man, I must take you to my world to stand trial and face justice!"

Ryan sighed, slumping his shoulders in defeat, knowing that when a man, right or wrong, pisses off a woman, any woman, young or old, rich or poor, homely or beautiful, from any race, from any spot on Earth, and at this moment, from outer space, that man is in a whole hell-of-a-lot of trouble.

A see-through dome, with an intricate instrument panel projected on it, dropped over her seating apparatus. The extraterrestrial waved her hands as though conducting a great symphony and the craft whirred faster. Ryan felt a mild vibration. She motioned another panel into view and touched the inside of her dome, manipulating navigational coordinates amidst what looked like Egyptian hieroglyphics. The spacecraft lifted straight up and Ryan watched the real-time view below the ship on the alien's dome monitor. He saw through the swirling fog, the crop circles of toppled corn, his glowing flashlight, the lonely road, his car with its headlights beaming, and as his world became smaller, his heart sank and he again thought, *I'm so totally screwed.*

The space ship, high above the cornfield, hovered for only a second and then streaked like a meteor across the night sky over lighted homes, highways with roaming headlights, lit-up towns, and past jolted pilots flying commercial jets. The she-being, flew the spaceship like a drummer in a heavy-metal, rock band, thrusting out her hands, in and out, up and down, from side to side, rhythmically, speedily, changing screens and views, responding to data, all the while abducting Ryan to an extragalactic world.

On the data-dome, amongst the hieroglyphics, the words *Los Angeles* appeared and a myriad of blending lights and landscapes blurred past beneath the craft. Within seconds, the craft hummed over another large city far below and the blip on the screen read, *Phoenix* and after another half minute, the screen read, *Mexico City*, where the ship changed its orientation to the skyline and rocketed vertically, beyond the clouds, through the atmosphere, in-between satellites, and outside the Earth's celestial sphere.

Ryan, inside his domed seat, felt no g-force or shifts in orientation. He gawked at the being, piloting the ship. She glanced back at him and glared with fury, sending a psychic directive of pain, punishing him with an excruciating headache. He squeezed his head with his hands, groaning, apologizing, begging forgiveness, and with wincing, squinting eyes, he saw the data-dome transform from a planetary view of the Earth into peculiar symbols of coordinates and trajectory followed by a three-dimensional layout of a churning, whipping tunnel, writhing like a cosmic snake in a realm of infinite stars. A count down of what seemed to be an approach-sequence flashed across the screen and the spaceship plunged into the tunnel's portal in an immense splash of light enveloped by a burst of electromagnetic energy. Inside the tunnel, comparable to the squirming bowels of a river-size serpent, replete with dips, rises, turns, and spirals, she deftly maneuvered the craft, dodging chunks of cosmic matter; some one-tenth the size of the craft; others ten times its size. Unlike Ryan, she never flinched, cringed, or gasped at the near misses; for her, it seemed to be just another day at the office. A horrifying minute passed and the shiny, streaking ship, barely evading a flaming meteor, blasted out the opposite end of the galactic worm in an explosion of multicolored sparks. A chart of a star system appeared on her dome and with ease and experience, she waved her hand, setting a new interstellar course across the alien galaxy.

Ryan laid his head back on the dome lid and resigned himself to his fate, knowing that he would miss his birthday party: a nice quiet evening back on Earth, dining on his favorite meal, blowing out candles, and eating birthday cake with his wife and son. Tears ran down his cheeks as he thought about Summer and Justy living their lives never knowing what happened to him. His wife, crying, wondering, speculating, unable to move forward with her life, hoping, he would return someday. His son, missing his daddy, trying to understand, wishing he had a dad to play catch with, wrestle with, and go fishing with. No celebrating Christmas, Easter, and Fourth of July. No birthdays, anniversaries, or graduations. No little brother or sister for Justy. Ryan would never again see his brother and sister, parents and grandparents, nor his friends and coworkers. All of them, back on Earth, a distant planet in another galaxy. He had no means of return, no way to communicate, and no hopes of ever seeing Earth again. He drew in a deep breath and sobbed as the ship rocketed across the black, star-blotted fabric of the universe abounding with clusters, constellations, quasars, comets, and nebulas.

Another minute passed. He wiped away his tears as a planet appeared on the she-being's data-dome and the ship changed trajectory and slowed, preparing for entry into a colossal space station orbiting a brown, thirsty planet.

He saw on her screen the real-time view of the space station. The huge, gleaming ship, the size and shape of a superdome stadium revolved slowly, revealing countless portals and docking stations. Amongst innumerable flashing lights, he saw windows and through the windows, he saw short beings in shiny spacesuits. All around the small spaceship in which Ryan rode, similar crafts (some larger, others smaller) entered into a docking bay or exited into space. His craft approached slowly, carefully, precisely, and within a few seconds, it alighted at a docking station, the domes lifted into the ceiling, the door opened, and the ramp slid down.

The she-being and Ryan climbed out of their seats and departed the craft to stand in a voluminous, oxygen-filled hanger. He peered across its vastness and saw five, silvery beings, hustling soldier-like in a V-formation toward him. Again, he thought, *I'm so totally screwed.*

The she-being glared up at him and said in a much calmer, but still angry, audible voice, "They are coming for you, Earth-man. You will now face justice for killing our great star pilot."

Ryan whined again, "It was just an accident and I'm very—" and again, she raised her fist, silencing him.

Another spaceship, larger than the one Ryan arrived in, landed at a docking station next to them. Its hatch opened, its ramp slid down, and two luminous beings stepped out with a third being in-between them. Ryan gawked at this third being. It had the same elongated, smooth head as all the others, but did not wear an iridescent spacesuit. Shocking to Ryan, this being was dressed in blue jeans, a black sweatshirt, and white sneakers. It had pale blue skin, short stature, lanky limbs, skinny neck, small nose with two small nostrils, lipless mouth, and the same cat-like eyes, plus without wearing its shiny suit, two small ear holes could be seen. Also odd, this he-being looked strikingly muscular, like maybe, he was the *Mr. Universe* of their universe. His sweatshirt stretched across his barrel chest of defined pecs and abs, and squeezed his bulging biceps while his tight jeans exhibited his firm buttocks and thick quads. Like the rest of his kind, he still sported a rangy neck, skinny forearms and lanky lower-legs.

Suddenly, the swank alien glanced directly at Ryan, winked an eye as if they shared a secret, knocked down one shiny escort, tripped the other, and bolted toward Ryan. Before the V-formation of aliens, now running, reached Ryan, the cotton-clad being, raced up to him and yelled in English using a deep commanding voice, "Back into the ship!"

The she-being, trying to stop the defiant he-being, leapt into a freakish, karate stance and started twirling her long, skinny hands above and around her head using some sort of alien mind-bind on him, but he stepped up, twirled his hands in the air and put a mind-bind on her, causing her to cease and stand at attention. She started to screech, but he raised his fist into the air and instantly silenced her.

Ryan dashed up the ramp, hustled into the spaceship, and jumped into his seat as the dome lowered around him. The buffed-out alien in the Wal-Mart clothes followed, raised the ramp, shut the door, dove into the pilot's seat, lowered its data-dome, revved up the craft, undocked, and launched out of the space station's portal; all in less than ten seconds.

Ryan, impressed, raised his eyebrows and exclaimed, "Sweeeeet!"

On the data-dome's screen, Ryan watched in real-time, two vessels launch out of the space station behind them. The screen changed to navigational data and the stylish he-being and Ryan zipped across the galaxy to back inside the squirming serpent tunnel where this top-gun alien, dodging fiery meteors and cosmic matter, flew superior to the she-being. On an upper section of the data-dome, there appeared the two radar bleeps of the chase ships, dodging obstacles of space matter as well. Suddenly, one of the pursuing ships hit a meteor and its blip vanished off the screen. The other ship remained in hot pursuit as both ships burst out of the squirming worm gate. Ryan saw a view of the Earth displayed on the data-dome and exhaled a deep sigh of relief, thinking, *Maybe, I'm not so totally screwed.*

The two ships evaded satellites, but after many close calls, the chase ship grazed a weather satellite, causing it and the satellite to spiral out of control, disintegrating to Earth in streaks of fire.

The spacecraft shuttling the he-being in tight jeans and Ryan re-entered the Earth's atmosphere, zooming over Mexico City, past Phoenix, beyond Los Angeles, and back to hover over the cornfield, whirring silently, camouflaged, mirroring the fog and the starry night. The domes slid up into the ceiling. Ryan and the alien climbed out of their seats, the door opened, the ramp slid down, and they stepped down to stand amongst the fallen cornstalks.

The alien faced Ryan and peered up at him. In the starlight, Ryan saw the he-being's cat-like eyes twinkle and his slit for a mouth shift into a grin and the being said in his Earth voice, "I have brought you home to the precise coordinates of where you were abducted."

"Thank you so much," gushed Ryan, "but why on Earth did you help me?"

"I only have a minute," stated the alien, "but hopefully, if I explain it to you, you will be my friend and keep my existence secret."

"First, you rescued me, saving my life, so I owe you. Second, I'd sound crazy telling other people about you."

"Okay," said the alien. "I was once an extraterrestrial from another world, however, now, I am an inhabitant of Earth, for this planet, your home, is now my new home. You and I are now brother-terrestrials. That is why I rescued you."

"How'd you wind up on our planet to begin with?"

"I am a star pilot and not long ago, on a solo mission to Earth, my ship crashed. Although, injured, I immediately vaporized the ship and waited rescue. With my face shield damaged, I feared I would suffocate. After a few hours of labored breathing, my body adapted to Earth air. While waiting, hidden in an old barn, I was discovered by an Earth woman. My world frowns at contact with any humans unless there is a plan to abduct them. She did not fear me, but found me fascinating and kept silent the secret of my existence. I had studied Earth languages for many years and spoke English very well, so while she doctored my wounds, we talked of the differences and similarities of our worlds. She shared of her lonely life and I spoke of mine. Her mate had died and I had always been too busy as a star pilot traveling the universe to find one. During one of our many conversations, she told me that Earth men found her ugly and boring, but I found her exotic and remarkable. Eventually, she invited me out of the barn and into a guest room at her farmhouse. It was very comfortable and I felt at home like never before. We spent many nights eating delightful Earth food, especially, what is called *pizza*, and listening to older, romantic Earth songs sung by a man named Frank. I fell in what earthlings call 'love' with her. Interplanetary relations are forbidden by intergalactic law and punishable by life in prison."

Ryan listened, his eyes wide in the starlight.

"One night," the he-being continued, "after we drank many containers of fermented barley and hops, she invited me into her bedroom, where I committed the supreme crime of the universe; a severe offense in my world, because, I am an alien to this world from where she originated. We made 'love' and it was glorious, but now she is with my child."

"You had sex with her?" Ryan asked. He visualized the nude, blue, muscle-bound alien with a naked, homely Earth woman and shuddered at the thought.

"Yes, we had sex," replied the alien. "Every day. Many times a day. On our planet, we simply interlock our bodies for procreation; it is quick and unfeeling, however, she showed me many pleasurable things and taught me that it is not only for producing offspring, it is fun too. We had infinite fun."

"So, she's going to have your baby?" asked Ryan, shaking his head in disbelief, imagining what the infant might look like with bluish skin, an elongated head, skinny arms and legs, a human torso, and sporting ears, lips, a nose, and hair.

"Yes, but if we are captured, the authorities on my planet will execute her, our baby, and me. On another night, when we were sleeping in our bed, a starship, hovering above the farmhouse, dispatched a scanner probe that entered through our open bedroom window. In a flash, the probe collected data, relaying it back to the ship that I was one of them, she was of Earth, and in her womb, our baby was both. We awoke at the flash of light and scrambled to flee. In the night sky, United States, military helicopters arrived. The craft streaked away pursued by them. We quickly packed supplies and escaped to hide in an abandoned cabin in the woods. The next night, I was on my way to prepare a remote hiding spot for us in a place called Montana when star pilots found me, captured me, and took me back to my galaxy for execution. You and I escaped and now, I will return to the exact coordinates of when I last saw her and hopefully, find her waiting for me. If we must, we will travel to another planet in another universe to find our peace and happiness. No matter what happens in this entire cosmos, I must be with my Rhonda."

Ryan smiled and exclaimed, "Wow!" shaking his head with amazement and then said, "My name's Ryan. What's your name?"

"My name in my language is too difficult for Earth people to pronounce, so Rhonda calls me Myway, after my favorite Frank song. Goodbye, Ryan and be careful what you say to your kind, for they may think you are crazy, but most importantly, keep an eye on the stars, for my kind may come for you."

"Okay, I will," said Ryan, "and Myway, thanks again for bringing me home." Reaching out a hand, Ryan gripped the alien's hand with the long spindly fingers and he shook it heartily, saying, "Welcome to Earth, my friend. Good luck!"

Myway smiled, shook Ryan's hand with a strong, squeezing grip, and said, "Thank you, friend."

Ryan stepped back and away from the ship. Myway spun and scurried up the ramp, the door shut, the craft whirred up into the night sky, and vanished in a streak of blue light.

Ryan tramped through flattened cornstalks, picked up his beaming flashlight, and made his way through the cornfield. He emerged onto the dark road, walked around to his idling car, climbed in, and shut the door. The warning dings stopped. He looked on the floor, spied his cell phone, picked it up, and started to call his wife, but decided not to call her and just hurry home. He glanced at the clock in the dash; his abduction to an alien galaxy and his return back to Earth had taken only twenty-four minutes. Twelve minutes there and twelve minutes back. Insane. He shifted the car into drive and drove in the patchy fog the rest of the way home.

Justin, bouncing on the sofa by the window, waiting, peeking through the blinds, saw his daddy's car pull into the driveway of their country home. He leapt off the couch and ran to tell his mommy.

Summer expected Ryan much earlier and though wondering why he was late, she quickly lit the candles on the birthday cake.

Ryan, pondering his intergalactic experience, sat silent in his car for a half of minute, then, shut off the car, climbed out, and shuffled up the walk to his front door illuminated by the porch light. He turned the doorknob, stepped inside, closed the door behind him, and gasped, cringed, and blurted out, "Oh, my God!" while recoiling, horrified, up against the door as a short alien in a shiny spacesuit attacked him. The iridescent being wrapped its arms around him and clutched Ryan's waist. Ryan couldn't believe that the extraterrestrials had returned for him so soon.

The squatty alien hugged Ryan and hollered with excitement, "Daddy, daddy, you're home!" Justin shoved his reflective, alien mask up onto his head and said, "It's me, Daddy. Don't be afraid."

Ryan peered down at the smiling face of his son who was dressed in a silvery, alien costume.

"Do you like my Halloween costume, Daddy?" asked Justin, grinning.

"You bet, son," he said, chuckling uneasily, "it looked so real, you scared me."

Justin giggled with delight and said, "I'm wearing it tomorrow for trick-or-treating."

Justin ran over and climbed into a chair. Summer stood next to him. Together, smiling, they held the birthday cake with the flaming candles. They both broke out singing Happy Birthday with Justin singing off key at the top of his lungs.

Ryan, looking weary and disheveled, grinned as a tear ran down a cheek.

At the end of the song, Justin whined, "Daddy? What's the matter? Don't you like our surprise?"

"I love your surprise, but most importantly, Justy, I love you and mommy. I'm just very happy to be home."

Summer studied her husband's face and asked, "Ryan, what's the matter? What happened to you?"

"I'll tell you later, hun," he muttered, wondering if he should tell her the truth, bringing her fear or should he just fib to protect her, telling her that he had hit a coyote, putting a dent in the car's grill and bumper. He walked over to the flaming birthday cake illuminating the happy faces of his darling wife and adorable son, made a silent wish to be always near them, and blew out the candles.

THE SCREAMING SKULLS

A bloodcurdling scream pierced the dead silence of the frosty, autumn night. From inside the wrought-iron gates of the secluded cemetery, from deep within a forgotten grave, and from the inescapable darkness of a rotting casket—the scream rang out. It was a blaring, manful scream, sopped with desperation, dripping with horror. A flock of crows, roosting in the gnarly branches of an ancient oak tree, cawed while scattering into the cloudless, moonlit night. A field mouse scurried down its hole beneath a pitted, granite marker and a barn owl perched on a towering tombstone spun its head backwards and stared unblinking at the grave. The resounding shriek lasted as long as a man's deepest breath and again there was dead silence.

I know, because I was there, hiding behind the oak tree, standing amongst the spindly weeds of a parched grave. It was just after midnight and just a moment before I heard the terrifying scream. By the eerie glow of the three-quarter moon, my eyes searched the small family graveyard and I saw it—the weathered tombstone of Perry William Wedworth. Though skeptical about the tale of the screaming skull, I hung around, watching, listening, panting with anticipation, hoping to hear a scream; praying I wouldn't. My breath billowed with condensation and though my teeth chattered, I was as still as the corpse beneath my feet. An icy gust of wind, like a congregation of rioting spirits, moaned through the tombstones, swirling fallen leaves as it passed. I flipped up my coat collar. Something brushed my leg and I jumped! In my fright, I imagined that it was a bony hand escaping from the grave beneath me, but to my relief, it was a gangly, dried-up dandelion rustling in the wind. How ridiculous, I thought, to be all alone and chilled to the bone in a dark, mournful cemetery, anxiously waiting for the dead to scream. I glanced at my wristwatch; the foretold time for the scream had passed. The screaming skull story was bogus, so I turned and took a step to leave, but then, I heard a man's muffled cry and froze in my footsteps. My watch must have been fast. I whipped back around and again focused on Perry Wedworth's grave. The smothered yell grew louder and louder until it blasted through the suffocation of dirt and blared like a siren into the soundless night. My eyes widened, every hair on my body raised on end, and just when I wondered if the pealing scream would ever stop—it ran out of breath and ceased. My eyes scanned the cemetery; not a living soul to be seen. If it had been a prank, it had been a damn good one. I'd heard the scream with my own frostbit ears; the outrageous tale was outrageously true. More important, as a freelance writer, I had an intriguing story; the kind of story I like to write; the type of story my readers like to read; a money-making story to buy some groceries and pay my past due rent; and a story worthy enough to place below its title, my name, Newton Cuff.

With the creep show over, the startled crows alighted back into the oak, the timid mouse stuck its twitching nose out of its hole, the stoic owl twisted its head to the front, and I hurried the hell out the squeaky gates, dove into my car, and locked the doors. With the engine running, the heater blowing, and the dome-light on, I scrawled down some notes in my pocketsize, writing pad. I then shifted my decade old, blue *Jeep Cherokee* into reverse, whipped it around, dropped it into drive, spun the tires, and raced away from the dead-end at the graveyard. Just past the cemetery, I glanced out my window at the scowling, century-old Wedworth estate waning up on the stark hill. The collapsed hay barns, the toppled feed silo, and the condemned two-story, wooden house all looked like spooky, sideshow attractions to the haunted cemetery. A 'possum darted onto the road in front of me. The ugly beast, trapped in the headlights, bared its teeth and hissed at me. I had had enough of being creeped out, so I swerved around the animal, punched the accelerator, and sped like a bootlegger pursued by the cops back down the two miles of deserted dirt road, turned right on the dark, two-lane highway, and hauled-ass down the ten miles of winding road back to the California foothill town of Mariposa. Once inside my *Super 8* motel room, I jotted down some more notes, ate one of my crunchy peanut butter and apple jelly sandwiches from my travel stash of twenty p.b. & js and washed it down with a glass of tap water. I'm broke for now, but no sympathy needed—I like p.b. & j sandwiches. To resurrect my mind from the grave, I watched a few minutes of *Comedy Central*, laughed a couple of times, and zonked off to sleep.

The next morning, I awoke to the enchanting sounds of shouting truckers and their noisy, idling diesels. I checked the Internet on my laptop regarding the wedding and funeral of Perry Wedworth, but found nothing. I ate another p.b. & j, washed it down with a cup of jarring, motel-lobby coffee, and stepped outside. The sun beamed bright, so I slipped on my sunglasses, but the air was cool, so I jammed back into my room for my jacket and then walked down a block and crossed the street to the local newspaper, the *Mariposa Gazette*. I followed some nerdy guy carrying a pink box of donuts through the front door. He set the box down on a counter top and went directly to his desk. I grabbed two donuts: the maple *and* the chocolate bar, and headed down the hallway to a door that read, *Archives*. The department didn't open to the public for fifteen more minutes, so while I waited, I ate my donuts, flipped back in my writing notes from a couple of weeks ago, and thought about the night when I had first heard the dubious story about the screaming skull.

It was on a Wednesday evening, my twenty-seventh birthday, when I had left my small rented loft above an antiques store in the California beach town of Cayucas and cruised a half-hour inland to the picturesque wine region of Paso Robles where I stopped by my folk's house for my birthday dinner. Mom made me my favorite meal: fried chicken, green beans, and real mashed potatoes.

My dad, 5'11" and 180 pounds with thick, dark hair and blue eyes, who I'm a younger more muscular mirror image of, said to me, "Remember son, every birthday, you look more and more like me."

"Yeah, Dad," I joked, "but you got to remember—every year you keep looking more and more like Grandpa."

We finished dinner, Mom and Dad sang me Happy Birthday, and I blew out the candles. I ate a hefty piece of birthday cake, told my folks I loved them and they told me, and then, I headed to downtown Paso where I parked my car across the street from *Pioneer Park* and walked a half block to the *Hair-Trigger Saloon*. My college buds, Denny, Tommy, and Eddy were already inside the bar and on their second pitcher of beer. We're not cowboys, in fact none of us have ever ridden a horse, but at the *'Trigger*, the beer is cheap and ice cold. The place was like most cowboy bars: a long sticky bar with brass trim, a nonchalant bartender, bowls filled with cheap, crunchy snacks, a few tall tables with barstools, a wide-open back door, two ragged pool tables, a smelly bathroom, and country-western stuff hanging on the walls. An old jukebox only played two kinds of music: Country and Western. My friends wished me a happy birthday as I grabbed a frosty mug, filled it with beer, and started chugging to catch up.

A few brews later, a leathered old-timer, a former rodeo bull-rider by the name of KaBob, slid off his stool at the end of the bar and limped over to our table. He walked bowlegged with a tilt to the left side and sported a wide, tobacco stained, jack-o-lantern smile with a few teeth missing. He wore a soiled, straw, cowboy hat with his silver hair hanging down to his shoulders, a long-sleeved, plaid shirt buttoned up to his neck, faded blue jeans with a large gleaming belt buckle, and a scuffed-up pair of rattlesnake boots. He was a regular at the *'Trigger*, we knew him well, and he was an interesting character. His name was simply Bob, but he had been nicknamed KaBob after a bull named *Destruction*—one of the meanest bulls on the Pro Rodeo circuit—skewered him with a chipped horn. After his near fatal injury, he worked the chutes and followed the rodeo around the country until he retired in Paso Robles.

KaBob dragged a stool from another table up to ours and asked, "How you fellers doin'?" Without waiting for a reply, he said, "Newt, I gimped over here to wish'ya, Happy Birthday."

I replied, "Thanks, KaBob."

"I also wanted to tell'ya some stories so you can write'em down. One story I had in mind is about screamin' skulls and the other is about my amigo, Drive-up Bubby—a five hundred pound hero, who toured America in a modified VW bug. I ain't got time to tell'ya both 'cause if I'm late gettin' home, my mangy-mutt, Bite-u will start barkin' and sure enough wake-up the whole gol-darn trailer park. The tale of Bubby is gonna have'ta wait, cause I'm commencin' to tell'ya about the screamin' skulls."

"Bring it on, KaBob," I said, filling his empty mug with cold beer, "tell us a tale."

KaBob guzzled a few swallows of beer, wiped the suds from his gray stubble with the back of his rawhide hand and said, "Thanks for the beer, son," and speaking in cowboy twang, began his story.

"Back in '58, I was a strappin', twenty-four-year-old wrangler out at the Wedworth's cattle ranch. I was tough as tires. The spread covered five square miles of range between Mariposa and Bootjack in the Sierra foothills about fifty miles from Yosemite. Most of my days were chock-full of cow-pies, rattlesnakes, and barb wire. For supper, I mostly ate pork and whistle-berries with slices of skunk eggs."

"Whistle-berries? Skunk eggs?" Denny inquired.

"You know, pork and beans," said KaBob, "with cut-up onions. So listen up you tinhorns—I lived in a twenty-foot tow-trailer smack-dab between the Wedworth's ranch house and the family cemetery. The homestead had been in the Wedworth clan for over a hun'ert years, so there were about fifty graves out in that graveyard. In the dead center of that boot-hill stood an old oak tree packed with cawin' crows. Believe you me, I hated them noisy, damn birds. Now, you tenderfoots probably think livin' next to a cemetery was creepy—well hell, it was—and then it got creepier, once I heard the screamin' skull."

"You heard a screaming skull," I said incredulously, "in the cemetery."

"Yep, I heard a screamin' skull," Kabob stated with confidence, "in the cemetery."

"Who screamed?" asked Eddy.

"It was Perry Wedworth's head—only his head—that was hollerin'—hollerin' from a deep, dark grave."

"Only his head?" asked Denny.

"Yessir—only his head."

"Why only his head?" asked Tommy.

All of us at the table had a screwy look, wondering, *why only his head?*

"Just mind your beers boys," said KaBob, "and I tell'ya. I first heard the scream on a frigid, October night—the night of that god-awful, sad day when the Wedworth's had to bury their only son, Perry. It had only been three days before, when I had gone to the weddin' of Perry Wedworth and Cindy Goode. Ever' since kindygarten them two youngin's had been smitten with each other and even as little whippersnappers had vowed to get hitched. Over all them years growin' up, ever'where you looked, them two were holdin' hands. They were good kids and folks all over the county loved'em. He'd been the star quarterback for the Mariposa Grizzlies—the high school football team that went all the way to the state championships and she had been head of the chearleadin' squad as well as singin' solos ever' Sunday in the First Baptist Church. Hell, Perry could chuck a football sixty-yards and hit his receiver in the numbers ever'time and Cindy, goodness, gracious that purty little gal sang like an angel. Well, not long after them kids graduated from high school, they got married on a bone chillin' October night. Since Perry's father, John, my cow-boss at the time, was a well-to-do rancher and Cindy's dad, Bill, was the Baptist preacher, well hell, most of the county showed up at Perry and Cindy's weddin'. Now, since both them kids were the only children of their parents, their weddin' was all out fancy with one-hell-of-a reception. I ain't never seen the likes of such a joyful celebration since. After the newlyweds cut the cake, a country band named *Hog-tied*, fired up and everyone started two-steppin'. I danced as if I had fire ants in my skivvies. It got to be after eleven when amidst flyin' rice, the newlyweds jumped into Perry's '55 Chevy Bel Air and what a beaut' that car was: a red and white, two-door hardtop with a wax job so shiny, you could see yourself to comb your hair. They sped off down the road, plannin' on stayin' the first night of their honeymoon in 'Frisco and then flyin' to How-why-ya the next day. Well, on that fateful night, as they drove down highway 140 out of the hills and then steered north on the 99 at Merced, a truck and trailer rig was headin' south on the 99, haulin' half-inch thick sheets of steel bound for *No-Theft Safe and Vault Manufacturing* down in Fresno. *No-Theft's* production had stopped, waitin' for that steel, so the truck driver had driven all the way to San Joe-see to get it and bring it back the same long day. Just as Perry and Cindy decided to give each other a long smooch, the truck driver fell asleep at the wheel, veered across the median, woke up, panicked, and jackknifed his rig across northbound traffic, smack-dab in front of Perry's Bel Air. When the lovebirds' kiss smacked and they looked out the windshield, the sideways truck was point-blank. Perry slammed on the brakes. The trucker looked down and saw a screamin' young man wearin' a tux and sittin' right next to him, a screamin' young woman in a white weddin' gown and veil. On impact, the strappin' on the load broke and a sheet of half-inch thick steel slid off the top of the stack, slammed onto the hood of the Bel Air, raked through the car's windshield, sheared off the dashboard, sliced through the steerin' wheel, and ....."

KaBob abruptly stopped talking, raised his mug of beer, and chugged down half of it like he was trying to swallow something stuck in his throat. I filled his mug again. He cleared his throat and continued.

"Well, in a flash, them sharp edges on that thick, metal sheet cut-off the heads—" Kabob snapped his fingers twice, "of both screamin' newlyweds."

Denny, Tommy, Eddy and me listened with our mouths opened, mugs suspended in the air, ready to take a drink, but not taking a drink.

"You might think I'm lyin'," spouted KaBob, eyeballing our twisted faces, "but it's true. Then the car's top, the shattered glass, and the severed heads—Perry's with a black bow-tie still strapped under his chin and Cindy's still wearin' the white weddin' veil, landed on the asphalt as both vehicles exploded into a fiery ball. The truck driver bailed safely out of his cab as Perry's body in the tux and Cindy's in her weddin' gown incinerated in the hot, molten fire."

Kabob took another thirsty drink of his beer, became somber, and in a low, respectful voice, said, "Everyone in the county mourned their deaths and most of those folks attended their double funeral held at the First Baptist Church. Cindy's father gave the eulogy. I'll never forget all the loud, wailin' grief. The Wedworths and the Goodes both wanted to bury the heads in the same casket, but the Wedworths demanded that they be buried in the Wedworth family cemetery while the Goodes insisted that the heads of the newlyweds be buried in their family plot in the town cemetery. The parents argued without resolution until they finally agreed that Perry's head would be buried in a separate casket in the Wedworth cemetery and Cindy's would be buried ten miles away in the town cemetery."

"They should have buried them together," I said.

"You're darn-tootin'," spat KaBob, "What they did, didn't make no sense a'tall. Since Perry and Cindy had been sweethearts since kindygarten and they were betrothed, they would have wanted their heads buried together. Well, every night since, beginnin' with that first dreadful night after the funeral and I suspect to this very day, at eight minutes after midnight, the exact time of their deaths, there's a bloodcurdlin' scream comin' out of Perry's grave. Well, way back then, with me bunkin' out in my trailer next to the cemetery, it wasn't too many nights of hearin' that scream that I quit the Wedworth ranch. Workin' the Wedworth ranch had been a good ride, but it was time to vamoose. That's when and that's why I started my rodeo profession ridin' bulls. Since then, I've heard cowboys scream after a bull stomped their nuts, but none of them painful screams could out scream that terrifyin' scream that arose from that grave."

KaBob stopped talking and shuddered as if someone had poured ice water down his back. Denny, Tommy, and Eddy rolled their eyes at the suspicious story. I believed him.

"I never went back to the ranch or that ghostly cemetery," said KaBob. "Perry's folks, the poor souls, every night could hear the ghastly scream of their only son. Eventually, Perry's mother, Joan, wound up in a crazy ward down in Merced where she died a few years later of a broken heart and his father, John, stayed on at the ranch until he died of a heart attack not long after Joan died. Ol' Wace Needles, another Wedworth ranch hand, my best good buddy and one hell of a bullfighter, found John's body sprawled out on top of Perry's grave. John had started diggin' his son up when he collapsed and died with his shovel in his hand. Both of Perry's folks are buried in a double grave next to him."

"What happened to the ranch?" I asked.

"Perry had been the last of the Wedworths and the only heir to the ranch. With him dead, the cattle were auctioned and the ranch sold for chicken-feed, but because of Perry's screamin' skull, the house was never lived in again. Eventually, it fell into disarray and it was finally condemned. Accordin' to his will, John Wedworth bequeathed the money from the cattle, land, and house to build a new sanctuary for the First Baptist Church. I recollect that the Goodes, both Bill and Wanda are gone too, buried next to Cindy. What I told'ya might sound crazy fellers, but it's true, and Newt, you're welcome to write it if you want. I got'ta git." He snatched a can of *Grizzly* wintergreen chew from his shirt pocket and put a pinch under his lower lip. He then slid off his stool, said, "Thanks for the beers," tipped his hat, and limped out of the bar.

An elderly voice said to me, "Good morning sir," and my wondering mind left the *Hair-Trigger Saloon* and returned to waiting at the door to archives at the *Mariposa Gazette*. I wiped the maple and chocolate icing off my face with the back of my hand and said, "Good morning," to a grandma looking woman with a Helen nametag pinned to her pink sweater that she wore over a long, pink dress. She wore thick, bi-focal glasses with oversized, pink frames and she had twirled her long, gray hair into a bun with a rosy-pink hairpin to keep it on top of her head. She unlocked and opened the door. We entered a large, drab room with its bare walls lined with wide, metal, file cabinets.

"Let me set my pocketbook down," she said as she set it on her desk. "Now, how can I help you, young man?"

"I need to find information," I said, "on the wedding and deaths of Perry Wedworth and Cindy Goode—October 1958."

"Oh my. Really? Perry and Cindy Wedworth. For goodness sake, those names haven't come up for a long, long time, but I know which cabinet the newspapers are in." She shuffled directly over to the cabinet, slid open the drawer, and like a magician pulling a rabbit out of his hat, retrieved the newspapers. She handed me the old, yellowed papers and said, "Someday, I'll have all these old papers transferred into the computer, but for now, handle them as little as possible."

"Thank you so much," I replied. "I'll be very careful." I sat down at a table next to her desk and laid out the four dailys in front of me. They covered the day of Perry and Cindy's wedding announcement, the day of their wedding and deaths, the day of their obituary, and the day of their funeral. I read every article about them and wrote in my notepad all the info I needed on family history, dates, times, and burial plots. Strange thing, I couldn't seem to take my eyes off their wedding photos. Perry had a chiseled, handsome face with a slight cleft in his chin, compassionate blue eyes, and wore his sandy hair in a crewcut. Cindy was petite, Hollywood gorgeous with curly blonde hair, twinkling green eyes and a perfect smile. Beyond their good looks, they just looked so incredibly happy. Their love for each other leapt off the page and shot me right in the heart. When I read about their death and funeral, I felt the grief and nearly shed a tear, and then, I got pissed, thinking, *how could fate steal them away from each other at their moment of bliss?*

I asked the matronly woman, "Helen, did you live in Mariposa at the time of the their wedding and funeral?"

"I did," she replied as her smiling face collapsed into sadness. "I attended their beautiful wedding and then, three days later—" she sniffed, pulled a pink embroidered handkerchief out of her purse, dabbed her nose, and continued, "three days later, I attended their sad—very sad funeral. They were such a lovely couple. Over all of my life, I've never seen two people more in love than those two. When they were growing up, no matter what was happening in this little town, whether a pizza party, an ice cream social, a birthday party, a dance, or a church meeting, those two sweethearts were never apart. Horrible shame they died how they did and at the time they did—it being on their honeymoon and all. Also a pity—it just didn't seem right that those two lovers …," she turned her hanky over and dabbed her teary eyes, "were buried in separate graves."

Helen told me all she knew about Perry and Cindy and their incredible love for each other and by the time she finished, I damn near needed to borrow her soggy hanky. I thanked her and left the Gazette, grabbing a glazed donut as I walked out the door. Hoofing it back to my motel, I kept thinking, life's not fair, which most people agree on, but what I couldn't accept was that for Perry and Cindy, life had been murderously mean. I couldn't just forget about it, go on my merry way, and write their story. I had to do something; for Perry; for Cindy; for love. Though their plight was ghostly and beyond the grave—I didn't care. Though graverobbing was a crime—I didn't care. All I cared about was helping find peace for the eternal souls of Perry and Cindy Wedworth. My quest: reunite the heads of the Wedworth newlyweds.

I arrived at my motel room and called KaBob on my cell phone. "KaBob. It's Newt. How you doing?"

"I'm always good as long as I'm still breathin'. I'd bet a three dollar bill that the screamin' skull's got you callin' me."

"You're right. I went out to the Wedworth cemetery and just like you said, just after midnight, at 12:08, Perry Wedworth screamed from the grave."

"Did it make you mess your skivvies?"

"Almost—but hey, I checked the story out at the Gazette's archives and I need your help."

"I know—I know. Bring a lantern, a pick, and some shovels."

"That scream—it's so horrible, so pathetic, so filled with anguish, we've got to help him."

"Since Perry was like a little brother to me, I'll help'ya ta help him."

"Great! How fast can you be here?"

"All I hav'ta do is unplug the electrical cord, uncouple the water hose, unhook the sewer line, and unchain Bite-u, and we'll hit the road."

"Can't you leave Bite-u chained to a tree in Paso Robles?"

"No, he's my pard. He's comin'."

I expected to see KaBob in five hours, but after I watched nauseating, daytime TV for six, KaBob arrived at my motel. Like he was dismounting a bullride, he sprung down out of his dented, chalky-white pick-up with the bulky camper shell on top, spit a brown splat of tobacco juice on the asphalt, and strolled over to me. Bite-u, his fuzzy, gray dog, leapt out of the truck, lunged at me, and nipped at my leg. I kicked the ornery mongrel in the teeth and he never tried to bite me again. The dog shook off its bruised pride and puttered over to a flowerbed of colorful pansies. The bowwow sniffed the dainty flowers, lifted its leg, peed on their bright pedals, sniffed again, squatted, hunched, and took a big, log-stacking dump on them. We jumped in KaBob's truck and while we headed out to the Wedworth cemetery, all three of us, including Bite-u whoofed down two p.b. & j. sandwiches each.

We rumbled down the curvy, two-lane highway, which in the daytime was incredibly scenic with all the crooked trunks of the wispy digger pines, the red and green leaves of the manzanita bushes and the stately black oak trees. The lonely dirt road leading to the cemetery wasn't so scary either, but what was bizarre, was that all the silky-black crows from the cemetery oak were lined up wing to wing on the weathered fence rail. They twitched their heads and ruffled their feathers, but not one of them cawed or flew away. With their beady black eyes, they silently watched us drive by. As we passed, KaBob cussed as Bite-u barked at every single one of them.

Arriving at the Wedworth ranch, Kabob gazed out at the ruins and muttered, "What a pity. That heap of rubble used to be a nice home." He pointed a leathery finger at a tall patch of weeds and said, "My roamin' bunkhouse used to be right over there just outside the cemetery. After a hard day ridin' the line', I'd be sleepin' like a baby, and then, like somebody tossed a pail of freezin' water on me, that scream would jerk me out of bed."

We arrived at the dead-end and squealed to a stop. I opened the door and Bite-u leapt out of the truck. The half-cocked mutt ducked under the gates and ran as if he was chasing a rabbit, directly to the grave of Perry Wedworth. While Bite-u yapped at the grave, we grabbed up the lantern, the pick and shovels, pushed open the gates, and hiked around the tombstones over to the headstone of Perry Wedworth. The flock of crows had left the fence rail, flew overhead in the darkening twilight, and roosted in the oak tree.

KaBob took hold of the pick as I took hold of the shovel. Bite-u sniffed around. KaBob spat some chew juice between two graves, eyeballed me like he was staring down a gunslinger, and asked, "You ready?"

I said, "Yes—No." If I had been that gunslinger, I would have dropped my gun and bought him a whiskey. "Well—yes, I'm ready."

"Let's dig," he said.

Pick, scoop, and toss. Pick, scoop, and toss. I accidentally pitched a shovel full of dirt on Bite-u and he growled. The sun slinked away and hid behind a foothill, so we lit the lantern. It was as cold and as quiet as the night before when I had been there alone. The only sounds were our heavy breathing, KaBob spitting, my teeth chattering, Bite-u sniffing and ever so often, the wistful hoot of an owl. Behind me, the lording oak tree with its bare branches full of crows was silhouetted against the three-quarter moon. Though we shivered and our hands were raw with blisters, we dug, racing against time to reach the casket before the bloodcurdling scream pierced our eardrums.

After a few hours of digging, KaBob said, "I'm plum tuckered out. We need to take a break, so I can fetch us some grub."

I kept digging. Ten minutes later, KaBob returned to the grave with a couple of forks and three plates of steaming, hot food. He set a plate on the ground for Bite-u and handed me a fork and a plate. I peered down at the food and inquired, "Pork and whistleberries with skunk eggs?"

"You bet'ya. Best chuck for toughin' out the cold. Keeps your belly warm and your rooter on fire."

"Much obliged," I said in KaBob speak, as I raked the pork, beans, and onions down my throat. Bite-u licked his plate halfway across the graveyard as we resumed digging. At ten minutes before midnight, there was a clunk with my shovel. We had struck wood. I checked my watch and knowing the scream was approaching fast, we kicked up our digging pace until we uncovered the top half of the coffin. The wood was rotten so we cracked it open with the edge of the shovel and peeled back the splintered wood. I checked my watch, seven minutes after midnight. One minute until scream time. I threw my shovel out of the grave and held the lantern closer. Both of us stood in the grave peering down at Perry's skull—just a skull—no decomposed torso dressed in a tattered, Sunday suit. The skull lay nestled into a blue velvet pillow. Time and bugs had picked it clean. Under his chin—a stiff, blood-soaked bow-tie. Although both of us had heard the scream before, we were still in denial that the skull would actually scream. So we waited. 12:08 ticked off, but nothing happened, but then, I remembered my watch was fast. Both of us sucked in a deep breath and exhaled slowly, trying to remain calm. The lower jaw of the skull dropped open and we watched and heard an intake of air as it drew in a long breath and then between the bare teeth of the skull and from deep within the dark hole of its mouth—the scream rang out. It started loud, grew louder, and without the wooden coffin and the heavy dirt deadening the sound, it was ten times louder than the night before. A cold wind crashed through the cemetery like a drunken bar fight and I shivered. I glanced at KaBob. He clenched his chew tight in his mouth and held his pick in the air ready to smack the skull into the afterworld if it did anything but scream. Bite-u, with his nose in the air, yipped and howled in concert with the skull. Cawing crows scattered into the night sky. An owl swooped in front of the glowing moon. Mice scampered about. I placed my hands over my ears and just when I thought I would scream— the scream stopped.

Bite-u kept howling, until KaBob yelled, "Bite-u! Shut-up!"

The dog yelped and with a wagging tail, kowtowed over to KaBob. The crows circled back to the oak tree. I reached down, grabbed up Perry's skull, and set it next to the grave. KaBob and I climbed out of the grave and I set the skull on top of the headstone. We started back-filling, which was a hell-of-a-lot easier than digging. We padded down the earth with the back of our shovels and kicked some dry leaves over it. I started to scoop up the skull, when I saw it draw in another deep breath. Both KaBob and I snapped, "What the hell?" and the scream started all over again. Again, the crows scattered, the owl swooped, mice scampered, and Bite-u howled. While Perry screamed, we loaded the lantern, the pick, and the shovels back into the camper. I returned to the grave, picked up Perry's screaming head like a football, tucked it under my arm, and ran out of the cemetery like I was running for a touchdown. KaBob, Bite-u, and me all covered in grave dirt dove into the truck. As KaBob started and revved up the engine, Perry's skull stopped screaming. I set it between us on the seat next to Bite-u growling at it.

Just as we turned around at the dead-end and sped away from the graveyard, Perry's skull started screaming again. It was unnerving. I tried to hold the skull's jaws shut, but it snapped at my fingers. With Perry's skull wailing, we sounded like cops with blaring sirens, chasing bootleggers down the dirt road.

KaBob tried calm persuasion, "Now, Perry, you're like kin to me. Like my baby brother. Ya'see, we're tryin' to help'ya, so maybe you could pipe down a bit."

Perry kept screaming.

KaBob had had enough racket, so he yelled, "Dagnabbit, Perry! Shut-up!"

Perry kept screaming.

When we made the fast turn off the dirt road and onto the highway, I swore KaBob's top-heavy camper was going to flip over and we'd skid down a slope into a tree. We whipped and bucked around the curves. KaBob gripped the steering wheel and cinched his cowboy hat down as if he was riding a bull. As we raced through the quiet town, lights snapped on in all the houses as Perry's hair-raising scream passed and awoke the residents. We arrived at the town cemetery, sped through the open gates, and screeched to a stop on a narrow, asphalt driveway in the middle of a century of graves. I jumped out of the truck and held Perry's skull in the air. KaBob and Bite-u stayed in the idling truck. Perry drew in the longest breath yet and let rip with an earsplitting scream. It was so loud, I feared it would not only wake the entire town, but also wake the dead. When Perry finally quieted, I heard a shriek, off in the distance, across the cemetery. It was a high-pitched scream. A woman's scream! Cindy's scream! Goosebumps covered my body. Bite-u jumped out of the truck and ran off. I chased after the dog over the nicely manicured grounds, zigzagging between headstones and monuments adorned with plastic flowers. In the moonlight, I saw Bite-u halt at a grave. He yapped and howled as a blaring scream rang out from it. As I, cradling Perry's skull, rushed closer to the noisy grave, both Perry's and Cindy's alternating screams grew louder.

KaBob drove the truck up the driveway and parked near the earsplitting grave. He jumped out of the truck, carried the lantern over and lit it. We saw the gravestone of Cindy's parents, William and Wanda Goode and next to it, the much older and weathered headstone of Cindy Anne Wedworth.

I set Perry's skull on Cindy's tombstone. KaBob and me dashed back to the truck and returned with the pick and shovels. Though we were cold and our hands were sore with blisters, we were by now experienced gravediggers, so we shoveled through the dirt like there was a piping hot breakfast and a cup of joe waiting for us in China. The entire time we dug, Perry screamed, Cindy answered, and Bite-u howled, giving both KaBob and me pounding headaches. We were about halfway down and I had just tossed a scoop of dirt out of the grave when I heard the blurp of a siren. I whipped around, peered out of the grave, and saw a sheriff's car pull up with flashing red lights. The patrol car stopped and captured us in a blinding spotlight.

"You men! In the grave!" an officer barked over his loudspeaker. "Throw down your shovels and come out with your hands up."

KaBob cursed under his breath as both of us threw down our shovels and crawled out of the grave. Bite-u ran and hid under KaBob's truck where he remained through the rest of the ordeal. The skulls stopped screaming.

In the midst of the spotlight, two silhouetted deputies, one tall and lanky, the other short and chubby, both with their guns drawn, walked toward us. One officer, the skinny one, mumbled in his country drawl to the other, "What do we got here? A Frankenstein thing or some kind of voodoo ritual?"

"No idea," replied the overweight deputy in a nasally voice, "but with that skull sitting on the headstone, they got to be up to no good."

The deputies stopped and stood a few feet away, sizing us up. KaBob spit a wad of chew and I worried what my parents would think about their graverobber son.

"What you boys up to?" asked the tall, thin officer.

"Was that a woman's scream we just heard?" added the stocky cop, who most likely ate a plate of biscuits sopped in sausage gravy every morning at the local diner.

I stretched my hands in the air like a captured criminal and asked, "Have you guys ever heard of the screaming skull of Perry Wedworth?"

"Yeah, but that's just hearsay," said the deputy with his biscuits and gravy belly hanging over his utility belt.

"And a long time ago," added the gangly officer.

"Well—" I said as I looked over at the skull of Perry and saw that he was drawing in a deep breath, "brace yourselves deputies, because the story is not just hearsay, but true, and not just a long time ago, but now!" Just as I finished speaking, Perry's skull let rip with a deafening scream. The trembling deputies pointed their guns at it. Both scrunched up their faces as if they were developing an excruciating headache. As soon as Perry's jaw slammed shut and he stopped screaming, Cindy's scream from the grave shattered the cold night air. The quaking deputies shifted and pointed their guns at her grave. When both skulls stopped screaming, I said, "You see, I'm Newton Cuff, a freelance writer and this is Kabob, an ex-bullrider who used to work for the Wedworths. We're trying to reunite Perry and Cindy and end their screaming torment."

"My word, the story is true," muttered the slender deputy.

"Tie me to a hog and roll me in the mud. It sure is," added the pudgy deputy.

A stream of cars with beaming headlights pulled into the cemetery. The piercing screams had woke-up the town folks and word had spread throughout the county. Men dressed in shotguns, women wearing bathrobes, and children with jackets over their pajamas surrounded the grave and they all held a flashlight. Helen, from the *Gazette* archives, stood there in her rosy slippers and a pinkish coat over her pink bathrobe. The nerdy donut guy stood next to her. Perry's skull in the spotlight of flashlights, screamed from its stage on top of Cindy's tombstone.

When people arrived and for the first time saw Perry's skull and heard the blaring screams, they panicked and backed away, but as they became used to them, some of them pitched in and helped dig. As soon as one digger became tired, another digger jumped into the grave and shoveled. It was only a short time before we reached the casket and removed the load of dirt from on top of it and around it. I climbed down into the grave and with just enough room for my feet, stood next to the coffin. All the bystanders crowded around the grave. Those up close watched in silent awe as those farther back in the crowd murmured, "What's happening?"

Deep in the grave, I glanced up into the bright beams and saw the contorted faces gawking down at me. I was about to open a coffin, a coffin with a skull, only a skull, a screaming skull like the one on top of the tombstone, crying out, demanding an eternal peace, a harmony, and a happiness that only their reunion could provide. I unlatched Cindy's coffin while both excited skulls screamed simultaneously. The lid was stuck closed, so KaBob climbed down in the grave and with our combined strength, we jerked on it.

The lid flew open and there was a loud gasp from the onlookers as numerous, crisscrossing flashlights converged on her skull. In the bright light, her skull rested, snuggled on a red, velvet pillow. Just like Perry's skull, insects and time had polished her skull too, but it was more petite than Perry's and she had perfect teeth. Her bloodstained, white veil encircled her head and cascaded alongside her cheekbones. She was almost pretty as far as skulls go. She looked peaceful, until her lower jaw dropped and she drew in a deep breath and let rip a spine-tingling scream. Everyone covered their ears with their hands. The sound unrestricted by velvet, wood, and dirt, echoed into the night. Perry's skull retorted with a scream as the wincing, chunky deputy handed him down to me. I placed the screaming skull of Perry Wedworth on the red velvet pillow next to the screaming skull of Cindy Wedworth. The skulls rolled in next to each other cheekbone to cheekbone. Best friends, lovers, husband and wife together now in death as in their short lives. Happy—they stopped screaming.

Again, for a moment, there was dead silence on the frosty, autumn night.

With KaBob and me still in the grave, we gently lowered the lid to the coffin, latched it shut, and climbed out of the grave. The young preacher from the First Baptist Church stepped in front of the speechless crowd. He had brown shoulder-length hair, a full beard, and standing there in his slippers and white bathrobe, he looked like a holy prophet. Breaking the silence, he cleared his throat and speaking loud enough for all to hear, he cried out, "Let us pray."

Everyone bowed.

"Dear Lord," the minister cried out, lifting his hands toward Heaven, "open the gates of your blessed kingdom and receive the souls of Perry William Wedworth and Cindy Anne Wedworth. The depth of their love was rare; a love beyond what most people will ever know, so I humbly ask that they be granted serenity, new bodies, and for the rest of eternity—they may sing and not scream. Amen."

The crowd echoed, "Amen," and then each town person stepped up, grabbed a handful of dirt, and tossed it on the casket. After the crowd dispersed, some of the men back-filled in the grave. The young preacher vowed that the church would purchase a new headstone with both Perry's and Cindy's name and dates.

KaBob, Bite-u and me rode back to my *Super 8* motel room. KaBob and Bite-u slept in his camper in the parking lot. In my motel room, I jotted down some notes in my notepad, took a long, hot shower, crawled into bed, and passed out.

The next day, in a special edition of the *Mariposa Gazette,* the headlines blazed: *The Screaming Skulls of Perry and Cindy Wedworth—Reunited!*

I wrote the short story, *The Screaming Skulls* and sold it to a magazine. It was an intriguing story; the kind of story I like to write; the type of story my readers like to read; a money-making story to buy some groceries and pay my past due rent. It was a story worthy enough to place below its title, my name, Newton Cuff.

A Pirouette of Souls

"Pleeease, Jason," begged Courtney riding in the passenger seat of their Saturn Astra hatchback, "don't get drunk tonight and embarrass me in front of my boss and coworkers."

"Stop nagging me!" snapped her husband Jason as the tires squealed around a tight mountain curve. "I've already told you a million times—I won't embarrass you."

"I'm still worried," she persisted. "If you'll recall at last year's Christmas party, you made complete fools of us. We were the office gossip for weeks." She flipped down the lighted sunvisor, checked her lipstick, and flipped it back up.

"Yeah, okay, I had a few too many last year," he said clenching his teeth, "but that's because your Drinkenstein boss was making passes at you all night."

Jason, thirty, almost handsome with brown eyes, dark, tightly trimmed hair and goatee, and mostly in shape except for a paunchy gut, sped through the next s-curve as the car's headlights swept past a forest of pines, shined on the mountain's granite face, and beamed back onto the double-yellow line of the two-lane road.

"He was *not* making passes at me," argued Courtney, twenty-eight, cute with blue eyes and short-styled, brown hair and petite with a shapely figure except for a bit of a ballooning butt. "He just gets friendly when he drinks, and Jason, please slow down on these curves. I'm getting carsick."

"I'm slowing down. Okay? Even though we're late and still

fifteen miles from the lodge. Anyhow, the drunken, old pervert didn't just get friendly, he tried to grope you every time you danced with him."

"He did not grope me!" she said, flushing with anger. "We were only dancing, but you—you had to go and make a pass at our bimbo receptionist, Ashley. "

"All I did was compliment her mini-skirt and besides, *she* was flirting with *me*."

"Then, why'd she slap you? Huh? And if that wasn't enough, while you were reeling from her slap, you stumbled and fell onto the dessert table. What an awful mess! The Christmas tree cake on the floor and you—you with that silly *I didn't do it* look on your face, standing in the middle of it, plastered with green frosting, and that little, peppermint ornament stuck to your forehead."

"That stupid cake had way too much frosting!"

"Then, while I wiped your face off with a napkin, you kept pointing and giggling like a bratty schoolboy at Bob's toupee. The poor man was mortified."

"It looked hilarious—like an old toilet seat cover."

"Real funny. Then, you snuck a bottle of tequila from the bar and chugged it while you danced like an idiot to that *Bee Gees* song."

"Hey, I was just stayin' alive."

"Oh really? Well, there's more! Then, you played your silverware like drum sticks on the table, plates, and glasses!"

"Cut me some slack! I was feelin' the groove."

"Stop being a smart aleck! And then, the worst thing you did—you peed on the shoes of old Fred, the bookkeeper!"

"That's because, he snuck up next to me at the urinal and I spun to see who it was."

"Oooh, you make me so mad!" she huffed, crossing her arms, turning away from Jason, and watching the roadside snowdrifts sparkle in the headlights.

"I'm sorry! Okay? I'm sorry," he growled. "I do stupid things when you treat me like crap! I was just trying to get your attention. That's all!"

Both sat silent for a moment thinking, knowing that their arguments were not really about Christmas parties, coworkers, and icy roads. Something more important bothered them, causing their emotional separation. Both loved each other and hated discussions leading to arguments, so they remained detached without addressing the real issue.

Jason asked calmly, "Remember, five years ago, right after we were married when you first started working at the company? We couldn't wait to come to this party. It was fun back then; the lodge, the Christmas decorations, the dinner and dancing, the nice bonus check, the woods, and you and me boinking each other's brains out in our cabin. Remember that morning when we just laid in bed and watched it snow outside? That was really cool. We were happy."

"I agree, it was fun and we were happy," said Courtney, looking again at her husband.

"We had a good time then," said Jason, "but the last few years, all we do is fight."

"That's because over the last few years, you've become a big jerk!" she said on the verge of tears. "And stop driving so fast, there's black ice on the road." She reached over to the heater control knob, muttered, "I'm cold," and turned up the heat.

They rounded a corner where the pine trees thinned and a panoramic view of the lake appeared. The distant, snowcapped mountains, a half moon, and a million glimmering stars reflected on the dark, frigid water. Lost in their argument, they didn't notice.

"I see the ice and I've slowed down," snapped Jason as the argument sped up, "and I can't believe you just turned up the heat when I'm boiling." He lowered his window a few inches, letting chilly air stream in and coldly explained, "I act like a jerk, because I know when we get to the party, you'll ignore me just like last year."

"When we get to the party, pleeease don't get drunk and act stupid!" whined Courtney. "And pleeease put up your window. I'm cold."

"You know, Courtney, you're becoming more and more like your nagging mom. I see the way she treats your dad; complaining all the time and never giving him any lovin'."

"My mom loves my dad! So don't even go there, but let's look at you—you're becoming a workaholic like your father. You started working for him right after we were married. That was five years ago. You work all day and into the night without as much as a small raise and when you finally do come home, all you do is drink beer and watch TV."

"Oh, please, you know I'm tired when I get home, and you know the company is struggling. To take from the company is taking from my folks. When dad retires, the company is ours. You hear me? The company is ours! I'm only paying my dues for now. I've got big ideas for our future."

"Whatever!" she said, crossing her arms and staring out the window.

"I hate it when you say that! You have absolutely no respect for me."

"Well, Jason, you have absolutely no respect for me."

"Oh, come on, now!" he yelled, pounding a fist on the steering wheel. "I listen to you moan and groan all the time. I try to make you happy. I work. I pay the bills unlike your unemployed, loser brother who depends on his wife's income."

"Leave my brother out of this!" screamed Courtney, glaring back at him. "And don't you forget that my income covers nearly half of our bills. Not to mention, I cook, I wash, and I pick up after you all over the house. You don't appreciate me at all, Jason!"

"Oh yeah?" growled Jason as he turned the heater knob

down. "Well, I bust my knuckles keeping our cars running. I mow the yard and I pick up after *your* damn dog. And another thing, I try like hell to be romantic. I barbecue every weekend, bring home your favorite girly wine, and watch those boring chick-flicks. I bring you chocolates and flowers and I'm always complementing how gorgeous you look. Yet, you still push me away. *You* don't appreciate *me* at all, Courtney!"

"If I push you away, it's because I'm exhausted from working all day or most likely, you've hurt my feelings by saying or doing something really dumb." She cranked the heater fan to high and yelled, "To tell you the truth, you'll never understand what I need!"

"When I hurt your precious little feelings, I always say I'm sorry. Don't I? Don't I? Besides, a wife shouldn't deny her husband sex! To tell you the truth!" he shouted, "y*ou'll* never understand what *I* need!"

Just as Jason stopped yelling and as Courtney crossed her arms and pouted, they rounded a hairpin curve. On his side towered a rocky hill. On her side loomed a steep slope studded with pine trees and a sheer, twenty-foot, drop-off into the chilly lake. On the shoulder of the road, caught in their headlights stood highway patrol officer, Trent Wilson throwing down a burning flare. Just beyond him was his patrol car with its red, yellow, and blue flashing lights and just past the patrol car was a white Buick LaCrosse smashed into a pine tree next to the road. The grill of the sedan wrapped around the tree as steam escaped from its damaged radiator. Its bright headlights illuminated the forest while its red glowing taillights jutted out onto the highway.

Black ice coated the road.

"What the …!" exclaimed Jason. Courtney gasped.

Coming out of the turn their Saturn ran over the glazed ice and launched into a three-sixty tailspin. Jason pumped the brakes and turned the steering wheel toward the slide but continued careening out of control. Across the ice, they twirled in a blur past the startled officer, his flashing patrol car, and the taillights of the crashed sedan.

"Oh nooo," moaned Jason. Courtney screamed.

Their car, captured in the headlights of the Buick, bounded off the road, slid over the snow-covered shoulder, soared between two tall pine trees, slammed onto the steep slope, vaulted off an earthy mound, and flipped into a deadly barrel roll.

Jason and Courtney screamed in horror and groaned in pain as their bodies whipped and banged inside the car. The airbags deployed punching them both in the face. The deafening sounds of crunching and twisting metal shattered the woodland silence.

As the car violently tumbled, the back bumper ripped off, the roof collapsed, and the hood flapped on its hinges. After nearly three crushing rolls, the vehicle catapulted off the embankment, plummeted twenty feet, and splashed upside down into the lake. The tires spun as the car's racing hot motor cast a cloud of steam into the frosty night.

Up on the shoulder of the road, Wilson, a veteran officer of twenty-two years, watched the car spin off the road, roll down the slope, and splash into the lake. He quickly tossed a second flare out around the curve in the road, raced back to his patrol car, and radioed for assistance. He opened the trunk, laid his utility belt and his revolver inside, grabbed a large flashlight and two thermal blankets, slammed the trunk, and dashed down the embankment to the lake.

Jerold and Vicki Brooks, the shaken, but uninjured, middle-aged couple in the smashed Buick, grabbed their coats, climbed out of their car, and followed the officer down the hill.

Another car approached the hairpin curve. Sisters, Lisa and Laurie Mercer, both in their twenties, both short and petite, and both wearing their blonde hair in a pony tail, were heading up the highway to their family's cabin when they saw the glowing flares. Lisa, the driver, slowly and cautiously rounded the curve. Both women peered out through the pines and saw the sinking car in a cloud of steam on the moonlit lake. Lisa parked on the shoulder behind the police car. The sisters grabbed their jackets and scrambled in the meager moonlight down to the lakeshore.

The crumpled Saturn bobbed for a few seconds and then sunk to the sandy bottom ten feet below. Escaping air bubbles ruptured the surface of the water warping the reflection of the snowcapped mountains, the half moon, and the glimmering stars.

Trapped inside the submersed car, both Jason and Courtney were conscious, but disoriented. As the frigid water rushed into their car, both sucked in one last breath. In the dark, Jason unfastened his seat belt, shoved the soggy airbag out of his face, and righted himself. The caved-in roof left him little room to maneuver. He reached over to help Courtney and felt her hands struggling to unfasten her seatbelt. Her crushed door had shoved her seat against the console blocking access to the buckle.

Courtney, still upside down and fighting her soaked airbag, tried to jerk the seatbelt loose. It remained fastened. She panicked, violently kicking and squirming. She felt Jason's hands trying to help her. Her lungs burned to take a breath. His lungs burned to take a breath.

Officer Wilson reached the cliff above the sunken car. Motorists, Jerold, Vicki, Lisa, and Laurie gathered behind him.

"You," Wilson ordered Jerold, "take my flashlight and shine it on the submerged car."

Jerold grabbed the flashlight and pointed it down into the water.

"You ladies," Wilson barked, as he pointed at an ice-covered, sandy spot, twenty yards down the shoreline, "Take these blankets and meet me over there. I'll try and get the people out of the car and swim them over to you." While ripping off his boots, he asked, "Do any of you know CPR?"

"We do!" replied Lisa and Laurie simultaneously.

"Good!" He turned and dove into the icy water. Jerold directed the flashlight on Wilson. The three ladies ran for the shore.

A bright beam of light pierced the dark water creating an eerie glow inside the sunken Saturn. Courtney wriggled free from beneath her seatbelt. She pushed the airbag away, righted herself, and held on to Jason. They held their breaths. Jason tried to push open the crushed doors, but they remained shut. They reached for the hatchback. Their lungs ached. The freezing water burned their skin. Jason found the handle of the hatchback and unlocked it. He tried to shove it open, but the weight of the upside down car kept it closed.

Wilson, swimming outside the car, tried the doors, but found them mangled shut. He stepped on the lip of the hatchback door and tried to pull up on the frame of the car. He ran out of breath, resurfaced, gulped in some air, and dove back down.

Courtney wrapped her arms around Jason and squeezed him tight as she ran out of air, thrashed a few seconds, and blacked out.

Wilson gripped the car's frame and tugged up on the car, lifting it just enough to insert his feet inside the hatchback and like a human Jaws of Life, he pried the door open. The front end of the car shifted in the sand and the hatchback opened wider.

Jason fought the overwhelming urge to take a breath. He wrapped an arm and his legs tightly around his wife and thrust his other hand out the open hatchback to the officer. He shook his head trying not to breathe. His oxygen-depleted mind screamed, *No! No! No! I don't want to die.* He succumbed, breathed in the cold water, and blacked out.

Wilson grabbed Jason's limp hand and pulled him along with Courtney out of the car. He kicked to the surface, thrust his head out of the water, and gasped for air.

"I've got them!" he shouted, his voice echoing across the

cold stillness of the lake. "I've got them both!" He rolled over on his back and cradling both of their faces above the water, he kicked toward shore. Up on the cliff, Jerold followed them with the beam of light. On shore, the ladies waited anxiously.

Above the sunken Saturn, in the faint, periphery glow of the flashlight, the ethereal, intertwined spirits of Jason and Courtney arose from the ripples on the water. Like a tranquil morning mist, their ghosts hovered just above the surface, slowly twirling in a pirouette of souls.

Jerold raced for the shore all the while shining the flashlight on Wilson swimming with the drowned bodies. At the lakeside, Jerold handed the flashlight to his wife Vicki and waded out a few steps into the chilly water to help Wilson. They dragged the limp bodies up on shore. The thin, icy snow crackled under their feet.

The wispy, woven souls of Jason and Courtney floated unseen over to the rescuers, stopped just short of the shore, and levitated, twirling together over the water.

As Wilson, shivering violently, and Jerold, with cold, wet feet, caught their breath, Lisa began CPR on Jason as Laurie began CPR on Courtney. They quickly rolled their victims on their sides, cleared their air passages, and began rhythmic rescue breaths and chest compressions. The lifeless bodies looked bruised and battered but there didn't seem to be any broken bones or deep lacerations. Vicki whispered a prayer while covering each victim with a blanket.

Suspended between two worlds—a world of mortality and a world of eternity—the ghostly spirits of Jason and Courtney celebrated a divine compassion for one another: an unconditional love void of trivialities and selfishness; a pure love stripped of stress and schedules; an exalted love teeming with patience, kindness, and gentleness; a perfect love, overflowing. The waltzing spirits waited, embracing, watching the valiant effort to save their bodies, but suddenly, they began to ascend into the starry sky and a portal of golden light appeared, dawning like the first starburst of sunrise, growing wider and brighter, inviting like the open arms of a grandfather, beckoning draw nearer, and they drew near, floating together toward the brilliant light, but then, they abruptly stopped, the portal vanished like the last starburst of sunset, and they twinkled as one star amidst a universe of stars while descending to the lakeshore to linger just above their lifeless bodies.

Unnoticed by the rescuers, the braided spirits of Jason and Courtney began to elongate as their vapory feet drew back into their bodies. Lisa and Laurie fervently continued CPR. Jerold and Vicki held each other and muttered prayers. Officer Wilson waited, hoping … minutes passed … and then, he moaned, "Okay, that's enough. They're gone. We did all that we could."

Lisa and Laurie stopped CPR, stood, and stared down at the bodies. Officer Wilson, Vicki and Jerold stared too. Jerold clicked off the bright flashlight. Faint moonlight lit their faces. A glistening tear ran down Vicki's cheek. All felt horrible over their failed attempt to save the couple. There was silence, except for sniffs and heavy sighs. A cold breeze brushed the lakeshore. Pine needles rustled. Ice crackled. The rescuers shivered.

The intertwined spirits of Jason and Courtney ebbed back into their drowned bodies. Life returned. Their hearts beat, their blood warmed, their skin glowed, as both raised their heads, choked, coughed the water out of their lungs, and gasped a long, life-saving breath.

Shocked, the rescuers took a step back, but then drew in close and knelt beside them. Jerold clicked on the flashlight and all peered at the faces of Jason and Courtney now flushed with the color of life.

"Save my wife," whispered Courtney barely audible. "Please … save my wife," and she again fell unconscious.

"What did she say?" asked Wilson, shivering from the cold.

"She said, 'save my wife'," replied Vicki.

"That's weird," said Jerold. "Are you sure she didn't say, 'save my life'?"

"She definitely said, 'save my wife,'" stated Lisa as Laurie nodded in agreement.

Jason, with his eyes still closed, coughed again, and moaned, "Where's my husband? Did you save my husband?" He too blacked out again.

"What did he say?" asked Wilson, not believing what he had just heard.

"He said, 'where's my husband? Did you save my husband?'" answered Vicki.

"That's weird," said Jerold again.

"Oh my," exclaimed Laurie.

"Man, that's strange," said Wilson.

"It sure is," said Lisa.

Both Jason and Courtney regained normal breathing, but remained semi-conscious. Officer Wilson moved in closer and said through his chattering teeth, "Both of you are out of your car and on shore. Hang on. Help is on the way."

Up on the dark highway, headlights and emergency lights appeared as an ambulance and another patrol car arrived on the scene. Flashlights lit up the woods. In less than a minute, two paramedics and another officer were at the lakeshore. They carried stretchers, blankets, and life-saving equipment. The paramedics checked for injuries and vital signs and hauled Jason while the two officers carried Courtney up the embankment.

Officer Wilson wrapped himself in a blanket and rode in the ambulance with Jason and Courtney out of the mountains down to the hospital. The other officer supervised clean up of the crash site. Additional patrolmen arrived. Vehicles traveling up or down the highway crawled past burning flares and flashing lights. A tow truck hauled away Jerold and Vicki's disabled Buick while an officer gave the shaken couple a ride up to their cabin. Lisa and Laurie continued up to their family's cabin. Courtney's company Christmas party was in full swing up at the lodge and her coworkers wondered why the couple had not arrived. The wrecked Saturn remained submerged while the quiet lake again reflected the snowcapped mountains, the half moon, and the glimmering stars.

At the hospital, Officer Wilson was treated and released for mild hypothermia. His worried wife brought him a change of clothes and drove him home.

Jason and Courtney stayed overnight at the hospital for observation. They didn't say much. Both slept peacefully. The next morning after additional medical tests, the doctors deemed them 'lucky' and released them. The couple's parents had stayed up all night in the waiting room and felt overjoyed that their kids were okay. Courtney's folks drove Jason and Courtney home, stayed a while, and feeling assured that the young couple were fine, they left.

Courtney withdrew to the bedroom and lay on top of the comforter on their king-size bed. Jason followed and lay next to her. They hugged for a long while. She cried. He cried. Face to face, they gazed at each other. He smiled. She smiled. Jason felt pain in his badly bruised shoulder and winced. Courtney felt his pain and winced too. Courtney touched a yellow-purplish bruise on her forehead and cringed. Jason felt her pain and cringed too.

"Jason," whispered Courtney, "I can't believe we're both alive. We were lucky, but I must admit—I still feel very, very weird."

"I feel weird too. Something bizarre happened at the lake. It was all so fast. I can't believe that both of us survived. You know, one of us could be planning a funeral."

Courtney hugged him tighter.

"It's horrible to think about," continued Jason, "so let's just be happy that we're still here for each other."

"Do you think we have brain damage from the lack of oxygen?" asked Courtney.

"No, babe, the doctors checked us out and said we were all 'good to go'."

"I don't feel like myself," she said. "I feel like I'm not only me, but—but you. I feel that I feel what you feel—and that you feel what I feel."

"Crazy, but I too, feel what you feel. I'm not just in your shoes; I'm in your body, mind, and soul. It's strange. I feel *your* happiness and *your* sadness. I want to laugh with you and cry with you."

"Me too, and I feel as though we're dancing; dancing as one."

The lovers lay together, hugging, kissing, and touching. They apologized with heartfelt sincerity for hurting each other. Their perfect love overflowed as their intertwined souls revealed each other's hidden fears and needs. They listened without any defensive or offensive attitude and they comforted each other with patience, kindness, and gentleness. They were deeply sorry that they had ever argued over Christmas parties, coworkers, each other's family, driving habits, money, household chores, and a dog. Full of humility, they asked each other for forgiveness, for they realized that compared to their love—all else was trivial. They thanked each other for all the good they give to the other. Respect and appreciation filled their hearts. He pledged to be a better husband and she promised to be a better wife. Most importantly, they forgave each other, they committed to meeting each other's needs, they again became best friends, and they vowed to remember always that they were given a second chance at life together. Their selfish selves and sinking relationship had drowned at the lake and they were brought back to life as changed people in a new relationship with a stronger bond.

As their souls and bodies hugged, Jason whispered, "There's something else that I feel you're feeling. You're worried about our marriage because you—you want a baby and I didn't realize just how important that is to you. I feel your soul bubbling with joy at the thought."

"Yes, ohhh yes, Jason," said Courtney, "I do want a baby; however, it's important to me—to us, that our relationship is strong and loving, and that we can provide for a baby. I feel that you want to start a family too. Your soul is smiling."

"Yes, I want a family too. I was just worried about being a good father and providing for us. I believe in us, as friends, as husband and wife, and as parents. In fact, I think we should begin making plans to start our family."

"That sounds wonderful and right now with your soul tickling mine," she whispered nearly breathless, "I desire you with all of my heart."

Jason rolled over on top of her and they kissed a long, wet, kiss. Soft lips; tender kisses. Touching tongues; passionate kisses. Hot breaths. Sighs. They paused for a moment, gazing into the other's adoring eyes and driven by raging desire, undressed each other and tossed their clothes on the floor. Both glanced out the bedroom window as both exclaimed, "Look, it's snowing outside!" They wrapped their arms around each other and pressed their naked bodies together. He felt her tremble. She felt his firmness. She understood his raging desire for her. He understood her deep need for tenderness. He whispered his devotion to her. She breathed her desire for him. Both wished to please the other. As one, their interlaced bodies and their crisscrossed souls made love unencumbered and uninhibited. Soft and slow: whispers and breaths. Hard and fast: shouts and sighs. They made love like first time lovers full of wonderment. They made love like long time lovers full of confidence. He felt what he felt but he also felt what she felt and she felt what she felt but she also felt what he felt. Hours passed as they ravaged each other's body with lust and love until both loudly climaxed in rapturous convulsions of ecstasy and at the peak of their pleasure—their wispy, ethereal souls untangled as each enlightened soul whisked back into its rightful person.

Jason and Courtney lay naked as one. They gazed for a long moment into each other's eyes while their heated bodies melted any lingering chills from the icy water of the lake. After their harrowing brush with death when their souls had danced as one, they became, quite literally, soul mates. The happy lovers sighed with contentment, crawled under the covers, cuddled in each other's arms, and watched the snowfall.

Mirror Me-Man

My life was fairly routine until three weeks ago on a Saturday morning around nine-o-clock. For breakfast, I wolfed down a crispy waffle sopped with maple syrup and gulped down a cup of coffee. My breakfast, however, had nothing to do with my undoing. You see, I am who I am but I am *not* who I am. I do my best *here* as I am certain I do my best *there*, even though, I know—no, *we* know—I am not one but two.

Before you think I'm crazy, hear me out. My name is Adam Twain. I'm thirty-two years old and I don't smoke, do drugs, or booze it up. Okay, once in awhile, I booze it up. I'm five-foot-nine, have brown hair and blue eyes, and I'm fairly in shape. I've been married to my sexy wife, Melanie for ten years whose thrilling hobby is piecing together picture puzzles. I play first base on a city-league softball team and watch a lot of baseball on TV. We have two kids, six-year-old Brandon and four-year-old Brittany who are exceptionally bright except at bedtime when they act like escaped monkeys from the zoo. We live in a small home in Paso Robles, California, we have a terrier named Barky that our neighbors hate, and for my job as a civil engineer, I draw plans for converting stop signs to traffic signals at busy intersections. Believe me, I'm a normal guy. Let me tell you what happened.

On that particular Saturday, while my wife cleaned the kitchen and the kids watched cartoons, I stood in my boxers at my bathroom sink and brushed my teeth. My reflection in the mirror looked rabid with toothpaste foaming out of my mouth. But, I wasn't rabid—remember, I'm not crazy. The bathroom, an extension of our master bedroom, had an enclosed tub and shower, a walk-in closet with a full length mirror hanging on the outside of its door, and a little private cubicle with a toilet and copies of Reader's Digest and Sports Illustrated. Sunlight filtered in between the blinds of a small window. I spit out the toothpaste and rinsed out my mouth, soaked my morning stubble with a hot, wet, wash cloth, slathered on shaving lotion and shaved, grabbed a hand towel hanging next to me, dried my face and hands, and hung the towel back on the rack. I then combed my hair, set the comb down, glanced in the mirror, and turned to leave, but stopped, spun back around, and again faced the mirror. Something had caught my attention. On my forehead, above my right eye, there appeared to be a pea-sized black dot. I leaned over the sink and scrutinized this new addition to my face. My reflection scrutinized me back. I tried to wash off the dot with the washcloth, but the dot remained. I examined it closer and determined the small alien blemish to be a mole. It looked harmless: round and black, not irregular or discolored. I raised up my hand and rubbed the mole with my index finger—but felt no bump. Odd. I looked again; felt again. My finger felt nothing. Bizarre. How could this be? A normal-not-crazy guy like me wakes up one morning with an invading mole that is seen but not felt. I quickly dressed in my weekend, yard-working clothes: a T-shirt, shorts, and grass-stained tennis shoes. I then hustled out of the bathroom, through the master bedroom, past my kids watching TV in the family room, and into the kitchen to see Melanie.

"Sweetie," I said, "will you look at something here on my forehead?"

She leaned over, loaded a dish in the dishwasher, stood up, and replied, "Sure. What is it?"

"Right here," I said, pointing at the spot where I'd seen the mole, "do you see a black mole?"

She stood on her tiptoes, examined my forehead, and muttered, "No hun, I don't see a mole."

"Are you sure?" I asked, pointing again, "Right here?"

She examined my forehead again and stated, "I'm sure of it. There's nothing there. No mole, sweetie."

"Okay. I thought I saw something. Thank you."

I gave her a kiss on her forehead. She grabbed up the waffle iron to clean as I strolled out of the kitchen, past the kids, through the bedroom, and back into the bathroom. I stood in front of the full-length, closet-door mirror and stared at myself. What the hell? There it was—the mole. I drew in close. With my face clenched in concentration, I studied the mole. Again, I felt for a bump. Again, it felt smooth. Engrossed by it, I took a step back, crossed my arms, and pondered it. Surely, my wife could not have *not* seen it. Was the mole there or not?

Since I had a yard to mow and because the summer heat would soon be overbearing, I shrugged my shoulders and turned to leave. As I moved, my mirror image moved, move for move with me, as one would expect of a mirror image, but then, out of the corner of my eye, I noticed as I took a step away from the mirror, my mirror image did *not* move, move for move with me, but moved, move for move a split second behind me. No way. My mind reeled. How, with a reflection, could there be a lapse in synchronization? Inconceivable. I tensed. I breathed hard. I leapt back in front of the mirror. Now, my reflection mirrored me, move for move again. Uniformity returned, but I stared myself down. The seconds ticked by ... 15 ... 30 ... 45 and then, the unbelievable occurred. I—no—not I—but my mirror image sniffed. Not a long, glottal, phlegm-coagulating snort; not a wet sniffle or a lengthy whiff. Just a sniff. Only the mirror me-man with the creepy mole sniffed; sniffed alone on his own. Not just scary, but scary as Hell. I sprung back, startled, never taking my eyes off me. My reflection did as I did as I did it. Our eyes narrowed. Our brows creased. We brooded. How could a reflection do something independent of that which it reflects? Impossible. Cautiously, I stepped up to the mirror; my face so close, my breath condensed on the glass. I glared never blinking. My image glared back never blinking.

"Come on, you me-bastard," I demanded, "do something different!"

As I spoke, he demanded word for word from me.

I waited. The mirror me-man with the mole waited. He was probably wondering who I was: the me-bastard that didn't sniff; the me-he without a mole on his forehead; the me-bro staring him down, challenging him to do something different.

Suddenly, I felt an inexplicable tug toward the mirror. I tried to resist it as my reflection did the same. The tow increased. We both placed our hands on the glass and tried to push away. With all of our combined strength, we could not escape the pull. My face slammed into my reflection's face as both of our bodies hurled up against the glass. Panic gripped us; our eyes darted; our teeth clenched; our faces contorted in horror. The suction grew stronger and just as I thought the mirror would crack, I heard the deafening discord of a congested intersection. Horns blared, motors revved, and brakes squealed mixed with crashing metal, breaking glass, and wailing sirens combined with angry shouts and horrific screams. Blinding red, amber, and green lights of countless traffic signals repeatedly flashed. One of my arms, one of my legs, and half my torso burst through the glass, however, to my astonishment, the mirror didn't break. Then, half my face plunged through with one eye, one nostril, and one ear on one side of the mirror while the other half of my matching set remained on the other side. I quite literally straddled the mirror fifty-fifty. With one eye, I saw on my side of the mirror, my bathroom with vanity, window, tub, and shower. Out of my other eye, I expected to see our shoes, clothes, and storage boxes in the closet, but I saw my bathroom with vanity, window, tub, and shower—but opposite—a mirror image. My skin crawled. My innards twisted. My underwear felt tight. I was not alone. There was I—and there was me, the other I. We were like two drops of water now forming one. Two replicate beings with two feelings, two beating hearts, and two souls with two inner voices having the same reasoning, formulating identical conclusions, and reacting exactly alike, but now, doing so, not in hidden reflective worlds, but at the same time and in the same space, straddling our closet mirror at my house, which also, was my reflection's diametrical house. Two alike people with only one miniscule difference: a mole.

Simultaneously, it became clear to the both of us that we stood at an intersection of two worlds; parallel worlds, like two trains running on the same schedule toward the same destination running side by side on separate tracks. Both worlds usually hidden from the other and separated by a gap; a ribbon of independence; a hint of individuality; a buffer zone that absorbed any and all autonomous quirks and instantaneously converted them back into a perfect reflection. My reflection was not only a reflection of me, but also, I was a reflection of my reflection, who was unequivocally another me and incontestably equal in all aspects. When our side by side worlds drew too close, our mutual awareness of each other caused the gap to narrow dangerously to the point that the two worlds not only touched, like in cases of déjà vu, but the worlds actually crossed and at this crisscross, they mysteriously merged like two trains choo-chooing at the same time on the same track. So there we stood, at the intersection of our worlds, both my reflection and me straddling our closet mirror.

The tug spiked tremendously and propelled me forward casting me out the other side of the mirror. My reflection shot out the opposite side of the mirror as both of us landed onto the bathroom floor. The noise and the flashing lights abruptly stopped. We laid there stunned for a few seconds and then both of us jumped to our feet and scanned the room. We saw the vanity, window, tub and shower, but to our mutual horror, I was on my reflection's side of the mirror and my reflection was on my side. Everything was situated opposite of what we knew in our daily lives. All that had been on my right was now on my left. As for my mirror image, all that had been on his left was now on his right. We both panicked and with the same idea of crossing back over to our respective worlds, we slammed ourselves up against the mirror and mashed ours faces against the glass, trying desperately to squish ourselves back through to our former realm. Nothing happened except an oily face smudge on the mirror. We took a step back, exhaled slowly, gave each other a reassuring look, and with greater force, slammed our bodies into the mirror again. Unfortunately, our worlds had disconnected and the gap between them had widened back to the ribbon of parallelism they had always been, sadly, sealing our fates. Furthermore, our combined impact shattered the mirror sending reflective pieces of our cherished domains crashing to the floor into a jagged mosaic of us looking forlorn. We panicked. He ran one way and I ran the other way. I turned left instead of right out of the bathroom, sped the opposite way through the bedroom, zoomed past my kids and the TV facing the wrong way, and burst into the backward kitchen.

"Melanie! Melanie!" I yelled.

My wife, wiping off the counter top, jumped and exclaimed, "Oh my, Adam, you startled me. What is it? What's the matter?"

Instead of rattling on about my reflection, the me-man with the mole, and the intersection of two parallel worlds, I simply blurted out, "I accidentally broke the closet mirror."

"Are you okay?" she asked with concern and compassion.

"I think so," I said, still trying to calm down and catch my breath.

"Well, come closer. Let me look at you and make sure you're not hurt."

I stepped up to her as she stood on her tiptoes and scrutinized my face.

"Hmmm. That's odd," she said.

"What's odd?" I asked.

"Your forehead."

"What about it?"

Speechless with her hand over her mouth, she shuffled back a step, glared at me with suspicion, and uttered, "You seem strangely different. Besides, you've always had a mole on your forehead, but now—it's gone."

So, you see, I am who I am but I am *not* who I am. I do my best *here* as I am certain I do my best *there*, even though, I know—no, *we* know—I am not one but two.

DRINK AND DIAL

B rett Fulbrite ran out onto *Friant Dam*. In a frenzy, he
slipped on the wet cement in the drizzling rain, landed
hard in a puddle, sprung to his feet, and raced over to a parapet
wall. He peered over it and saw sixty-feet straight down, the
cold water of the *Millerton Lake Reservoir*. Ravenous, man-
sized catfish swam along the dam. He raced to the opposite wall
and looked down six-hundred-feet at the concrete spillway.
Raging water churned into the *San Joaquin River*. He glanced
over his shoulder, saw his pursuer, panicked, and scrambled to
the middle of the dam. A chain-link barrier blocked his retreat.
Trapped, he searched wild-eyed for an escape. The only ways
out were to splash into a fish-feed, splat onto the spillway, or
smash through Harmon.

Harmon, a monstrous man, stomped up to him and stood
before him like a warring gladiator. His soggy leathers appeared
as dead animals hanging from his body and his long, wet hair
stuck to the side of his clenched face.

The rain stopped, but a howling wind kicked up over the dam
as Harmon bellowed, "Where you going to run now, wimp?"

"Listen," pleaded Brett, an inch shorter than an average guy
and moving about defensively like a wrestler, "I never knew
Heather had a boyfriend. We've been together six months and
she never ever mentioned you."

"You've been with my girlfriend for six months!" growled
Harmon. "Oh man, you are so dead!"

Harmon lunged. Brett dodged. Harmon grabbed. Brett punched. Harmon laughed, got a good grip on Brett, and heaved him off the dam.

The night before the day Brett was tossed off the dam, he sat on a barstool at the *Elbow Room*, a classy restaurant with an upscale lounge. The famous, local hangout stood amongst other gourmet eateries, specialty shops, and apparel boutiques in *Fig Garden Village*, a charming, outdoor mall located in Fresno, California. He licked the back of his hand, sprinkled salt on it, licked the salt off, slammed down a shot of *Cuervo* gold tequila, winced, and quickly sucked on a lemon wedge. The burst of sour scrunched up his face as he grabbed his bottle of *Corona* and chugged a few swallows of cold beer, all the while motioning the bartender for another tequila.

The bartender, Corey, a clean-cut, college student tending bar part-time, served him another shot along with a small bowl of fresh lemon slices. For the fourth time, Brett licked the salt, slammed the tequila, winced, sucked a lemon, scrunched up his face, and chugged his beer while signaling Corey for another round, but the bartender was busy at the other end of the bar, mixing cocktails for a flirtatious pack of *cougars*: seasoned, wealthy women, divorced or widowed who prey on virile younger men. While Brett waited for his fifth round, he drew in a deep breath, exhaled a long sigh, and thought about Heather, his twenty-five-year-old girlfriend who had long strawberry-blonde hair, kiwi-green eyes, very-berry lips, Chiclets teeth, a gumdrop nose, creamy apple-blossom skin, a voluptuous body fashioned of succulent fruits, and who, as of thirty minutes ago—had broken up with him.

Corey served the cocktails to the tittering ladies, fended off their advances, and placed another shot of tequila in front of Brett. The young bartender leaned in and cautioned Brett in a hushed tone. "Hey, bud, you might want to slow down on the *Cuervo* and totally think about how you're going to get home."

"Okay, thanks," Brett replied softly. "Oh and, Corey buddy—" Brett grabbed up the shot glass of Mexican firewater, gulped it down, shuddered, leaned in toward Corey, and whispered soundly, "please—bring me another *Cuervo and* another *Corona.*"

Before Corey returned with the sixth round, all five downed shots of the tequila hit Brett like a *Cinco de Mayo* celebration as his brain danced the *Salsa* and he nearly fell off the stool. He gripped the bar with both hands, steadied himself, and stared straight into the mirror behind the bar. His woeful image, seated between fifths of *Chivas Regal* and *Dewars Scotch*, glared back, pondering why Heather had dumped *him*, Brett Fulbrite, a damn good catch.

Corey brought Brett his sixth shot of gold and another frosty brew and asked Brett, "So tell me bud, why are you poundin' down drinks and lookin' so bummed-out?"

"Well," slurred Brett, pointing across the restaurant, "see that table over there? Less than an hour ago my girlfriend Heather and I were having dinner and then—" Brett tilted his head back, slammed down his shot of tequila, cringed, and continued, "she broke up with me. Me—can you believe it." He took a sip of beer. "I mean, come on, look at me, I'm twenty-eight, single without any baggage and healthy as hell with the toned body of a gymnast."

One of the cougars, attractive, but smeared with make-up, overheard him say the word *single*, so she flashed a teethy smile, batted her eyes, and gazed hungrily at him.

Brett smiled cordially at her, but kept talking to Corey. "I own *Fulbrite's Lights*, a successful lighting store. I make damn good money and the ladies have told me that they love my sincere blue eyes, my winning smile, and my dark wavy hair.

It's sad. I really thought that I had found my Mrs. Fulbrite, but to Heather—I'm her Mr. Friend."

"Dude, I'm sorry you're hurtin'," said Corey, "hang on while I help the ladies at the end of the bar."

Brett sipped his beer while thinking about earlier that afternoon. Since it was Sunday, both Heather and he had the day off. She had stopped by his house where they had made love. The sex wasn't wild or kinky and she had been very aloof, but as always, he had had a fantastic time. He decided to rev up their romance and take her out to dinner to a romantic, low-lit place with flickering candles on the tables, but she really didn't want to go; nevertheless, with his persistence, she finally agreed. All during dinner, she'd been quiet, so during dessert, over a slice of raspberry cheesecake, he had boldly asked her, "What's the matter?"

"Nothing," she had responded with obvious angst on her face.

Maybe, he had been in denial about the depth of their love and now that he thought about it, she had been acting distant for months; however, what manly-man truly fathoms the three primary mysteries of a woman: her feelings; her diet whims; and the most perilous enigma of them all, her infamous 'nothing is the matter' response.

Right after she had replied, "Nothing," he had responded, "Oh, okay, it just seems that something is on your mind. That's all. Maybe we should plan a trip to the beach."

"No, Brett," she said resolutely, "we need to talk." Which really meant that she needed to vent her feelings about him without any mutual discussion and since ravaging her body of luscious fruits was worth a pummeling to his ego, he set down his fork, gazed into her eyes, readied himself to hear all about his shortcomings, and listened intently.

"Brett, the last six months have been good," she acknowledged, "but I've never really stopped loving my ex-boyfriend and I know, I haven't been fair to you, but I've been seeing him on and off since you and I started dating six months ago. Lately, I've been seeing him more and more and we've decided that we want to give our love another chance."

Before Brett could utter a word, her cell phone beeped and she peered down to read a text message. While the faint light of her phone lit her angelic face, Brett stammered, "C-c-can't we talk about *us*?"

"No," she said, as she typed a reply text, "but hopefully," she added, while snapping closed her cell phone, "you and I can remain friends. But for now, I have to go. Thanks so much for dinner." She stood up, gave Brett a quick hug, said, "Goodbye," and sashayed out of the restaurant.

Brett watched her pert tushy in her tight jeans wiggle-walk out of his life. His pride stopped him from chasing her. Her bewitching perfume lingered as he sat there in silent shock. He ate his last bite of cheesecake, paid for dinner, and trudged across the restaurant to the bar.

At 8:45, after having sat on the barstool for just over an hour, he paid for his bar tab of six shots of *Cuervo* and three *Coronas*, tipped Corey generously, and staggered outside to the parking lot. A howling rainstorm had blown in, so he stood under the entrance awning of the restaurant and contemplated whether to, number one, risk driving drunk the three blocks home; or choice two, stagger home in the pouring rain; or option three, call a taxi. He visualized handcuffs, a jail cell, heavy fines, and months of traffic school for the first option. He imagined tramping home, drenched in the rain, catching a cold, and weeks of coughing for the second. He chose the third and called a cab. While he waited, he felt an overwhelming urge—an emotional impulse propelled by his intoxicated lack of discernment—to phone Heather. He knew better than to *drink and dial*: an outdated term used when telephones had a rotary dial and a drunken fool called someone and freely expressed heart felt feelings whether they were amorous, anguished, or angry. Usually, the next day, the *drink and dial* caller—nursing a hangover—regretted having made the call. Even so, Brett opened his cell phone and searched his contacts for Heather's number. Lightning streaked across the sky and he glanced up. Thunder clapped and he shuddered. With a pickled mind and blurry vision, he found Heather's name and punched the send button. She probably wouldn't answer her phone and he hoped she *wouldn't*, because he didn't so much want to talk to her, he just wanted to leave a message, pouring his soul out to her in a sentimental proclamation of his love. Her phone rang repeatedly and just as her voice greeting answered, the pack of boisterous *cougars* paraded out of the bar, crowding under the small canopy with him. It was like being in a cage made of raindrops with a flock of squawking parrots. One of them opened an umbrella nearly poking Brett in the eye. She scampered off in the downpour to get her car while the other women cackled loudly as lightning flashed, thunder roared, and rain splattered. Over all the clatter, he didn't hear a word of Heather's voice mail greeting except the vague beep to start talking.

"Hey, uhh, Heather baby, it's me," he slurred. "I was just thinking about you and how much I already miss you. You know how much I love you and ...."

Harmon Dagger sat on the yellow, daisy-print sofa at Heather's apartment and waited for her to come home. She provided bookkeeping and tax services for small businesses, so she had told him that she was out at a night class, learning new tax laws. Also, earlier that afternoon, she had called him and had told him to let himself in with her hidden key, take a shower, change clothes, and help himself to the twelve-pack of beer she had bought for him. Furthermore, he just received a text message from her on his cell phone that after tax class, she would stop and buy some groceries for tomorrow's breakfast.

While he waited, he guzzled a can of beer and watched *World Wrestling Smackdown* on TV, all the while shouting at the savage wrestlers as if he brawled in the fight ring with them.

Harmon had worked overtime all weekend operating a bulldozer for a road construction company, so kicking-back on the couch, drinking beer, and watching violence on TV felt relaxing and since it was raining, he would have tomorrow off. This meant, he could get drunk and stay up all night having sex with Heather. He thought about those icy cold beers on the nightstand next to her hot, naked body sprawled out on the bed and he grinned, sliding his tongue slowly over his dry lips. He felt thirsty, so he got up off the sofa, headed into the kitchen, and grabbed his sixth cold beer out of the fridge. He opened the beer and gulped down half of it as though he was still trying to wash down the road dust from the construction site. At six-foot-six and two-hundred-ninety-eight pounds of human bulldozer, he looked bigger than the refrigerator next to him. He wore faded Levi's, a tight, 3X, black T-shirt with the red words *Insanely Jealous* printed across his square pecs, and a tattoo of a laughing skeleton riding a fiery *Harley* inked on the bulging biceps of each arm. He had stormy gray eyes, an overcast face, and a boxy nose with a healing scar—from his latest bar fight—across its bridge. He donned a barbula beard, a small tuft of dark hair under his lower lip and black, heavy-metal-rock-star hair dangling down to his mammoth shoulders.

He grabbed a king-size bag of nacho tortilla chips out of the cupboard and took a step toward the living room when the telephone rang on top of Heather's work desk in the next room. He heard a man's voice on the answering machine, so he stuck his head into the room and listened as the stranger slurred, "Hey, Heather baby, it's me. I was just thinking about you and how much I already miss you. You know how much I love you and ...."

Harmon stomped in his size fourteen bare feet over to the

machine, hovered over it, and listened as Brett continued his mushy soliloquy. Harmon scribbled on a sticky note Brett's number from the caller ID and shoved it into a pocket of his pants.

Back at the *Elbow Room*, beneath the awning, the rowdy ladies clamored into their girlfriend's car as Brett continued whining to Heather. "You know how much I love you and I know you still love me. That's why I'm calling. I can't get you out of my mind and every time I think of you, I see your sexy walk, I hear your sweet voice, and I crave your hot body and all those nasty things you do to me. You are such a bad little girl, especially in the hot tub. Mmmmmm! I had fun tonight until you left. In your eyes, I might not deserve you, but there's no way that loser boyfriend—who never treated you good—deserves you either."

As Harmon listened, his face tightened, his fists inflated, his tattoos flared, and the words *Insanely Jealous* on his T-shirt swelled in font size. Just as he grabbed up the phone to blast Brett—Brett's taxi pulled up in front of the *Elbow Room*. Brett hastily begged Heather, "Pleeease baby, please see me soon. I love you with all my heart. Call me." He shut his cell phone and jumped into the taxi.

Harmon snatched up the phone, but all he heard was the click of the hang-up. He crashed his boulder of a fist back onto the answering machine, disintegrating it all over the room and burst the bag of chips against the wall. At that same explosive moment, Heather, carrying a bag of groceries, sauntered into the apartment through the front door.

"Harmon, I'm home," she hollered as she set the bag down on the kitchen counter. "Sorry, I'm late, but the tax class lasted longer than I expected."

Harmon stamped into the kitchen and silently glared at her. His wild eyes twitched as his giant body quaked with jealous rage. He chug-a-lugged the rest of his beer never taking his laser-beam eyes off her, crushed the empty aluminum can with his hand, and hurled it against the refrigerator.

Startled, Heather jumped and gasped. Standing a foot shorter than the monstrous man, she shook with fear and stammered, "W-w-what's the m-m-matter Harmon. Y-y-you look angry."

'Look angry' was an understatement. Harmon looked like a crazed rodeo-bull about to stomp her into the dust. His contorted face looked like a clenched fist and his clenched fists looked like sledgehammers. He breathed so heavily, he snorted. He took a step toward her. She trembled and took a step back. He lunged at her, wrapped his huge, leathery hands around her small, delicate throat, and pinned her up against the refrigerator. Little magnets of flowers and kittens fell to the floor.

"Please Harmon!" she screamed in terror. "Tell me, why you're so angry?"

"I know about your panty-waist boyfriend," he boomed in his baritone voice, "and I know you've been doing nasty things to him in his hot tub."

Heather grabbed Harmon's wrists with both hands and struggled with all her strength to pry them from her neck. His murderous grip only tightened. She stared at his rock hard biceps and the bulging tattoos of the laughing skeletons riding flaming motorcycles. The skulls laughed in her face.

"Pleeease baby," she wheezed, "I don't know what you're talking about."

"Stop lying," he snarled, and then bellowed, "you filthy slut, you cheated on me! You were supposed to be at tax class, but you were out with him!" He hoisted her up to where her feet dangled a foot above the linoleum floor. She hung there horrified, an inch from his homicidal face. She could feel his hot breath and see the red blood vessels in his maniacal eyes.

"I didn't cheat on you," whispered Heather, now feeling

dizzy from lack of air. "I was at tax class. I don't know who or what you're talking about."

"How can you deny it, when he just called and left a lovey-dovey message for you. You and me been together for two years and now—you skank, you cheated on me!"

"Please Harmon," she sobbed, "I love only you. Please, I beg you, put me down. You're choking me."

Seeing the tears in her eyes and her face turning blue from lack of oxygen, moved him to lighten his grip. "Okay, okay," he snapped, "I'll put you down, but tomorrow—" he growled as he lowered her to the floor and released his clamp of death around her throat, "your lover is dead meat!"

She breathed in large gulps of air and started drumming Harmon on his burly chest with both of her petite fists while she screeched, "Harmon, you big, mean creep! You scared me to death and hurt me! I hate you! Just leave!"

"No—I'm not leaving!" he shouted, grabbing her wrists and shoving her away from him.

"Leave now, you big jerk!" she demanded crossing her arms.

"I'm not a jerk. I only got pissed off, because *you* lied to me and cheated on me!"

She boldly pushed her way by him as he staggered back a step to let her pass. She ran into her bedroom, locked the door, and screamed, "Harmon, go away! I don't want to ever see you again!"

He remembered the last time they had broke up and how he had desperately missed her, so he muttered through the door, "I'm sorry I scared you Heather and I'm sorry I hurt you, but you—you deserved it. You should not have made me jealous."

"I said—go a-way!" She walked over to the telephone on her nightstand and picked up the handset. While listening to the dial tone, she shrieked, "Harmon, I'm calling the cops!"

"Don't call the cops. I'm still on probation."

"I—don't—care!" she yelled.

"All right. Okay. I'm out of here. But you shouldn't have cheated on me, because tomorrow—your boyfriend is hamburger!"

Harmon shoved his feet into his socks and boots, slipped on his black leather jacket and gloves, and snapped on his black *Nomad* dome helmet. He bellowed toward Heather's room, "This ain't over!" and he stomped out into the dark and the downpour, fired up his chopper, a crimson red *Harley-Davidson Rocker*, and roared down the slick streets home.

Heather heard the front door slam, cautiously unlocked her bedroom door, locked the front door, and stepped into her office to listen to the answering machine. Pieces of it and nacho chips were strewn all over the room. She wondered what the message had said. She cleaned up the mess, took a long, steamy shower, and crawled into bed. She thought of Harmon's jealous outburst and cried herself to sleep.

Arriving at his own apartment, Harmon removed his wet leathers and hung them up to dry. He snatched a fifth of *Jack Daniel's* out of the cupboard, twisted off its cap, and swigged a couple of gulps. He visualized his naked girlfriend in the arms of this other man and he snarled with rabid jealousy. He set down the bottle, plucked the phone number out of his pants pocket, and called the number. The phone rang and rang. He breathed heavily anticipating his verbal, nuclear blast in the man's ear.

Brett couldn't answer his phone. After the taxi had dropped him off at home, he had stumbled inside where he had passed out on top of his bed. He slept still wearing the clothes he had worn when he was out earlier that evening with Heather.

The phone finally stopped ringing and Harmon heard the soon to be dead man's recorded greeting. "Hi, this is Brett Fulbrite, owner of *Fulbrite's Lights*. You have reached my voicemail, so please, leave a message and I'll call you back as soon as I can. Thank-you."

Harmon crushed shut his cell phone, gulped a mouthful of whiskey, wiped his mouth with the back of his skillet-sized hand, and wryly grinned. Tomorrow, he would Google, *Fulbrite's Lights*, obtain the address, and pay a visit to soon to be dead, Brett Fulbrite. Yes, even Harmon, a beer drinking, Harley riding, leather clad, ape of a man had a PC. He fell asleep on his couch while watching *WrestleMania*.

Monday, the next morning, the storm had stopped, but the sky threatened more rain. Brett hiked the three blocks back to the parking lot of the *Elbow Room* and picked up his blue *Nissan Maxima*. The fresh air and exercise helped to alleviate his hangover, but his heart still ached from losing Heather. Hopefully, *whatever* he had said—because he *couldn't* remember what he said—last night to her answering machine would create a change of her heart toward him. He drove to his store located in a multi-business shopping center on the southwest corner of *Herndon* and *Blackstone Avenues*, unlocked and opened the front door, and flipped on the wall switches turning on hundreds of dazzling lights. Chandeliers, ceiling fans, stained-glass, and directional lights hung from the ceiling. Below the hanging lights stood rows of floor lamps next to countertops crammed with table and desk lamps. One wall displayed bath, vanity, and hallway fixtures while the opposite wall exhibited outdoor and landscape lighting. On the back wall, shelf after shelf stockpiled boxes of bulbs in all sizes and watts: fluorescent, halogen, krypton, xenon, incandescent, globe, flicker-flame, landscape, and floodlights. Brett walked over to the purchase counter next to the front door, stepped around a sale display of four-foot fluorescent light bulbs, turned on the computer, and unlocked the cash drawer. He checked his watch, 10:00 a.m., time to do business. The phone rang and he answered, "Good morning, *Fulbrite's Lights*. This is Brett, how can I help you?"

"What time do you open?" growled the caller in a deep guttural tone.

"We're open now, so come on down and shop our great selection of ...,"

Before Brett finished his sentence, the caller hung up. He shrugged it off, picked up a feather duster, and began dusting off lights around the store. After about twenty minutes of dusting, he heard the loud roar of a motorcycle in the parking lot. He stepped over behind the counter, peered out the window, and saw his first customer of the day, park in front of his store. He watched the huge, leather-clad man climb off his red motorcycle, remove his helmet, set it on the seat of the bike, and stomp toward the entrance.

Harmon shoved open the door, saw a man behind the counter, and barked, "Are you Brett?"

"Y-y-yes, I am," stammered Brett, a bit taken back by the gigantic, intimidating man.

Without saying a word, Harmon walked over to the display of four-foot long fluorescent light bulbs and dragged out a tube.

Brett thought, *Okay, no problem, nothing to fear, he's here to buy some industrial light bulbs.*

Harmon held the bulb like a club, swung, and smashed it over the counter. Glass exploded as Brett jumped back and instinctively covered his face with his hands. When he opened his eyes, he saw the gargantuan man, like the *Sultan of Swat,* swinging another bulb at him. Although Brett's head was the intended strike zone, he barely ducked as the bulb brushed his hair and crashed into the sales monitor. He darted, amidst a shower of glass, from behind the counter and bolted down an aisle toward the back of the store. Harmon followed. Brett yanked down floor lamps behind him, crisscrossing them on top of each other, obstructing Harmon's path. Brett glanced behind him and saw the murderous brute, wielding another long tube in his massive hand, stepping over the lamps in relentless pursuit.

"Why are you trying to kill me?" yelled Brett, out of breath.

"You left a message on my girlfriend's phone last night," hollered Harmon, advancing step by step on Brett. "I heard it and I'm Harmon—her boyfriend!"

"No friggin' way," Brett muttered, "Just my luck. Heather's boyfriend is a *Manzilla*." He tried to escape out the back door, but he hadn't unlocked it yet. He reached in his pocket for the store keys, but they were on the front counter. He grabbed for his cell phone to call 9-1-1, but it was next to the keys. Trapped, he lunged at the shelf next to him and yanked out a box of round, sixty-watt light bulbs. Grab and toss. Grab and toss. With rapid fire, he hurled the grenade-size bulbs at the charging behemoth. Harmon dodged and ducked the airborne assault, but one zinging bulb shattered on his forehead. He stopped in his tracks, felt his head with his free hand, and gawked at the blood on his fingertips. Seeing blood made him crazier. He let rip a battle cry and ran at Brett. Brett persisted with his barrage of bulbs. With bulbs bursting in air, Harmon advanced within striking distance and then, like *Darth Vader* wielding a lightsaber, he swung the long fluorescent tube.

Brett ducked as the glass cylinder swooshed over his head and crashed into a two thousand dollar chandelier, hanging low so that customers could appreciate its dazzling beauty. Frosted glass and gleaming crystals exploded everywhere. Beneath a shower of glass, Brett dropped the box of bulbs, dashed for freedom over to the wall display of patio lighting, and grabbed a six-foot bamboo tiki pole. Harmon plodded a step behind Brett and snatched up a bamboo pole. Both men gripped their tiki-stick, holding it lengthwise in front of them. Harmon swung. Brett stopped the blow with his pole. Clack! Harmon swung and swung again. Brett fended off each blow. Clack! Clack!

Brett shuffled backward in front of the table lamps as Harmon bore down on him.

"Heather never told me about you until last night!" shouted Brett.

"It doesn't matter," growled Harmon. "You touched my ol'lady and now you're gonna die. She broke up with me last night over you."

"No—she broke up with *me* last night over *you*," asserted Brett.

Harmon snarled and fiercely attacked Brett. Their poles whistled through the air, launching lampshades and crashing porcelain lamps to the floor. Harmon thrust and jabbed. Brett blocked. Clack! Like *Shaolin* monks adept at *Wing Chun Kung Fu* they engaged their dragon poles in fierce combat. Harmon's pole became stuck in track lighting overhead, providing an offensive opportunity for Brett to thrust the end of his tiki pole into Harmon's beer-barrel gut and force him backward. Harmon lost his balance, tripped over a broken lamp on the floor, and crashed backward, tipping over a table loaded with lampshades. Brett raced to the front counter, grabbed his keys and his cell phone, and scrambled out the front door. Harmon jumped up wearing a lampshade on his head, tore it off, crushed it with his hands, and chased after Brett.

Brett, racing to his car, nearly bumped into Amy, his part-time helper.

"I'm sorry, I'm late," gushed Amy, "but—"

"Call the police!" screamed Brett, dashing past her to his car, "and watch the store!" He jumped into his car, locked the doors, started it up, and sped out of the parking lot onto *Blackstone*. Thunderclouds darkened the sky.

Harmon stormed out of the store practically trampling Amy too. She jumped out of his way and watched as he snapped on his helmet, pounced on his bike, fired it up, and chased after Brett.

Brett made a U-turn and sped north toward *Riverpark Shopping Center*. Harmon made a U-turn right behind him. Brett, weaving around slower vehicles, fumbled with his cell phone to dial 9-1-1, but dropped the phone between his car seats. He made a sharp, squealing turn onto *El Paso Street*, leading into the *Riverpark* complex of twenty-three stores and sixteen eateries. Harmon stayed on his tail. The street lead onto a brick-paved circle with traffic feeding in from four directions. Brett screeched around the circle five times merging in and around incoming and outgoing traffic and then, without signaling, whipped out of the circular drive and back on *El Paso* to *Blackstone*. Harmon cussed, trapped behind two leisurely, merging vehicles.

Brett made a quick turn on *Blackstone*. Harmon exited the circle not far behind him. Brett headed north, speeding around traffic and squealing around corners, and then cranked a right turn into *Woodward Park*: three hundred acres of redwoods and picnic tables. He glanced in his rearview mirror. No Harmon on his *Harley*.

Harmon lost sight of Brett's car, but rode straight to *Woodward Park,* suspecting that's where Brett would flee and hide.

At the entrance station to the park, Brett pulled his wallet out of his pants pocket, fumbled for three dollars, and paid the attendant. He heard the roar of a motorcycle, gawked into his rearview mirror, and saw Harmon on his bike nuzzled up to his bumper.

Harmon smiled maliciously, slipped his bike's gears into neutral, revved up the engine, pointed with a hotdog-sized finger at Brett, and raked his hand like a sharp knife across his throat.

Brett spun his tires and sped away down the narrow, one-way street as Harmon accelerated past the booth without paying. The attendant called park security and a wanna-be cop in a small, wanna-be cop car with flashing lights, followed in pursuit. Brett, Harmon, and the frumpy security cop raced around the hilly course, zooming past the lake, a bird sanctuary, an amphitheater, the fenced dog park, and the *Shin Zen Friendship Gardens*. If Brett, Harmon, and the security guard could have only strolled through the peaceful park together, maybe they could have all gotten along. They zoomed past the exercise course, three children's playgrounds, and four sheltered picnic areas when Brett jerked his car onto a two-mile equestrian trail that snaked along a scenic view of the *San Joaquin River*. All three vehicles bounced and bottomed out on the muddy off-road trail. Brett gunned it up a hill slinging muck onto Harmon's bike and leathers. Harmon cussed and cranked his bike faster. Brett rumbled along the bluffs and rocketed back down hill to the manicured park. Harmon stuck with Brett and the security guard adhered to Harmon. Brett bounded back onto the asphalt road, zipped past a gazebo, a stream with three small ponds, two more covered picnic areas, and accelerated out of the park's exit. Harmon relentlessly followed. The security cop stopped at the exit.

Brett turned on *Friant Road* speeding toward *Friant Dam* and *Millerton Lake*. Harmon remained on Brett's bumper. Brett accelerated up to a shaky and blurry speed. So did Harmon. The dark clouds burst as rain hammered the valley. They sped in the downpour on the slick road past the gravel pits, *Lost Lake*, the fish hatchery, and the *Dam Diner*. Brett glanced out through slapping windshield wipers and saw the looming dam. His car's dashboard started dinging—out of gas. He zipped through the small town of *Friant* and turned left on the narrow, winding road up to the dam. Just as he pulled into the dam's parking lot, his car coughed and ran out of gas. He coasted to a stop near the walkway leading out on top of the dam. Harmon slid to a stop behind him, removed his helmet, wiped the rain from his face and stomped over to Brett's disabled car.

"Get out!" yelled Harmon, through the driver's side window.

"No!" shouted Brett, peering out through the rain drizzled window. "I didn't know Heather had a boyfriend!"

"Doesn't matter! You're still gonna die!" Harmon took a step back. Lifted a leg, and kicked in the window with his huge, wrecking-ball boot. Brett, reached down between the seats, grabbed his phone, scrambled out the other door, and ran toward the dam. Harmon pursued.

As Brett ran, he called 9-1-1 and shouted, "Hello, this is Brett Fulbrite. A man is trying to kill me up here at *Friant Dam!*"

"Does he have a gun?" asked a lady with a calm voice.

"No, just his bare hands! But he's huge!"

"Assistance is on the way."

Next, Brett called Heather. Her voice mail answered.

"Heather!" he screamed, "It's Brett. Your ex-boyfriend who is now your boyfriend is trying to kill me your ex-boyfriend!" He's trapped me up at *Friant Dam*. Call him off me." He glanced over his shoulder and saw Harmon tramping after him, talking on his own cell phone.

While Brett called Heather, so did Harmon. He too got her voice mail and left her a message. "Heather, I just wanted to let you know, I've cornered your whussy lover up here at *Friant Dam* and I'm going to toss him off it. By cheatin' on me, *you* killed this guy—not me! I can't live without you. After I throw him over, I'm jumping off. Goodbye."

Brett ran out onto the slippery walkway of the dam. He fell in a puddle, sprung to his feet, and ran to the parapet walls. On one side, he saw the lake with huge, hungry catfish and on the other side, the raging spillway. Halfway across, a chain-link fence stopped him. He spun and searched for an escape. There was no way out, except to crash through Harmon.

Harmon, with murderous intentions, stomped up to Brett, and stood ready for battle. He snarled with every breath. His wet leathers hung from his body and his stringy hair stuck to his face. The rain ceased, but a vicious wind whipped up over the dam, causing both men to shudder.

Harmon taunted, "Where you going to run now, wimp?"

"Listen," said Brett, moving about defensively. "I never knew Heather had a boyfriend. The last six months we've been together, she never ever mentioned you."

"You've been with my girlfriend for six months!" growled Harmon. "Oh man, you are so dead!"

They scuffled. Harmon grabbed Brett, picked him up, and flung him over the dam.

Brett, falling, grabbed the parapet wall and dangled six-hundred-feet above the cement floodway, raging water, and certain death.

Harmon climbed up on the wall and with a crazed look in his eyes, stood up, and was about to jump.

"Wait!" yelled Brett, desperately hanging on to the wall next to Harmon's boots. "Listen to me! Don't jump!"

Harmon peered down at Brett and shouted, "Why not?" and almost lost his balance.

"No woman is worth dying over," reasoned Brett, "even one as hot and sexy as Heather. She cheated on you, but you know, she cheated on me too. I didn't know she was still seeing you. You didn't know she was seeing me. We're like brothers now."

"Like brothers?" repeated Harmon.

"Yeah, like brothers. We both belong to the ex-Heather club. Hey, I've got an idea. How about you step down, pull me up, and the two of us will head out on Friday night, drink a few beers, and meet us a couple of new Heathers. Heathers who'll love us and not cheat on us."

Harmon, thinking about what Brett had said, gazed out at the stormy view across the valley, down at the river, and at the surrounding foothills. Just as the giant of a man made a move to step down, a California Highway Patrol officer raced up to the dam's parking lot next to the walkway. His car slid to a stop on the wet pavement and he jumped out, brandished his weapon, and approached Harmon and Brett. Right behind the CHP car, another car squealed to a stop and Heather sprung out. The officer positioned himself close to the two men and in a loud, commanding voice, ordered, "You—in the leathers—get down off the parapet!"

Harmon saw Heather approaching and growled, "No," and yelled, "Just shoot me!"

"I will if you make a move," said the cop. "For now, you just stay up there, so I can help this guy."

While the officer kept his gun pointed at Harmon, he wrapped an arm around Brett and hoisted him back over the wall to safety. Brett moaned a sigh of relief and stood behind the officer.

The cop, still pointing his gun at Harmon, again demanded, "Get—down—off the parapet!"

Heather hastened up on the scene and stood next to Brett. She trembled in fear for Harmon's safety. The wind shrieked over the dam.

Brett spun with a look of surprise and asked her, "Heather, what are you doing up here? It's not tax season."

"Harmon's my boyfriend," she said and with teary eyes, she peered up at Harmon and pleaded, "Harmon, please get down. I love only you. I never cheated on you. Please, I want you to come back home with me."

"You cheated on me with this guy!" he pointed at Brett.

"No, she didn't," defended Brett, "I only call her once a year, in April, when she does my taxes."

"Liar! You called her last night!" yelled Harmon.

"No, I—" Brett started to argue and then, it dawned on him. He shook his head and moaned, "Get down Harmon and let me explain and if my explanation doesn't clear this up, then we'll both jump off the dam in a hail of bullets."

"No, I'm not getting down. I'm jumping to my death," asserted Harmon.

"Nooo, please no!" wailed Heather.

"Well, before you do," stated Brett, "hear me out."

As Harmon peered down at Brett and as the CHP officer and Heather looked on, Brett pulled his cell phone out of his pants pocket, flipped it open, scrolled down his list of contacts, found Heather's name, held it up for Harmon to see, and said, "You see, Harmon, last night, Heather broke up with me and so I got drunk and called her. I was hurt over losing her and poured my heart out, but as you can see in my list of contacts …."

At that moment, interrupting Brett, a sexy woman in tight jeans and high heels, who had just a moment before parked her car next to the cop car and who now scrambled out on the dam, stopped and stood with her arms crossed next to Harmon's girlfriend, tax-preparer Heather: a skinny lady, who wore no make-up, had stringy brown hair parted down the middle, and who's brown eyes peered out of thick glasses set in purple frames.

Heather scrutinized the voluptuous woman as if she was adding up receipts for a tax refund.

The gorgeous lady with kiwi green eyes, a body shaped of luscious fruits, and strawberry blonde hair blowing in the wind, glanced up at Harmon, glared at Brett, and spat, "That monster on the wall is *not* my ex-boyfriend and is certainly *not* my boyfriend now. What the hell is going on Brett?"

The cop, Harmon's homely girlfriend Heather, and Harmon all sang out in a chorus, "Yeah, Brett! What's going on?"

Brett sighed and moaned, "I was trying to explain. Last night after Heather …," he pointed to strawberry-blonde, sexy Heather, "broke up with me, I slammed down a bunch of tequilas and beers. When I left the bar …," Brett peered at the cop, "I decided *not* to *drink and drive*, but I did decide to *drink and dial*, so while I waited for my cab, I pulled out my cell phone

and at the time, I thought I had called my ex, Heather here …,"
he pointed again at his stunning ex-girlfriend, "but there was
a lot of noise around me with the storm and a pack of loud
ladies leaving the bar, so I didn't hear her voice greeting. All I
heard was the beep to start talking and when I did, I poured my
heart out to who I thought was her …," he pointed again at sexy
Heather. "But unfortunately and it's obvious now—I called the
wrong Heather listed in my contacts. I called Heather, my tax
accountant, instead of Heather my ex-girlfriend."

Harmon shook his head, sighed heavily, and climbed down
off the wall. His girlfriend, skinny, homely, tax-preparer Heather
dashed over to him and hugged him. He hugged her lifting her
off her feet and with tears in his eyes, he groaned, "I'm so, so,
sorry, babydoll."

Sumptuous Heather huffed, turned, and stomped away in
her tight jeans and high heels. Brett watched her perfect tushy
wiggle-walk for a second time out of his life.

The CHP officer arrested Harmon and took him to jail.
Tax Heather dropped Brett as a client and drove away. Snooty
Heather sped away too. A tow truck hauled off Harmon's *Harley*
and another CHP officer assisted Brett with putting gas in his
car. All the while, the hungry catfish swam by the dam, the
raging water churned into power, and the rushing wind howled
over the dam.

At Harmon's trial, Brett testified on behalf of the biker.
The court reduced the charges against Harmon, however, he
remained on probation and had to pay full restitution for the
damages at *Fulbrite's Lights*.

Months later, on a Saturday night, Brett drank only two
beers at the *Elbow Room.* On his way out to his car, he noticed a
man in the parking lot who kept dropping his keys and fumbling
with his cell phone.

"Hey man," said Brett, "you okay to drive?"

"Yeah, I'm good to go," he slurred.

"It might not be any of my business—but you're not calling your *ex* are you?"

"Yeah, matter a fact, I am," he mumbled. "How'd you know?"

"I just know. So come on dude, first of all, don't *drink and drive*—call a cab; and second, and trust me, I know what I'm talking about—put away your cell phone, it's not a good idea to *drink and dial*."

LUCKY NUMBERS

At last, after three long hours of grueling concentration, I foresaw the six lucky numbers. Did I cheat? Not at all. The lucky numbers appeared to me as I sat comfortably on my couch. How did I foresee them? Well—I'll tell you the story and maybe, just maybe, *you'll* win a mega-million-dollar jackpot.

You see, we've all heard that most people only tap into ten percent of their brainpower with the rest of it stored in self-imposed ignorance. I wholeheartedly believe this. Textbooks call the utilization of this unused mental power "genius." Whenever an individual exhibits genius, we are amazed, but unfortunately, we become frightened by that which we don't understand. Just like the saying: When someone pokes their head above the crowd, someone else cuts it off just to keep things even. Similarly, certain sects of our society call it taboo and quickly crucify it. Nevertheless, our sublime genius is integral to our vigorous nature and if empowered will soar amongst the heavens. Too bad we keep it earthbound like a snared bird with clipped wings. As for me—I freed my genius and it streaked across the sky.

So how did I predict the lucky numbers? Well, first, I believed that I could. No, not just hope or wish that I could. I believed with all my heart, mind, and soul that I could—a determination void of all doubt, like when you turn on a faucet, you just know the water will flow. Oh, and just for the record, I'm not a psychic. I'm just a regular, twenty-seven-year-old, single guy. I work, eat, sleep, and I love pepperoni pizza. Another thing, I didn't burn candles at the witching hour or cast spells over a boiling cauldron of blood and bats. It was three-o-clock on a Saturday afternoon, warm sunbeams filled the room, and I relaxed on the sofa with my socked feet resting on the coffee table.

Okay, second, I found an outdated newspaper and locked my eyes on the previous *Super Lotto* numbers. Next, I found a No. 2 pencil and erased the old numbers, leaving an inky smudge where each winning number used to be. After that, I closed my eyes, breathed deeply, and cleared my mind of all worries and wishes, all fears and doubts, and all hobbling emotions. I concentrated and tried to visualize the first lucky number that would appear in the next day's Lotto section.

All of a sudden, a psychic tornado of numbers assailed my mind. I sat up straight with my feet firmly on the floor. With my eyes still shut, I watched the upright funnel spinning counterclockwise with a continuum of numbers whirling about its circumference. They circled up close and then orbited out of sight. I watched, concentrated, and believed with such zeal that beads of sweat formed on my brow. Then, one of the numbers—a number seven—emerged on the periphery of the cyclonic wind. Other numbers flashed past, 'round and 'round until the number seven gyrated out onto the very cusp of the tornado, escaped the turbulence, and floated down like an autumn leaf before my mind's eye. I blinked open my eyes, confidently smiled, and with my No. 2 pencil, wrote the lucky number seven in the first inky smudge in the newspaper. Again, I closed my eyes, breathed deeply, shut out all distractions, and searched the whirlwind for the next number. A quarter of an hour passed and I glimpsed the number 12 whisk by numerous times and it tumbled out and floated down. Again, I snapped open my eyes and scribbled the lucky number 12 down on the second inky smudge. Since my novice mind lacked mental stamina, each additional number took longer to isolate out of the churning chaos. Nevertheless,

I persisted. I concentrated. I believed. After three demanding hours of meditation, all six numbers had fluttered out of the whirlwind. Ending the cognitive spectacle, I scrawled down every lucky number: 7, 12, 19, 27, 39, and 43 on their smudgy spot in the newspaper. Feeling famished, I ordered Chinese food. I felt so confident about winning the lottery that while I waited for my delivery, I wrote my resignation from my job, checked *Realty.com* for a beach home, searched *Cars.com* for a new car, and pulled up *Travelocity.com* to plan a trip.

Forty-five minutes later, there was a knock at the door. I paid and tipped the delivery guy, set the food on the coffee table, and dove headfirst into my orange chicken, sweet and sour pork, and shrimp chow mein. I ate it all, down to the last noodle. I was so full, I couldn't eat the fortune cookie. After I tossed the empty boxes in the trash, I jumped into my car, drove down to the corner convenient store, and bought a lottery ticket with the lucky numbers—7, 12, 19, 27, 39, and 43. I smiled all the way home. Back home, I set the glorious ticket on the coffee table next to the leftover fortune cookie. For the rest of the evening I remained on the couch and surfed three hundred satellite TV channels. Every few minutes, I glanced down at the ticket and grinned. At ten-o-clock, I crawled into bed and dreamt of my new life as a millionaire.

The next morning, like it was Christmas, I awoke with a start, sprung out of bed, hurried outside in my boxers, and snatched up the newspaper. I rushed back into the house, plopped on the couch, yanked off the rubberband, peeled open the paper, and with tremendous expectations, peered down at the six lucky numbers, comparing my whirlwind numbers to the winning Lotto numbers. My face collapsed into disbelief and scrunched up into disappointment. I moaned as I visualized the leisure, the beach home, the new car, and the trip, all of them blow away in a whirlwind of *sorry, you can't have*. I crumbled up my resignation and tossed it across the room. I whined out loud,

"You stupid, lying tornado, I believed you. I thought I'd have everything I've always wanted. Now, instead of thinking I'm a genius, I feel stupid and instead of being wealthy, I'm still strapped. Thanks a lot!"

As you now know and most likely suspected from the beginning, I missed all of the Lotto numbers. I confess, my genius had not soared; it had never left the ground. Not only could I *not* see the future, I had wasted three hours of my weekend trying. I sat on the sofa for a few minutes, got up, made a cup of tea, and sat back down on the sofa. I tried to forget my failure, but since my powers of mental concentration sucked—I couldn't—so I watched TV. During a commercial, I glanced down and saw the fortune cookie. My empty stomach gurgled from the tea, so I grabbed up the cookie, unwrapped it, cracked it open, and put a morsel in my mouth. It tasted good. I slipped out the fortune and read its inscription, 'Never use your talents to satisfy greed.' I thought, *No kidding. Thanks for the lesson.* I ate the rest of the cookie and tossed the fortune down on the coffee table, however, when the little strip of paper landed, it flipped over, and I noticed the words 'Lucky Numbers' and six numbers printed on its backside. I snatched up the fortune and peered at it closely, laying it next to the six whirlwind numbers from the day before—my predicted numbers—the numbers I had written on the inky smudges in the newspaper. I gasped, my heart raced, and my breath quickened. I read the numbers that I had foreseen and read the numbers from the fortune cookie. I chuckled. My genius had indeed soared. The numbers on the fortune were 7, 12, 19, 27, 39, and 43.

SNOW CONE CATCH

Eleven-year-old, Kerby Speck, skinny and shirtless, sporting a Tampa tan, paced about like a caged tiger out in left field on the baseball diamond at Gidden's Park. Eager to snag a hot grounder or catch a high fly-ball, he pounded his fist two times inside his glove (an old, ragged *Rawlings*, he'd re-stitched with a white shoestring) and hollered in his Southern twang, "Heyyy batta, batta, batta!"

Kerby, not the shortest or the tallest kid going into sixth grade, wore cut-off, blue jeans, loose, white socks, abused *Converse Allstars*, and his short brown hair combed straight back gleaming with hair-oil. He crept up closer to the infield, his twinkling blue eyes scheming with his spontaneous grin, and taunted the batter, shouting, "Come-on sissy batta! Knock it over my head! Heyyy, sissy batta! You got no bat!"

Every kid on and off the field, shook their heads in disbelief, gawking at Kerby like he was stupid or suicidal for calling this big kid, this big thug, this big stick at bat, a 'sissy batta.'

The batter, thirteen-year-old bully, Denton Kramly stood scowling in the batter's box (a square scratched in the dirt by a kid with a dull pocket knife). Tall, oafish, and freckle-faced, he wore a faded, baseball cap smothering a wildfire of red, curly hair. He was outfitted in his outgrown, last season's little-league uniform consisting of a too tight, blue, pin-striped jersey, too short, white, high-water knee-breeches, blue stirrup stockings stretched over dirty white socks, and beat-up *PF Flyers*. This playground menace, who picked on, made fun of, and terrified every kid younger, shorter, fatter, dumber, and poorer than him, growled, swinging his favorite wooden bat (a thirty-three inch, *Louisville Slugger*), warming up like he was up to bat against Sandy Koufax. He pounded his bat on home plate (a flattened fried-chicken bucket) and taking Kerby's jeering bait, called his shot like the *Babe*, pointing out to left field where Kerby stood hollering. Denton swung the bat with a few more warm-up swings, locked into his batting stance, glared at the pitcher, and spit as if he chewed tobacco.

Kerby's friends, Ira Wyndale, a brawny kid with wavy, dark hair, played third base and Paul Rellons, a scrawny kid with uncombed, blonde hair, covered second. Both motioned Kerby back, yelling in unison, "Kerb! Back up! This guy can hit!"

Kerby slammed his fist into his mitt and bellowed, "I know that! You guys cover your bags! I got left field!" He hit his glove again and resumed yelling, "Heyyy, sissy, sissy batta!"

On the pitcher's mound (a scrape in the dirt made with the heal of a sneaker) stood a short kid named Jamie Humminger, a little-league ace-pitcher with a bazooka arm. A long brown mullet dangled out from under his *Dodgers* baseball cap that he wore tight and low to shade his eyes and though his clothes were casual: a tank top, shorts, and ratty shoes, his face was stone serious. Every time he pitched, he chewed *Juicy Fruit* chewin' gum that he had swiped from his mom's purse and before every wind-up, he did three things. First, like most pitchers, he gripped the baseball in his mitt hiding his finger placement on the seams, so the batter wouldn't know whether to expect a fastball, curveball, changeup, or slider. Second, he moved his mitt in front of his face and for a few intimidating seconds glared out at the batter through the shady slit between the top of his mitt and the bill of his cap, and third, he clenched his teeth and stopped chewing his gum. He did all three things, wound up like Drysdale, and ignoring his fear that Denton would pound him if he struck him out, fired a heater through the strike zone.

Behind home plate, playing catcher, squatted a chunky seventh-grader named Chucky with the nickname of Chucky Fried, which was shortened from Ken-Chucky-Fried-Chicken, a nickname that Kerby had given him because his family ate chicken out of a red and white bucket almost every night for supper. He wore his catcher's mask over his backward baseball cap that covered his flattop haircut and he wore a padded vest over his rolls of belly fat. He had an arsenal of two weapons that he used without mercy to distract batters causing them to strike out. One, he would holler in his *Daffy Duck* cartoon voice, "Thhhwiiing batta!" making them bust up laughing and two, he would rip a fart; some silent; others sounding like air bubbles escaping out a bucket of mud; smelling like spoiled broccoli, rotten eggs, and rank fried-chicken; all of them, eye tearing, nostril burning, stomach turning, noxious fumes, discombobulating the best of batters.

As Jamie's fast pitch crossed the plate, Chucky Fried started to yell, "Thhhwiiing batta!" and tilt to cut the cheese as he did with every batter, but didn't. He shut-up with butt shut, worried that he might rattle Denton, making him miss the ball, provoking the bully with the bat to pummel him right there and then.

Denton, snarling, gritting his teeth, hungry for a homer, swung like Micky Mantle at that first pitch and meeting the ball with the sweet-spot of the bat, belted it into the stratosphere as if it were a missile launched from *Cape Canaveral.*

Chucky Fried jumped up, ripped off his mask, and staring starry-eyed up at the sailing ball, called it like a sportscaster, "And off it goes into the wild, blue yonder!"

All the players on both teams cranked their heads back with their mouths open, awestruck, gawking up at the soaring space-ball lingering high above Gidden's park, a neighborhood playground with four trashcans next to four picnic tables under four tall shade trees. It had one tall metal slide, two seesaws, three chain swings with leather straps that hugged the seat of your pants, and a baseball diamond with dandelions in the outfield, dirt clods in the infield, and bases concocted from whatever the kids found in the trashcans: greasy red and white chicken buckets, crinkled, brown paper bags, or paper plates smeared with potato salad. A small, chain-link backstop stood behind home plate and a waist-high, green wooden fence with peeling paint encompassed the outfield. With every step infield or outfield, small, brown grasshoppers sprang up from the ground and twittered to another spot. Though the summer heat and humidity of Florida bothered dogs, cats, and parents, the kids didn't complain at all; it was another day of sunshine and baseball.

During that summer of 1966, the ballplayers, consisting of nearly every kid nine to thirteen living in the vicinity of Nebraska and Hillsboro Avenues, met for a pick-up game every day at two-o-clock, showing off their skills swinging a bat, scooping up grounders, and catching pop-flys, all the while pretending that someday, they'd be in the majors, slamming a homer, rounding third base, and waving their cap to the roaring fans in the ballpark. Every game, the same older kids picked the same kids, so every game, the same kids played on the same teams. On this muggy afternoon with the humidity warping everything into a mirage, it was the bottom of the ninth, there were two outs with a runner on second and third, and the team Kerby played on led by only one run. Just one more out and his team would win or one more hit by Denton and Kerby's team would lose. Denton's slam-ball soared high in the sky toward the homerun fence. It would be close. It might or might not go over. It was up to Kerby now.

Just before the crack of Denton's bat, Kerby, respecting Denton's batting power, darted backward and when Denton smashed the ball, Kerby burst into top speed all the while concentrating on the baseball rocketing into the sky.

Denton, confident that he had hit his second homer for the day, lackadaisically tossed the bat into the dirt and jogged toward first base.

The ball vanished into the blazing sun. Kerby blinked, blinded for a second, but spied the ball again when it reappeared in front of a stray cloud. He dashed toward the homerun fence; his eyes locked on the ball, smacking his fist two times into his mitt as he scrambled beneath the arching, plummeting orb.

Every kid in the park peered up at the galactic ball, then at Kerby, his feet churning in a blur, and then at the homerun fence, wondering, guessing, and calculating whether Kerby could get under the zinger before the ball dropped over the fence.

Denton, halfway to second base, stopped in the base line, shoved back his baseball cap, placed his hands on his hips, and watched, now wondering too, if the ball would make it over the fence. The runners from second and third, waiting at homeplate, wondered the same thing.

Kerby, with talent and dexterity, sporting an all-star smile, spun to face the oncoming ball, bumped up against the fence, leapt into the air, reaching, stretching, and inching his glove out onto his fingers tips, and plucked the ball out of its homerun trajectory, catching it in the very tip of his mitt's pocket and robbing Denton of his homerun.

Kerby landed on his feet, peered at the baseball sticking out the end of his glove, and with a wide grin, held in the air for all to see his glove cupping the ball and hollered, "Whoohoooo! Snow cone catch!"

Ira yelled, "Snow cone catch! Way to go, Kerb!"

Another friend of Kerby's, a deaf-mute kid playing first base, who Kerby nicknamed Yoohoo because he liked to drink *Yoohoo*, a cold chocolaty drink in a bottle, silently jumped up and down, threw his mitt high in the air and caught it again.

Paul pointed in Denton's face and shouted, "You're out! We win!" and immediately realized, he just snubbed a bully and scurried away to stand next to Ira.

The kids on the losing team moaned while a few good sports yelled, "Nice catch Kerb!" "Good game!" "See ya tomorrow!"

Not Denton. He threw his cap into the dirt, kicked second base (a plastic picnic plate), pointed at Kerby, and yelled, "Kerby, when I get my hands on you, I'm so gonna hurt you!"

Kerby knew hotheaded, sore-loser Denton meant every word of his threat, so Kerby shouted, "Nice game guys! See ya later!" He threw the ball to Ira and popped over the fence like a homerun that didn't happen for Denton.

Kerby eluded the infuriated bully and hustled around the ball diamond and out of the park. He scampered three blocks over and down another half block to his home on Caracas street, a shady lane lined with oak trees dripping with moss like beards in a synagogue. He lived in an older home built in the thirties with three small bedrooms; a room for his mom and dad, although his dad was off fighting an unwinnable war in Vietnam; a room for his older sister, Susan, thirteen; and a room which Kerby shared with his two younger brothers, Roger, nine and Ricky, five. Kerby bounded from the sidewalk up the cement steps to the front porch, yanked open the screen door, slid in next to Ricky into a '50s diner' style table and booth, and slurped up a plate of spaghetti while rattling on to his mom, sister, and brothers about how he caught the snow cone catch and won the game.

After supper, with three hours of daylight left to burn up on fun, Kerby dragged out from under the porch his *Pogo Stick*, a heavy duty one with two handles for bigger kids. He bounced down the steps, off the curb, and up and down the street. Ira and Paul showed up and took turns bouncing for a half-hour until they all decided to ride bikes to buy nickel candy down at a small market on the corner of 12th and Osborn. Paul and Ira climbed on their *Sting-Ray* bikes complete with the apehanger handlebars, banana seats, and sissy bars, and rode off down the street. Some creep had stolen Kerby's bicycle out of his front yard, so the only bike available was his sister's, a ghastly contraption because the *Schwinn*, a purple, girly bike without the ball-breaker bar, didn't have any tubes or tires on its metal rims. Correct: no rubber; just the metal ring holding the spokes. Riding on the bare rims jarred Kerby horribly, especially when riding over rifts in the street and cracks in the sidewalk. Ignoring all the sissy-bike ridicule from his pals, he rode off, knowing that the only way to ride the screwed up bike was to stand up on the pedals so his knees took the impact not his butt, back, and balls, and ride on the grass. So as Ira and Paul rode in the street, Kerby rode across lawns.

Around the block, a few streets down, and on the corner of 12th and Ellicot, Denton, still angry over his pinched homer and losing the game, sat brooding on the steps of his front-porch while impatiently waiting for supper. He lived in a small, older home like Kerby's, but his house needed paint, the grass needed mowing, and in the backyard, up on jack stands, sat a rusty, old car needing tires. Denton glanced down the street and low and behold saw Kerby riding across lawns heading for his yard. The bully grinned, popping his fists full of knuckles.

Paul and Ira saw the red-headed ruffian lurking on his porch and sped past him.

Kerby tried to keep up with Paul and Ira but peddled slow, maneuvering around flowerbeds, sprinklers, plaster lawn-dwarfs, and plastic, pink flamingos.

Denton noticed Kerby's sluggish locomotion and sprang up, ran out, and leapt in front of Kerby's bike, straddling its front wheel, gripping its handle bars, and stopping the bike with a jolt, ejecting and dumping Kerby to the ground.

"I told you, I was goin' to hurt you," threatened Denton, pointing at Kerby laying flat on his back.

"Oh, come on Denton, it's just a game," said Kerby, standing up and brushing himself off. "Don't be such a poor sport!"

Paul and Ira turned their bikes around, rode back, and stopped at a safe distance across the street from the showdown. They watched, without saying a word, not wanting Denton to turn his wrath on them.

"That's the last homer you'll ever steal from me," yelled Denton as he reared back and socked Kerby in the stomach.

Kerby bent over absorbing the punch. The punch not only knocked the wind out of Kerby, but it also knocked out some of the pent-up anger he held inside over missing his dad in Vietnam, over his stolen bicycle, over losing his lawn mowing jobs making two bucks a yard because the mower's blade blew up on an old lady's backyard with a metal pipe sticking up in the tall grass. More so, over the fact that he was too shy to talk to Gail Matterson, a petite, sixth-grade goddess with big, brown eyes and long brown hair; a girl he had a crush on, who sat next to him last year in fifth grade, and who, he followed a half of block behind every day walking home from school.

He glared up at Denton, straightened up, drew in a deep breath, stepped up, and more angry than scared, let out a battle cry like G.I. Joe storming an enemy bunker and slugged Denton in *his* stomach.

Denton wheezed, dropping to his knees, but jumped to his feet as both he and Kerby put up their dukes and began circling each other.

Kerby snarled, "Now, we're even."

"No we're not," barked Denton. "We're even when I'm done thrashin' you!"

Fists flew. Kerby dodged and ducked, nevertheless, he received a few grazing punches and oddly enough, at the time, due to adrenaline and anger, he didn't feel any of them. After about twenty seconds of throwing blows and as Ira and Paul rooted Kerby on, Denton's haggard mom with a shock of dyed, bright-red hair, wearing tight jeans, a purple halter-top, and pink flip-flops, staggered out of the house and over to the boys. In one hand, she held a smoldering cigarette and in her other, she gripped a can of bargain beer. Trembling with rage, she screamed in a grating voice, "Stop! You boys stop fightin' now!" She jammed her cigarette between her lips, slapped her son across the back of his head, yanked the cigarette back out of her mouth, and scolded, "If your daddy weren't locked-up, he'd smack you 'round for fightin'! Now, git your sorry behind up on that porch and stay there! You hear me! Git! And you boys, git on home!" She took a long puff of her cigarette, nervously flicked the ashes, and with a scowling, hardened face portraying a life of abuses, she again said, "Git on home!"

Denton, ashamed of his intoxicated mom and embarrassed for the way she treated him in front of the fellas, hung his head, shuffled over to the porch, and muttering and cussing under his breath, demanded, "When's supper?"

"I'm fixin' it, soon as I drink this damn beer," she spat, staggering back inside the house.

Before the screen door shut behind her, Denton yelled, "You said that three beers ago!"

Kerby rubbed his punched spots on his head and arms and climbed back on his sister's shabby bike without looking back at Denton. He rode to the store with Paul and Ira. They bought a few pieces of candy and ate them while rambling on about the fight.

Kerby commented, "Bullies ain't so terrifyin'. I held my own with ol' porch-boy, no-homer Denton. If he's the toughest kid around, then, who's there to worry about?"

Paul and Ira shrugged their shoulders unable to speak, both chewing on an *Abazaba* taffy bar. On the way home, they saw Denton still sitting on his front porch steps.

Denton saw them and cussed at them as his mother inside screeched, "Damn-it, Denton, stop that swearin'!"

Knowing Denton couldn't leave the porch, Kerby, Paul, and Ira rode in circles on Denton's neighbor's lawn, all the while singing stupid songs, enraging Denton even more. Dedicated to all the kids bullied by Denton and with Kerby belting out the songs the loudest, they sang, *"Denton is a friend of mine; he resembles Frankenstein. When he walks across the street; you can smell his dirty feet. And when he does the Irish jig, he looks just like Porky Pig!"* Then, the rowdy troubadours slid into an ongoing chorus of, *"Tra-la-la-boom-de-ay! I'll take your pants away. And while you're standin' there, I'll take your underwear!"*

Denton grew furious as Kerby and his pals repeatedly sang the rhymes until Denton burst off the porch as his inebriated yet watchful mother shrieked from inside, "Denton Jr.! You git your butt back on that porch!"

Denton stopped, returned to the porch, and hollered at Kerby, "While you bozos were at the store, I called some friends over to deal with you. I've been waitin' on 'em. They'll be here any minute."

Denton lobbed more insults at Kerby. Kerby hurled more back at him. Just as Kerby and his pals started to leave, they saw a pack of five kids riding their bikes down the middle of the street heading directly for them.

Kerby, standing, straddling his bike, shuddered with fear, recognizing the lead bike rider as Victor and the kid riding behind Victor as Cookie. He turned to Paul and Ira to say, "Let's get outta here!" but they were already a half a block away standing on their pedals, whipping their bikes from side to side, and pedaling like the finish line of the *Tour de France* was in front of their homes.

Kerby hollered, "Hey guys! Don't just leave me here!"

Without missing a crank of the pedals, they both shouted over their shoulders, "Sorry, Kerb!"

Victor rode up on a new *Sting-Ray*, which looked too small

for him, like maybe—no, like no doubt, he stole it from some terrified fourth grader. He locked up his brakes and slid up, bumping his bike's tire up against Kerby's front metal rim.

Kerby cringed, but stood his ground.

"You Kerby?" Victor demanded with disdain.

"Uhhh, Kerby's down at the store buyin' candy," replied Kerby, looking down at the ground. "If you hurry down there, I'm sure he'd be happy to share some with you guys."

"He's Kerby!" yelled Denton.

Cookie and the other three tough kids rode their bikes in circles around them.

Denton, delighted, laughed.

Victor, an eighth-grader, who should have been in ninth, but was held back a year, was a far worse bully than Denton; meaner, crazier, and utterly incorrigible. He excelled in truancy, shoplifting *Playboys*, flunking school, and defying authority. All the kids feared him because they had either been bullied by him or had heard another kid tell of being bullied by him. Not only did Victor's attitude scare Kerby, but so did his appearance. Strong and stone-faced, Victor wore his sandy hair in a crew-cut on account of, he had recently been released from juvenile hall. He had squinting, murky-blue eyes scheming how to hurt somebody and zits peppering his pallid face like he never ate a healthy meal. He dressed in soiled denim jeans, worn-out, high-top, sneakers, and a white, dirty, oversized, hand-me-down T-shirt stained with drops of spaghetti sauce or more likely blood from punching some poor, horrified kid in the nose. Compared to kids his own age, he wasn't that big, but to elementary school kids, he appeared monstrous.

Cookie, a short, seventh-grade, Cuban kid with bushy black hair and a maniacal smile gleaming with a gold front tooth replacing the tooth he'd lost in a fist fight, stopped and straddled his bike next to Victor. He dressed stylish, wearing colorful, button-up shirts with collars, clean pants, and new sneakers and spoke with a Spanish accent, parroting every sentence Victor spoke as if he were interpreting for his own immigrant parents. His bike looked exactly like Kerby's stolen blue *Sting-Ray,* but Cookie's was recently spray-painted red with over-spray on the handlebars, tires, and seat.

The other three gang members, one gangly black kid, called Cuestick, and two beefy, Cuban brothers, Augustine and Orlando, rode their bikes around Kerby, glaring, circling like a pack of hyenas after a lion's kill.

Victor lit a cigarette and with it dangling from his lips and looking demonic behind its smoky cloud, snarled, "I heard you were givin' our friend Denton over there a bad time."

"Yeah, a bad time," echoed Cookie, his gold tooth glinting.

Denton standing on the porch with his arms crossed and grinning, hollered, "See Kerb, I told you, you were dead!"

"He started it," claimed Kerby to Victor, "after I caught his fly-ball."

"You stole my homer!" yelled Denton.

"You ain't nothin' but a itty-bitty crybaby!" retorted Kerby to Denton, angry at the absurdity that Denton expected Kerby to miss a catchable fly-ball.

Denton launched more cuss words until his mother stomped out, pulling the pop-top on a new can of beer, and screamed, "Damn-it! Denton, you get your no good butt in the house right now!"

Denton flipped off Kerby, earning a smack from his mom on the back of his head and shuffled inside.

"You shouldn't have caught that ball," stated Victor, holding his cigarette and flicking the ashes at Kerby.

"Yeah, you shouldn't have caught it," said Cookie, wagging a finger at him as the rest of the circling gang nodded their heads in agreement.

Kerby frowned. He would never intentionally miss a fly-ball

and never throw a game for fear of a bully. Shouldn't, wouldn't, couldn't happen.

"Another thing," continued Victor, after he took a long drag on his cigarette and expelled a cloud of smoke in Kerby's face, "I heard, you called my friend, Denton, 'Frankenstein and Porky Pig'."

"Frankenstein and Porky Pig," repeated Cookie.

"So what?" snapped Kerby. "He was cussin' me."

"Doesn't matter what he does," stated Victor, "'cause he's our friend and you're not and you made him mad and that makes us mad, so we're goin' to have to hurt you and teach you that you can't mess with our gang."

"Yeah, don't mess with our gang," said Cookie.

"My fight's with Denton, not with you guys," said Kerby matter-of-factly.

"No! It's *now* with us," snapped Victor.

"Yeah, with us," growled Cookie.

Kerby swallowed hard and muttered, "Hold on fellas," as he slowly turned his sister's bike around and started pedaling across the grass, "I hear my mom callin' me. We'll have to take this up tomorrow."

"Stop!" shouted Victor.

"Yeah, stop!" yelled Cookie.

Kerby pedaled faster because his life depended on pedaling faster.

"What are you ridin' there?" yelled Victor. "That's the crappiest bike, I've ever seen."

Cookie hollered too, "Yeah, crappiest!" as all the gang burst out in laughter and pedaled in hot pursuit.

They chased and certainly could have caught Kerby and surely could have pounded him into the ground, but they rode on the street next to him, laughing, taunting, and teasing him like a cat does a mouse.

Kerby rode, thrashing flower beds, bumping over

driveways, curbs, and hoses, racing across weed covered yards and manicured lawns with spraying sprinklers, scratching rose bushes, and darting cats all the while he prayed, hoping that he could make it home before they seized him and pummeled him.

A German Shepherd asleep under a porch, awoke, and kicking up a cloud of dust, charged out, snarling, barking, and baring its teeth, chasing after Kerby and biting at his pedaling feet. Kerby jerked his feet up and away from the canine's snapping teeth, and placed them up on the handlebars until he coasted out of the dog's yard where he resumed pedaling like crazy.

Kerby turned the corner and saw the house of Paul Rellons and he grinned for he had a plan; a stunt he had practiced a million times. Just as Victor swooped in on his bike to knock Kerby off his, Kerby cranked his handlebars, turning off the grass down Paul's driveway. Victor and his gang slammed on their brakes and diverted down the same driveway. Kerby stopped pedaling, stood, balanced on his pedals, and coasting, released his grip on the handlebars. At the very instant Victor and Cookie swooped in on both sides of his bike and kicked Kerby's bike out from under him, Kerby reached into the air and grabbed an overhanging limb of an old oak tree. Kerby's bike crashed into a fence as he swung up, scurrying like a monkey high up into the tree, hiding in the thick leaves and moss covered branches.

The gang jumped off their bikes, letting them crash into the fence too. Cookie climbed up the tree and positioned himself on a limb below Kerby, determined to yank him out of the tree. Every time he tried to grab Kerby's foot, Kerby kicked him in the face. Cookie, feeling pain and not wanting his gold tooth knocked out, climbed down in defeat. All of the gang raced over to an orange tree and picking oranges off the ground or yanking them off the tree, bombarded Kerby.

Kerby, dominant at dodge ball at school, dodged them all. He caught one in mid-air, quickly peeled it, and laughing at his assailants, ate it. He caught a few more and hurled them back at them.

Suddenly, Mr. Rellons pulled his car up the driveway, saw the kids hurling a cannonade of oranges, screeched his car to a halt, parked it, jumped out, and hollered, "What are you boys doin'?"

"They're tryin' to kill me," yelled Kerby from the top of the tree.

Mr. Rellons cranked his head up, peered into the tree, saw Kerby, and yelled at the gang of rowdy boys, "You kids! Get out of here before I call the cops!"

Victor's gang scattered, grabbed their bikes, and scooted down the driveway. Just before Victor turned into the street, he stopped, straddled his bike, spun, and lobbed an orange, hitting tall, lanky, Mr. Rellons on the top of his bald head, causing him to cuss under his breath.

While Kerby climbed down out of the tree, the back screen door flew open and Paul and Ira raced out the house, asking at the same time, "Hey Kerb, you okay?"

Kerby swung from the lowest limb down to the ground and replied sarcastically, "Yeah, but no thanks to my 'best friends'."

Kerby went inside Paul's house, washed his sticky, orangy, sappy hands, and they all, including Mr. Rellons drank a bottle of ice-cold grape *Nehi*.

Kerby, after an hour of hiding out at Paul's and since it was getting dark and since the gang might still be lurking around, and since he could maneuver better on his feet in case they were, decided to walk the block home to his house. Ira wanted to hang out at Paul's for a while longer. Halfway home as Kerby approached a huge hedge that divided the yard between two houses, he peered down and saw through the leaves, five pairs of sneakers and five sets of bicycle tires. Kerby darted past the hedge like Willie Mays running to first base. Victor and his gang abandoned their bikes and chased after him. Kerby, sprinting just ahead of the pack, ran up to his house, jumped over the porch rail, grabbed the front door's doorknob, twisted it, but found it locked. The gang leapt over the rail as Kerby dove over the opposite rail, rolled on the grass, jumped up, and dashed to the back yard. They did the same nearly nabbing him. Kerby bolted to the back door, turned the knob, and shoved open the door as Victor and his cohorts tackled him and they all came rolling, sprawling, and fighting into Kerby's family room. Kerby's mom and siblings watching TV, all screamed in terror as Kerby kicking, punching, and thrashing, screamed, "Mom, call the cops!"

His trembling mother, a small woman with auburn hair, jumped up from the couch, ran to the phone, and called the police. The officers must have been in the area, because within less than a minute, twenty-two punches, and thirteen kicks later, Kerby heard the blurp of a siren out front. Victor and his gang heard it too, stopped kicking and punching, bolted out the back door, jumped the alley fence, and escaped to their bikes.

Kerby's mom filed charges. The police busted Victor and his gang, but unfortunately for Kerby, the bullies got madder and meaner.

The next week, the last week of summer vacation was peaceful; no bullies. Kerby's bumps, bruises, and pride healed and he evaded getting beat-up again, by avoiding Gidden's Park.

At the end of that safe week, on a muggy Saturday night after an afternoon of thunder showers, and with the wet streets glistening orange in the setting sun, Kerby's mom dropped him off at the *Fun Skate* roller rink down on Armenia Avenue past Hillsboro. The old rink had been in business since Kerby's grandfather had skated there as a kid. It needed paint and only half the neon sign lit up so in the dark the sign read *Fun*. He rented his skates, put them on, skated over to the waist high rail around the rink, and searched for her and saw her.

Gail skated past him twirling and gliding with the grace of a ballerina, her long, brown hair flowing like the wake of a ship with every turn and twist. Kerby fell into a trance; his heart pounded; his breath quickened. He thought, after surviving a beating from not only one bully, but from a pack of bullies, how bad could it hurt if Gail didn't like him. He beat-up his shyness like the bullies had beaten him and dodging others skaters, he made a beeline across the rink's wooden floor to Gail.

"Hi, Gail," said Kerby, smiling, blushing, and if he had a tail, wagging it like a puppy.

"Oh, hi, Kerby," she said, smiling, skating crossovers around the end of the rink, "how's your summer going?"

"Wanna skate together and I'll tell you about it?" said Kerby.

"Sure," she said, reaching out to hold hands with him while she pivoted to skate backward. While they skated, swerving to and fro, he told her all about the ballgame, the snow cone catch, his fight with Denton, his encounter with Victor, Cookie, and the gang, and how they crashed into his house and how he bravely fought them all off while his frightened mom called the police. She listened, enjoying Kerby's story telling prowess and then she shared of her vacation with her family in Saint Augustine, the oldest city in America, touring the *Fountain of Youth* and the Spanish fort, *Castillo de San Marcos*.

The song stopped and the lights came up to full brightness and one of the skating staff, a teenage girl announced over the PA system, "Okay, anyone who wants to participate in the *Bunny Hop* and the *Hokey-Pokey*, now's the time."

Kerby and Gail remained on the skate floor while other kids crowded around them. During the songs, Kerby showed off for Gail, acting silly, completely over-exaggerating all of his

Bunny Hop and *Hokey Pokey* moves. They laughed, enjoying each other, and as the lights dimmed and a slow ballad played, the teen announcer said over the loud speaker, "Okay now, everyone off the floor except pair-skaters."

Not a whole lot of kids skated in pairs, so Kerby and Gail had the floor nearly all to themselves. Gail leaned in and said, "I think you're a really nice boy and I've always liked you. I wondered why you followed me home from school, but never walked with me."

"I didn't think you wanted me too," replied Kerby.

"Well, when school starts next week, I want you to know—I want you to."

Kerby smiled and retorted, "This is the first time ever—I can't wait for school to start."

They skated around the rink a few times with her twirling like an Olympic skater and she said, "Those bullies are so mean and you are so brave." She pulled on his hands, drawing herself in close to him, leaned in, and kissed Kerby's cheek.

He grinned and boasted, "Well, one thing for sure—I ain't afraid of no bullies!"

"Is that right?" snarled someone skating in the dimness directly behind Kerby.

Kerby glanced over his shoulder and gulped, peering into the clenched face of Victor, and skating next to him Cookie, Cuestick, Augustine, and Orlando, glaring at him, pursuing him like they were hockey players and he was a puck.

Kerby let go of Gail's soft, dainty hands, and said, "You'd better get off the skate floor for now."

She shuddered and skated off as Kerby silently prayed for his life.

Victor skated up and latched on to Kerby's wrist. Next, he linked his other hand with his pals lined up next to each other with their hands linked together too, forming a human whip. The bullies, literally ran on their skates until they meshed into a rhythm, pushing, churning, chugging faster and faster, tugging Kerby along with them.

Kerby yelled, "Let go!" and tried to yank his wrist free from Victor's gator grip, but couldn't free himself. He thought to drop to the floor, but didn't, not wanting to be kicked by a bunch of roller skates.

Gail, worried, with her hand over her mouth, watched safely from behind the rail.

The rink's manager, a middle-aged man and all his teen helpers worked the busy snack bar during couple's skate, so they were unaware of Kerby's plight.

Victor's gang laughed, thoroughly enjoying the panic they saw on Kerby's face.

Nearly every kid in the place stopped talking, eating snacks, and drinking sodas and stood at the rail, watching the human whip increase in velocity around the rink.

The few couples skating, fearing for their own safety, left the rink and stood aghast at the rail.

Victor shouted, "Now!" and the line of skating bullies yanked to their left, transferring the speed down the bully-line to Kerby. Victor, with perfect timing, released his grip on Kerby, launching him ahead of them at break-neck speed.

Kerby, zooming across the rink and attempting to slow down using the toe stopper on his skates, slammed into the rail at supersonic speed, flipping head over skates and soaring over ducking kids scrambling to get out of the way. He landed on top of a table loaded with buttery popcorn, ketchupy hotdogs, sticky sodas, and cheesy pizza, bounced off the wall, back over the table, and crashed to the floor. Moaning in pain without any broken bones or loss of blood, he glanced up into the crowd of kid's faces and saw amongst them, Gail's angelic face peering down at him, asking, "Kerby, are you okay?"

Kerby, embarrassed by it all, sprung to his skates, and though still seeing stars, said, "I'm okay. Sure. You bet. I'm okay."

With pair-skating over, the manager left the snack bar and noticing a crowd of kids gathered in the corner of the rink, he investigated it. Kerby and Gail, as well as other kids, told him what had happened. He found Victor and his gang on the other side of the rink, terrorizing kids and stealing their snacks and sodas. He demanded that the gang leave immediately or he would call the police. After Victor took off his rented skates, put on his shoes, and turned to leave, he hurled a skate at the manager.

The man dodged it and hollered, "That does it Victor! You and your pals are banned from *Fun Skate* for life! Get out! Get out now! And never come back!"

Victor flipped off the manager, Cookie followed suit, as did Cuestick, Augustine, and Orlando and they stomped out the door into the sweltering night.

At ten-o-clock the rink closed. Kids left with their rides home. Kerby walked Gail out and stood with her until her dad picked her up. He waved to her father. Her father waved back. She climbed into the car, rolled down her window, and said, "Hey Kerby, thanks for all the fun skating around together. You sure do a crazy *Hokey Pokey*. You gonna be okay?"

"Yeah, I'm all right."

"Do you need a ride home?"

"Thanks, but my mom's comin' any minute now."

"Okay then, see you at school on Monday. Bye."

"Okay, see you there."

Gail left with her dad. A few waiting kids left with their rides. Kerby heard the rink's door lock behind him as the manager and his helpers cleaned up the place. In the dark and empty parking lot, Kerby stood alone, a sitting duck below the glowing entrance light under the neon *Fun* sign. He glanced around, nervous, leery, thinking that maybe Victor and his gang prowled about somewhere like panthers in the night shadows. The heavy, humid air squeezed Kerby like a python. He felt clammy and ached a bit from the gang's human whip. All was quiet except the sound of crickets and a huge sphinx moth flapping about the entrance light.

Just as Kerby thought, *Where's Mom?* he heard shuffling shoes. Frightened and thinking the worse, he spun and it was the worse. Victor and his cohorts rushed him from their hiding place around the corner of the building and seized him.

Victor shouted, "We are so gonna punish you for gettin' us kicked out of *Fun Skate!*" and they dragged Kerby, punching and kicking him into the dark around the side of the building.

At that moment, Kerby's mother pulled into the parking lot and saw the gang drag Kerby around the building. She sped up, raced over, and slammed on the brakes, screeching up to the gang and Kerby, the headlights illuminating the cowardly conduct of the shocked gang. She honked the horn, startling them, thus allowing Kerby to escape, dive into the car, and lock its doors. The gang tried to open all four doors, hoping to rip Kerby out of the car. His mom shoved the car into reverse, dropped it into drive, and sped home where she again called the police.

On Monday morning, the first day of school, Kerby dressed in new long pants, new *Converse Allstars*, a new button up shirt, and a new haircut all slicked back. He arrived early at Thomas A. Edison Elementary, an old, two-story, brick schoolhouse at Curtis and 17th streets; so old that his mother and grandmother had both attended there. Kerby, a junior safety patrol, met with other sixth graders in the cafeteria where Mr. Goodman, an older, gray haired, heavy-set teacher in charge of the program, gave them all an orange belt with a strap going around their waist and over their right shoulder. He pinned a shiny, tin badge to each kid's belt; a badge with *AAA* representing *American Automobile Association* in the center of the words *Patrolman School Safety Patrol*. Kerby stared down at his gleaming badge and after all the humiliation he endured by the fists of Victor's gang and after all their bullying around the neighborhood, he felt proud to help little kids cross busy streets.

The teacher had a wall map of the streets surrounding the school and assigned street corners to each crossing guard, appointing Kerby to Curtis and 15th, a T intersection with the most traffic and the most kids crossing. He left the school, raced down Curtis two blocks to 15th, and crossed the busy street to his station, arriving early enough, so not a single kid would have to cross alone. He dutifully stopped traffic and waved the younger kids, all decked out in their new school clothes, safely across the street. Ira and Paul arrived at the corner and acted like morons begging Kerby to hold their hands like babies when they crossed the street. Kerby, all business, stopped traffic for them and ordered them to go on to school. Gail, along with a few of her girl friends strolled up to Kerby's corner. Kerby puffed out his chest so the sunshine glinted off the badge nearly blinding them. He strolled out, stopped a huge, delivery truck, and escorted the girls across the street. Gail turned and smiled at Kerby; a smile brighter than his badge. Kerby, smiling, mesmerized, stood in the middle of the street and watched Gail saunter away. The truck driver honked. Kerby jumped, hustled out of the way, and waved on the traffic.

The flow of kids soon stopped and Kerby heard the school bell ring. Safety patrol kids were allowed to be ten minutes late for class so Kerby waited for a lull in the traffic and casually crossed 15th. As Kerby stepped out of the street and up on the sidewalk to stroll back down Curtis to school, a big kid came out of the shabby corner house; a dilapidated home with a dead yard and a dented, old pick-up in the driveway. The junior high boy, playing hooky from school, lit a cigarette, sat on the steps of his front porch, and listened to a small transistor radio poking out of his shirt pocket. He glanced up and saw Kerby crossing the street. He set his radio on the porch, sprang up, raced across his yard to the sidewalk, and blocked Kerby's path.

"Well, well, well," said Victor, smoking his cigarette, "if it ain't my punchin' bag, Kerby Speck, coming to visit me at my very own home. You're like pizza delivery."

Kerby started to run, but Victor yelled, "Stop! Or the next time I see you, I'm gonna kill you."

Kerby froze in his steps as Victor sauntered over to him.

"Oooh," teased Victor, "a big safety patrol. You wanna help me cross the street?"

"No!" spat Kerby. "Just leave me alone. I gotta go to class."

"No, you don't. You're goin' to be late," said Victor, as he reached out and snatched Kerby's safety patrol badge off his orange belt.

Victor gawked at it for a moment, held it up for Kerby to see, and said, "You like this badge a lot, don't you?" He knew it represented giving and helping, responsibility and pride, and he hated it gleaming in the sunshine when he lived a life under such a dark cloud.

"Yes, I do," admitted Kerby, "so give it back."

Glaring at Kerby's face, watching it to catch every bit of anguish, Victor dropped the badge on the sidewalk, stomped it, smashed it, and ground it with his foot.

Kerby cringed and hung his head in defeat.

Victor picked up the annihilated badge and again held it in front of Kerby's face, asking him, "So how do like your badge now?"

Kerby looked away, not wanting to see it.

Victor wound up, threw the badge, and it soared into the blue sky, across the street, and landed on the roof of a small church next to its steeple. Even with the scant amount of gleam remaining on the badge, it beamed like a SOS signal to God.

Kerby's lip trembled, his eyes teared, and his face turned

red, not from fright but from fury. He breathed heavily with every breath fanning the angry fire within. He believed, he was on that corner, at that time for a reason; to be there, not only to help little kids cross the street, but he, like David saving his tribe from Goliath, was there to save his neighborhood from Victor. He glanced up at his badge glinting on the roof of the church and he knew no matter what, that good would triumph over evil. He was tired of being bullied, beat-up, and scared to walk down the street or play baseball and he sorely missed playing baseball. As when he fought Denton, all of his anger surfaced; anger over the chance that he might never see his soldier father again; over his mom trying to raise four kids without his dad; and over feeling ashamed that he got his butt kicked at the roller rink in front of Gail, and now, the last straw, his safety patrol badge smashed to smithereens.

"Is the wittle baby gonna cry?" taunted Victor. "Huh? Him miss his whittle badge?"

Kerby didn't answer. He glared into Victor's eyes. Victor stared back, his bully power weakening, for his ability to terrorize fed on fear and there was no fear in Kerby's eyes, only flames of fury.

Kerby took a step closer into the smoky veil around Victor. He witnessed Victor's eyes blink, his nose twitch, and his shoulder flinch, and he blurted out, "You know Victor, just because you got it rough at home and in school doesn't give you the right to pick on other kids."

Victor remained silent, shifted his cigarette to his left hand, reared back, and with his right hand slugged Kerby down to the ground.

Kerby picked himself up; his bottom lip bleeding; his fists clenching; his face scowling at Victor and again, he saw Victor flinch.

Victor muttered, "Oooh, Kerby looks mad. I'm so scared."

147

He took one last drag on his cigarette and flicked it out into the street.

Kerby knew that Victor, for once, spoke the truth. The bully was scared. Without saying a word, Kerby, driven by exasperation and rage, swung his right fist, catching Victor on the cheek and as Victor reeled backward, Kerby punched him again with another right to the mouth followed by a left jab in the eye. Like a down and out prize fighter boxing in a dingy gym for food, room, and board, Kerby punched, never giving Victor a chance to put up his dukes.

Victor crashed to the ground and Kerby, well taught by his bully mentors, straddled him, and like Cassius Clay, punched him in the face until Victor's nose bled, his lips bled, and his confidence bled out. Kerby knew if he stopped punching before Victor was totally whipped, the bully would do worse to him, so he kept slugging, jabbing, and kicking until Victor cried out begging, "Stop! Stop!" like all his terrified victims had cried out.

"You might be older, bigger, and meaner than me," yelled Kerby, "but you and your gang ain't gonna terrorize me and the neighborhood no more," and like firing pistons in a V-8, he struck Victor again and again, slugging with endless energy, swinging without mercy, beyond revenge, striking until his flying fists would forever be stamped into Victor's memory.

Mr. Goodman, looking for Kerby who was late for class, walked down the street and saw him on top of Victor, pummeling him. He ran up to Kerby, jumped behind him, and yanked him up and off Victor, all the while, Kerby's fists swinging in a blur.

The teacher remembered when Victor had attended Edison and all the trouble he had caused, and said, "Victor, I know Kerby, and I know you, and I know *you* started this fight. When I get back to the school, I'm calling the truant officer on you and you son—are in a lot of trouble. And another thing, if you ever threaten any of my kids again, I'll come after you myself."

Victor, bleeding from his nose and mouth, jumped up and balling like a baby, ran up to the porch and slammed into his father stepping out onto the porch. The shirtless, barefoot man wearing jeans with the zipper down and with disheveled hair like he just crawled out of bed and rubbing his temples as if he suffered a hangover, glanced over at Kerby, surmised there had been a fight, and barked at his son, "You cryin' cause that wimpy kid whooped your butt? No kid of mine's goin' to be a crybaby." He reached out and slapped Victor two times in the back of the head, causing Victor to wail even louder and beg, "Please Pop, don't hit me anymore. I'm sorry."

"I only smacked you boy, to give you somethin' to cry about," he growled. "Now git in the house and how come you ain't at school?"

Victor disappeared inside their house as his angry dad picked up Victor's radio and threw it against the wall silencing it.

Mr. Goodman hollered at Victor's father, "I'm calling the truant officer, so expect a visit from him."

The barechested man lit a cigarette, yanked it out of his mouth, and yelled back, "You tell your Mr. Truant Cop that, I'll do the punishin' on my own kid!" and he stormed into the house.

Kerby and Mr. Goodman walked back to the school. The teacher gave Kerby a new badge, sent him off to class, and called the truant officer on Victor. Later that morning, a few kids heard Mr. Goodman tell other teachers the story of Kerby pounding Victor. The story spread like wildfire throughout the school and Kerby became a hero.

After school, without any sign of Victor or any of his gang, Kerby helped the kids back across the street as Gail waited for him standing under a shade tree. All the kids at the crossing, especially the victims of Victor, gawked at Kerby as if he was the village dragon-slayer for his gallant victory over the bully. Once the last kid crossed the busy street safely, Kerby walked

Gail home, telling her the story and of course adding a few embellishments. She listened with wide eyes while holding his hand. At her front door, Kerby asked her to go steady with him and blushing, she said yes. Her mother invited him in for fresh-baked, chocolate-chip cookies and he ate four of them washed down with a glass of milk.

On the bright and cheerful Saturday following that first week of school, all the neighborhood kids met at Gidden's Park for a pick-up game of baseball.

Denton, who had heard the story about Victor getting whooped, showed up, and acted civil.

Gail, smiling, stood behind the backstop and watched Kerby showing off making easy catches look hard and hard catches look easy. She carried a paper sack with two peanut butter and jelly sandwiches, two small bags of *Lay's* potato chips, and a couple bottles of cold, chocolaty *Yoohoo* for Kerby and her after the game.

Kerby, playing left field again, waved to Gail. She waved back and right after she did, he saw Victor ride up on a bike and stop behind the backstop next to her.

A kid hit a double bouncer to Jamie the pitcher who scooped it up and tossed it over to Yoohoo on first for three outs. Kerby and his team jogged in as the other team took the field.

Kerby glanced over at Victor who had a black eye and a scabby cut on his lip. He watched, ready for combat, as the bully strolled over and stood toe to toe with him. Kerby didn't back away but leaned in closer. Both boys made fists while both breathed heavily as both licked their dry lips.

Gail, worried, covered her mouth with one hand. All the players became silent, waiting, watching, and wondering if fists would fly. The humidity grew heavier. A crow cawed from the top of a tree. A brown grasshopper twittered by.

Muscles tensed, teeth clenched, and eyes narrowed. Seconds ticked off and like two gunfighters waiting for the other to draw, each waited for the other to throw a punch. Sweat trickled down Kerby's brow and just when he thought the standoff would escalate into blows, he saw a strange look in Victor's eyes. There was a sadness, a humiliation, a plea for acceptance and Kerby remembered a saying he had heard in Sunday school: *The only way to get rid of an enemy—is make him a friend.*

Kerby broke the silence and the standoff, saying, "So uhh, Victor, you wanna play ball?"

Surprised, Victor didn't answer while he tried to grasp this strange treatment. To him, compassion was a unfamiliar concept. However, it did feel good, so he gave up trying to understand it or even fight it, hung his head, and humbly replied, "I got no glove."

Without missing a beat, Kerby said, "How 'bout you play on the other team and when my team's up to bat, you can use my mitt?"

Victor looked shocked; his blue eyes defrosted, his face unclenched, and he grinned.

Kerby pulled off his mitt and tossed it to Victor. Victor caught it, slid his hand into it, and ran out to right field where they were short a player.

Kerby snatched up a bat because it was his turn up at the plate. Showing off for Gail with his twinkling blue eyes scheming along with his spontaneous grin, he pointed like the *Great Bambino* at Denton out in left field and clobbered the first pitch over the bully's head for a home run.

GO GET MOM

G rant stood next to the mangled car and gawked through the passenger window at his lifeless body trapped between the deformed seat and the twisted steering wheel. The deflated airbag, stained red, cradled his head against the door while a deep cut above his temple dribbled blood down his cheek and off his chin. It seemed so strange that he sat so still; so ghostlike, dusted with powder from the airbag; so silent, with dangling arms and contorted legs; so surreal, among sparkling shards of windshield glass; so terribly tragic; a half century of life; a head-on collision; gone.

After a long week of sales calls along California's Central Coast, Grant had left Paso Robles, heading east toward his home in Fresno. While driving through the rolling foothills, radio and cell phone signals are weak, so Grant slipped in a CD of mixed jazz and set his cruise control to just above the speed limit. He felt exhausted from all the driving, dealing with customers, eating at restaurants, and sleeping in motels, so he couldn't wait to get home, barbecue steaks, drink a glass of wine, and sleep in his own bed. He sorely missed his wife and three sons. Like every Friday afternoon, a procession of traffic coursed down highway 41: eighty-four gaunt miles of foothills, range-land, cotton fields, plowed dirt, and plain old dirt; boring miles of ground squirrels, coyotes, hawks, buzzards, and herds of cattle; and slow miles on two narrow lanes at 55 mph with fat motor-homes, long toy-haulers, and loaded semi-trucks. It was an extremely dangerous route where eager vacationers sped west to sun and fun at the beach, racing, crossing double yellow lines, reckless, passing on blind curves, assuming oncoming traffic would pull off the road and let them zoom by to arrive at their destination fifteen seconds sooner.

Cruising down out of the dry, golden foothills, Grant followed a sluggish semi-truck hauling two trailers each teeming with a load of carrots. He was still about twenty miles out from Kettleman City: a rest-stop halfway home for fast food, fuel, and a restroom. The tiny town, in the middle of nowhere, baked under the blazing sun in a dusty, desert terrain. During the hot summer days, a sign should be posted at the west end of town, *Beachcombers, Welcome back to the Central Valley where it's 112° and you'll have to go back to work*, because, when travelers reached Kettleman—vacation was over.

The heavy-laden semi-truck blocked Grant's view ahead of him, so he glanced at the scenery around him. Dried-up tumbleweeds and spindly, yellow dandelions mottled the shoulders on both sides of the highway. Beyond the shoulders, fenced rangeland ran all the way to the hazy horizon. Cattle grazed under the shade of scattered oak trees, buzzards circled overhead, red-tailed hawks perched on power poles, and ground squirrels scurried dangerously close to the road.

Instead of becoming impatient with the slow-moving truck, Grant adjusted the air conditioner vent to blow directly on his face and cranked up the sound of a jazzy saxophone playing a standard. He squirmed in his seat to get comfortable and took a sip from his water bottle. A little, white butterfly fluttered in front of his car and his eyes followed it. At the same instant that it splattered on his windshield, the rambling truck abruptly swerved off the road in a cloud of dust. Grant clutched the steering wheel with both hands and slammed his foot down on the brake pedal. Suddenly, out of the swirling dust, sped an oncoming car—head-on. The westbound car, passing a white motor-home, accelerated in Grant's eastbound lane, however, there was not enough time or highway for the car to pass the huge RV. For a second, Grant saw the driver in the oncoming car. The young man sat straight up in his seat, gripping the steering wheel; his eyes wide open; his face contorted in horror. In the passenger seat, a terrified, teenage girl recoiled, screaming, thrusting her hands in front of her face. The cocky, inexperienced driver expected the truck to pull off the road to let him pass, but he didn't expect another vehicle, Grant's car, behind the truck.

Terror and screeching tires possessed the highway. Grant yanked his steering wheel toward the shoulder—no time; an explosion of metal and momentum; deafening; disintegrating; a gasp; a groan; a flash of light; a thought—*I'm dead.*

The vehicles stopped in a sizzling, steaming, mass in the middle of the eastbound lane. The westbound RV and the eastbound semi-truck pulled off the road and stopped, followed by other stopping motorists in east and westbound lanes. People called 9-1-1, jumped out of their cars, raced to the horrific wreck in the middle of the hot asphalt, and encircled it. The sun blazed without the slightest breeze and glinted off a forming pool of oil.

Grant's spirit floated back a few feet away from the collision and peered at what used to be two vehicles: his silver Buick Century and the teen's blue Toyota Camry, both cars now one hideous pile of crushed metal, shattered glass, and gruesome bodies. He noticed his ghostly reflection in his car's window, no bruises or blood, and even though he felt twenty-five again, he still looked fifty with salt and pepper hair; his face portraying the lines and creases from forging a career and raising three rowdy boys. He didn't feel any pain or sorrow, but he really didn't expect to. During life, people had always said, 'Once you're dead, you're free of all physical and emotional pain.' It was true.

He turned away from his reflection and peered at the other mangled car. The trapped, teenage driver, barely alive, groaned in pain behind the steering wheel of the compacted mass of wreckage. On the crumpled hood amidst the escaping steam and smoking oil lay the maimed body of the teenage girl. She had not worn a seatbelt. Bluntly thrown through the windshield, she lay face down, silent, motionless; her white top and jean shorts stained red; her long, black hair, clumping with blood. Her arms were crisscrossed in front of her, while her straight legs stuck through the gap in the windshield; her feet, clad in pink sneakers, still inside the car.

The ethereal spirit of the young Latina girl stood next to Grant; her perfect, brown skin glistened in the sun and her long, black hair, streaming down to the middle of her back had a blinding sheen the length of it. She stared at her still, battered body, then slowly turned and faced Grant.

Grant looked into her large brown eyes and saw glints of bewilderment. She was maybe seventeen or eighteen; too young to be dead. They did not speak; no introductions, no questions, and no explanations. They knew that life as they lived it was over, but they also knew that life didn't end there on that desolate stretch of highway, for they felt a blessed assurance beyond human hope that it continued on to a new beginning, in a new place, with a new body, all strangely, but wonderfully different. Together, they watched a woman check the girl's body for vital signs as two men pried open Grant's passenger door with a tire iron. One of the men leaned in, quickly checked Grant, withdrew out of the car, sadly looked at the others, and shook his head. The woman, checking the young girl, also shook her head. Another man kept talking to the teenage boy, saying, "Hold on. Help is on the way."

California Highway Patrol arrived followed by fire trucks and ambulances. Traffic halted, backing up for miles in both directions. After two firemen carefully removed the body of the young girl from the hood, another firemen sprayed fire retardant on the smoking, metallic mass. Two more fireman extracted Grant's limp body from his demolished car. The rescuers laid the bodies on the shoulder as paramedics tried to revive them. A paramedic made desperate attempts to save the young girl, but finally sighed, covering her face and body with a blanket. The firemen brought out the Jaws of Life to rescue the teenage boy while another paramedic readied a defibrillator in an attempt to resuscitate Grant.

Grant and the Latina girl stood quietly, unnoticed amongst the rescue workers, onlookers, and commotion. Suddenly, she gasped, turned to Grant, and whispered, "I hear my grandfather calling my name. Strange. He died when I was eight. I must go now."

Grant spun around, away from the accident, and saw a bright light in the shape of an arched doorway in the pasture on the other side of the barbwire fence. Invisible to the living, the brilliancy framed the silhouetted image of a man standing with outstretched arms. Grant watched the young girl run unscathed through the barbwire, calling to the man, "Poppi, Poppi," and leap into the light and into his arms. Grant watched their silhouettes as the man swung her around, joyfully hugging her, and then, they turned, walking hand in hand away from the accident, away from Grant, away from an existence with a mortal shell and into an eternal world of peace and contentment. They vanished, the light waned, and just as the portal closed down to a pinhole of holy light, it beamed glorious again and Grant heard his name called. A silhouette of his deceased father stood amidst the light, calling out Grant's name. Grant smiled and took a step toward his father, but stopped as his father called out, warning, "Son, stay away from the light. Remember your pact." Grant stopped, remembering a promise, a strange pact that he had made with his older brother and sister. He could not go to the light. He could not embrace the spirit of his father.

He could not step into the heavenly afterlife. First—he must do something. Something ghostly.

Fifteen years had passed since Grant's mother, Joyce, had died from breast cancer at the young age of fifty-seven. Her children, grandchildren and anyone who had ever had the pleasure of meeting her, adored her. She planted love, nurtured love, and reaped love. She made her home a happy, welcoming place and she was always ready to cook someone a hot meal. Every color of flower grew in her garden inviting the hummingbirds at sunset. Her family and friends missed her. After her death, Grant's father, Bill, never the same after his wife's death, remained in their country home for many years, until after a long, debilitating illness, he died at a hospice facility.

A few weeks after his father's funeral, Grant had met with a realtor, an elderly man and friend of the family, who had recently nearly died from complications with prostate cancer. As they sat at the dining room table at the house of Grant's father, discussing the listing agreement of the property, the realtor stopped speaking and gasped, saying, "I thought we were alone in the house!"

"We are," replied Grant. "Why?"

"Well," said the realtor, a bit taken back, "I just saw a woman walking down the hallway and as she passed by us, she glanced at me."

Grant instantly jumped up from his chair, ran to the hall, and peered up and down it, half expecting to see a ghost, but quite relieved that he didn't. No one was there. He sat back down in the dining room chair and asked, "So what'd she look like?"

"She wore her reddish hair pinned on top of her head and a long white dress."

Grant could not believe what he had just heard and said, "My mother, who died fifteen years ago in this house, was buried in a long white dress, in fact, it was her wedding dress, and she always wore her auburn hair in a sort of short bouffant.

"Very weird; but I swear Grant, I saw her."

"I believe you. I just can't understand why her spirit would remain in this world. She had a strong faith and in her last days, she spoke often about spending eternity in Heaven."

"I don't even believe in ghosts," stated the realtor, "but I saw her. I can't imagine why your mother's ghost would linger in this house—but of course, I must disclose this in our listing agreement, not that I saw a ghost of course, but that your mother died in this house."

After the house sold, and after a few months had passed, Grant bumped into the new owners, Ross and Karissa Newly at the grocery store and asked them how things were going.

"We just love the house," gushed Karissa, thirty something, cute with a bubbly personality, "but there's something I'd like to ask you."

"Oh Karissa," huffed her thirty something husband, tall, with more of an analytical view of life, "don't ask him what I think you're going to ask him."

"I'm sorry dear, but I must, for the sake of the children."

Their daughter Ellie, eleven and skinny, and their son Mason, eight and pudgy, were standing next to them listening intently, wide eyed, gawking up at Grant, waiting for their mom to ask him and for him to answer.

"Kids," said their father, "go pick out a few boxes of cereal."

"Noooo, please dad," they both whined, "we wanna hear about the ghost."

"What ghost?" asked Grant. "What happened?"

"Well, one day," began Karissa, "when Ross was still at work, and the kids had just returned home from school and were playing inside, I was outside working in the garden, and by the way, you know, I just love all of those hummingbird feeders that your mother had hung in the garden."

"Karissa, please, stick with the story," chided her husband.

"Okay, you see, I always carry my cell phone with me and I received a call from my daughter on her cell phone. I answered, expecting that they wanted me to make them a snack, but she was screaming hysterically. I ran into the house and found the kids, frantic, hiding in her bedroom closet. After they calmed down a bit, they told me that they were on Ellie's computer when a woman walked past her room, stopped at the doorway, and watched them. They saw her reflection in the monitor and spun around expecting to see me, but I was in the garden. They saw a ghostly woman wearing a full-length, white dress with her hair pinned up."

"We sure did," chimed both Ellie and Mason and then Ellie added, "and she was a ghost. We're not making it up!"

"And we've seen her more than just once," added Mason.

"Well, first," said Grant, "I believe you and I want to remind you guys that we fully disclosed in the listing agreement that my mother had passed away in the house and ...."

"We remember," interrupted Ross, "and we do love the house and we're not getting legal or anything, we just want to know, what's going on?"

"I really don't know," admitted Grant, "however, I will say this, my mother was buried in a long white dress with her hair pinned up."

"It's her," whispered Ellie to Mason. "It's his mother and she's a ghost."

"Most likely—it is her," agreed Grant, "but there's something you must keep in mind—my mother was a kind and gentle woman who lived only to love her children and her grandchildren. She made her house the center of many happy memories." Grant looked down at the kids, gazed into their eyes, and softly said, "If the ghost in your house is truly that of my mother's, then you need not be afraid. No more screaming and hiding in the closet. You are safe. She loves family, especially kids, and she would never do anyone any harm in any way at anytime."

After Grant had bumped into the Newlys, he set up a visit with his older brother Dale and sister Cheryl to discuss the incidence of their mother's ghost wandering the halls at the old house. They met at his sister's house, sat around a small kitchen table, and drank coffee. Grant explained the sightings of their long gone mother as his siblings gasped in disbelief.

After much discussion, they finally believed him and Grant made a suggestion. "I think that the three of us should make a promise, a pact to each other, that whoever dies first, will go get Mom."

"How do we know it's even possible to 'go get Mom?'" spat Dale.

"I don't know," admitted Grant, shrugging his shoulders, "but if it's at all possible, we should try. I mean, you know, she seems to be *here*. Obviously, if she's still *here*, then maybe after our death, we can still be *here*."

"But why would she linger?" asked Cheryl. She took a sip of coffee and while her brothers thought over the question, she added another question, "Is she just some defiant soul unwilling to go to the light?"

"I wouldn't think so," replied Dale.

"Me neither," acknowledged Grant, "but I do know this, that one of us has to go and get her and push her or pull her into the great beyond. Let's make a pact—" He shoved his coffee cup out of the way and thrust his right hand into the middle of the table. They did the same, overlapping their hands, and made a pact as all three spoke the words, "Whoever dies first, will go get Mom."

At the time of the pact, Grant thought that since his brother and sister were older and both suffering from chronic health problems that they would most likely pass on first. He never imagined, he'd be in a fatal accident and be the first to go.

Out at the fatal, head-on collision on highway 41, Grant's spirit stood next to tumbleweeds and dandelions, a few feet from his battered body. He faced the arch and the image of his father standing at the cusp of light, a threshold between there and here. The effortless impulse to walk into the light and embrace his father conflicted with his promise to go get Mom. He took a step toward the light.

"No," called out his father again, "remember your pact with your brother and sister."

Grant stepped through and past the barbwire fence and stopped in the radiance of the arch. The light was not just seen, but felt. It surged through his spirit as compassion and he knew love. It imparted wisdom and he knew truth. There was peace and he knew happiness. It felt perfect and right. The light beckoned and he took a step closer.

Again, his insistent father spoke, "Grant, you must go get your mother."

By a son's love for his mom, respect for his father, and the strength of his word to his brother and sister, he turned away from the beckoning light and by the will of his spirit, he shot into the air untethered by gravity, unrestrained by time, and unhindered by the ascendancy of life or death. He flew in a flash over the rangeland: cattle and oak trees; past Kettleman: fast food restaurants and gas stations; above the farmland: cotton fields, furrowed ground, and a canal glinting with water; soared over Fresno: freeways, traffic, houses, and swimming pools and out to the country, drifting over the eucalyptus trees and the circular drive, hovering over the house full of memories and in a twinkling, he stood in the living room of his childhood home.

The new owners were not at home, but Grant's mom was, sitting in a rocking chair, in the same spot where her rocking chair had always sat, where every morning of life, she had sipped her tea and watched the sunrise over the Sierra mountains and where every evening at twilight, she had watched the hummingbirds hover at the bird feeders in her garden. He gazed at his mother as she, rocking contently in her chair, gazed at him and he said, "Hello, Mom. I've missed you."

"Hi, son," she said, "I've missed you too. I've missed all of my family." She stood, they hugged for a long moment, and still holding hands, they parted a step. She wore a long white dress and her auburn hair pinned perfectly on top of her head. She looked healthy, her face glowing, and she seemed vigorous without any signs of the ravages of cancer.

"Mom—why are you still here?" asked Grant.

The little lady gazed up at her tall son, her eyes twinkled and she smiled, saying, "Well, because, my family needs me."

"Yes, we do need you," said Grant, "but we're all doing okay. Well—except for me"

"I know why you're here," she said, "but first, I never wanted to leave my children or my grandchildren. I loved my life. My family brought me such great joy."

"Yes, Mom, you brought all of us great happiness too, but you passed away fifteen years ago. You must go to the light. There's another world, better than this one, waiting for you. Dad's waiting too."

"I know. I see the arch of light all the time, but time is different here in the *In-between*. It seems like just yesterday when I first heard my name called and I first saw the light. I've had every deceased relative that I'd ever known and some I didn't know, standing in the doorway of that arch and I ignored them all. Then, your father showed up, but he knew what I knew and he helped me stay away from the light."

"Why Mom? What's keeping you *here* between two worlds?"

"In the *In-between*, we see things and know things. I haven't waited long. It seems but a few moments since I entered this world. You see son, I was allowed to linger—to be here for *you* one last time."

"For me? I don't understand Mom. Why for me?"

"It is my love as a mother for her son that caused me to remain here. I tarried *here*, so you would come *here* to find me and *not* go to the light. I lingered—to cause *you* to linger, so that the good and courageous men out on the highway would have time to save your life."

"You lingered—so that I'd linger?"

"Yes, son."

"You saved my life?"

"Yes, son. So now, I'm ready to go, besides, I hear your father calling my name."

A blazing light in the shape of an arch appeared on the other side of the room. His father stood in the light with open arms, calling out to Joyce. She walked toward the light, stopped at its threshold, turned, and faced Grant. With a brilliance radiating out from behind her silhouette, she smiled and said, "I love you son. Someday, we shall all be reunited and what a glorious day that will be."

"I love you too, Mom. Thanks for lingering and saving my life. Someday, I'll see you on the other side."

She turned, stepped into the light, and embraced her husband. Both looked at Grant and waved goodbye. They vanished, the light dimmed, and the arch disappeared.

Grant stood there alone in his old house, in the *In-between*. He thought, *What now? I'm still dead*. Without warning, he felt a terrific tug and he shot out of the house and into the air. Within seconds, he whooshed over Fresno, farmland, Kettleman, and rangeland back to the accident, straight to his body, and he felt a jolt, a pain, an electrical energy, zapping his body. His face clenched. His body contorted. His arms and legs jerked. A heartbeat. A gasp. Alive! He heard mumbled voices and opened his eyes to a blur of people hovering over him.

"It's a miracle!" exclaimed a paramedic. "We've got a heartbeat! Hang in there, sir. You've been in a car accident and we're airlifting you to *Valley Medical* in Fresno."

They strapped his head, arms, and legs in a gurney. He felt hot sunrays on his face. He heard the throp of a helicopter and felt the wind of its blades. The men hoisted him inside and the craft lifted off in a swirl of dust. Grant lived, only because, he lingered long enough to go get Mom.

CASSIE'S CONTENTMENT

Delbert slapped off his buzzing alarm clock, sat up, grabbed his lighter and pack of cigarettes off the nightstand, and rolled out of bed. His wife, Cassie, sucked in a short snort, pulled the blanket over her shoulders, and kept sleeping. Usually, on Saturday mornings, after a long hard week with him busting knuckles as an auto mechanic and her baby-sitting their three kids plus a few others, they both slept in until around ten-o-clock, unless both needed a smoke or their kids started fighting. However, today, Delbert had set the alarm for nine. It was Cassie's twenty-fifth birthday and he had planned a big surprise.

As he shuffled out of the bedroom and down the hall, he tapped a cigarette out of its pack, placed it between his lips, and lit it. Arriving at the bathroom, he shut the door, set the pack and lighter on the toilet tank, lifted the seat, and stood there lanky and pale in nothing but his mullet haircut and boxers. With the smoldering cigarette dangling from his lips and his sleepy eyes shut, he held his boxer's elastic waist band down with one hand and with his other hand, he directed his raging stream that echoed inside the porcelain bowl. It was a long leak due to drinking a twelve pack of *Bud* the night before. When his stream dwindled down to a dribble and he gave a final shake, a welcoming relief shivered from his shoulders down to his knees. He let his boxers snap back around his waist, flushed the toilet, yanked the cigarette out of his mouth, tapped the ashes off into the swirling water, and then headed to the kitchen. On his way, he walked through the family room of his singlewide trailer, where his three kids sat on a food-stained, worn-out couch and watched cartoons on TV. All three of the youngsters—six-year-old, Joey, dressed in only his mullet haircut and boxers, his four-year-old sister Darlene, wearing her *Little Mermaid* pajamas, and three-year-old, Carly, in only her white training pants—held a cereal bowl in their lap, slurping and munching on spoonfuls of *Cocoa Puffs*. Joey looked like the kid-version of Delbert with blue eyes, stringy, blonde hair, and a small chin dent. Darlene favored Cassie with dark brown hair, brown eyes, and smiley dimples, while Carly, a tot-size version of both Delbert and Cassie had blue eyes, brown hair, and both chin and cheek dimples.

As Delbert shuffled between the youngsters and the TV, he muttered, "Hey, Sport—Princess—Baby girl."

"Hey Daddy," the little girls chimed as Joey, without glancing out of his TV trance and right after a huge spoonful of cereal, muttered, "Hey, Dad," causing milk to dribble down his chin which he promptly wiped off with the back of his hand.

"Hey son, how 'bout turnin' down the TV; your mama's still sleepin'."

Joey shoveled in another spoonful of cereal, grabbed up the remote, and turned down the volume.

Delbert stepped into the kitchen, took one last drag on his cigarette, and snuffed it out in an ashtray full of butts. He moved the box of *Cocoa Puffs* and a carton of milk out of the way, grabbed up the stained, glass coffeepot, filled it with water, and poured the water into the coffeemaker. He then put in a paper filter, dumped four scoops of *Folgers* into it, and pushed the start button. As the coffee maker gurgled, he glanced out the back screen door and saw his hungry dog with its face mashed up against the screen. At the sight and sounds of Delbert, the large, tan colored mutt wagged its tail and whined. Eager to eat, the dog paced up and down the wooden porch deck, dragging its chain that had scraped off the paint on the porch and carved a ragged groove around the porch post.

Delbert opened the screen door and stepped out onto the back porch. He picked up the dog's dish—a bent aluminum pie pan—and reached into a bag of dry dog food. While Tank yapped, Delbert scooped up a plastic cup full of chow, filled the tin, and slid it under the mongrel's nose.

"Now stop that barkin'," snapped Delbert, "and eat!"

The dog gobbled it up, munching, crunching, and spilling it all over.

Delbert stood on the porch next to his sooty, *Weber* barbecue, a plastic five-gallon bucket with sand for cigarette butts, and a garbage can full of crushed beer cans. He gazed out across his shadeless backyard at the scant patch of lawn and meager flowerbeds surrounded by treeless, brown prairie land. He squinted at the bright sunlight and grimaced at the already stifling heat. Chirps of grasshoppers and crickets filled the air. It was a typical, scorching summer day in the small, remote oil-town of Taft, California, about which people in nearby Bakersfield joked, "I only go to Taft, when I taft to." A baked, dusty breeze swirled by rustling the clothes on the rotary clothesline. He noticed that the flowerbeds needed weeding, that the lawn needed mowing, and that a spot of dry, yellowing grass needed watering, so he dragged the garden hose and sprinkler over to it, came back to the trailer, and turned on the faucet just enough as not to drench the clothes on the clothesline. At the end of the porch sat a plastic kiddie pool with a grasshopper swimming circles. In the yard lay a big orange plastic bat, a white plastic baseball, and a few floaty pool toys. He felt lucky to rent the trailer where they had some space and privacy between his noisy, fun-loving kids and his neighbors. He walked around to the side of the trailer, stopped and gawked at the broken down 1972 Dodge Challenger that someday, he would restore and just for a moment, he dreamed of racing it out at Bakersfield's *Famosa Raceway*. He walked back to the porch and patted Tank on the head, which prompted the feeding dog to snarl.

"Oh, stop that growlin'," ordered Delbert, "I don't want your food, you crazy, dumb dog."

Delbert strolled back into the trailer, cranked the knob to turn up the swamp cooler, and went into the kitchen. He poured two cups of coffee—left his black, but added a little cream and a lot of sugar to Cassie's—and carried the cups between the TV and his mesmerized kids back to the bedroom.

"Hey, baby doll, wake up," he said to his wife still snuggled in bed. "I brung you some coffee. Happy Birthday!"

Cassie moaned, opened her eyes, blinked a look at Delbert, and buried her face deeper into her pillow.

"Come on baby, wake up. I've got a surprise planned for you today since its your birthday and all."

"How 'bout, since it's my birthday, you let me sleep in for awhile, baby."

"'Cause, I got your mama comin' over to watch the kids while we take a little trip. Now, I'll just set your coffee down right here on your nightstand while you get to wakin' up. Then you need to pack some clothes for overnight and don't forget that black nasty-nighty I like."

"Well, speakin' of that nasty-nighty, Del, you must be thinkin' it's *your* birthday."

"You're right, every time you wear it, I think *I'm* a lucky birthday boy."

"*You* are—so where we goin', since I need to pack?"

"That's a surprise, baby. After you just threw me that beer and bowlin' party when I turned twenty-five, I wanted to do somethin' special for you."

"I like surprises, Dell, and it really don't matter where we go as long as we get away from the kids and the god-awful heat for a few days."

Cassie sat up in bed, fluffed the pillow behind her, reached over and snatched up her pack of smokes, tapped one out, lit it, took a long drag and asked, "How the kids doin'?"

"Oh, they're fine—eatin' cereal and watchin' cartoons."

She tossed the pack and lighter back on the nightstand, picked up her cup of hot coffee, took a sip, and said, "Mmmm, that's good coffee, baby. Thank you."

"Well, you just relax and take all the time you want, but your mama's goin' to be here in about an hour."

"All right Del, I guess I'll be gettin' out of bed right now then."

She sat her cup down on the nightstand and put her cigarette in the ashtray. She stood up and stretched, as her long, silky hair—tied in a ponytail while she slept—streamed down to her waist. She grimaced at a pain in the small of her back and said, "Hun, will you give me hug and while you're huggin', rub my sore back? Every time I lift up Carly, I get this backache."

Delbert wrapped his skinny arms around Cassie in her nightgown. She pressed her large breasts against his chest and laid her head on his shoulder while he massaged her lower back for a few minutes, and when he was done, he ran his hands over her large hips that buttressed a plentiful size butt that had stuck around after she had birthed three babies.

"How's that feel, doll?"

"It feels a lot better, so I'll get to packin', but—you think we can afford a trip?"

"Sure, 'member, I made some cash, puttin' a new tranny in your Uncle Ted's pick-up."

"Well—what about that ol' minivan—you think it'll hold up?"

"Hope so, after all, over the last couple of months, I put in a new starter, a new battery, and a rebuilt alternator. I also gave it a tune-up and changed the oil."

"How's the tires?"

"I just rotated them, so the back tires are lookin' a bit worn, but we got lots of road miles left on the front ones. Hell, all that minivan needs is new paint to cover that ugly, chalky blue and we'd damn-near have a new minivan."

"All right then," Cassie said with excitement, "Let's get to goin'."

Both showered and dressed. Both wore cut-off blue jeans, sandals, and T-shirts. Delbert's sleeveless, white T-shirt had a colorful print of a high-revving, tire-smoking race car on the back and on the front it read, *Nascar—Livin' Loud and Proud*. Cassie's baggy, pink T-shirt read in bold blue letters, *Hello—My name is Mommy*. They packed two small suitcases and while Delbert loaded them up in the minivan, Cassie cleaned up the kitchen and turned off the sprinkler out back.

Sally, Cassie's mom, drove her decade-old *Ford Escort* onto the gravel that covered Delbert and Cassie's front lot. She parked her car and climbed out with a cigarette in her hand. She had a chronic cough—but smoked anyway. The thin, forty-two-year-old woman, married and divorced four times, bore the creases and wrinkles of a much older woman. She wore skin-tight jeans, a bright yellow halter-top, and her short, bleached hair combed back. She never put on any make-up, except when she was out hunting for husband number five during happy-hour at the *300 Lounge* inside the *Strike-King Bowling Center*. Barely surviving off her last divorce settlement, she lived alone in a trailer park behind the *Lucky Burger* on Main Street. Her days consisted mostly of drinking coffee, smoking cigarettes, and watching TV. As she shuffled in her pink flip-flops across the gravel, she took one last drag on her cigarette, coughed, and tossed the butt on the ground. Tank barked from the back porch.

Cassie heard her mom's car pull up on the gravel, her car door slam, and Tank barking. She opened the front screen door and said, "Hi, Mama, thanks for comin' over," and hollered toward the back screen door, "Tank! Stop that barkin'!"

Sally, in her throaty, smoke worn voice, replied, "I don't mind helpin' out, it beats sittin' 'round that trailer of mine, smellin' charbroiled *Lucky* burgers all day."

"Well, I just appreciate you watchin' the kids for us, so me and Delbert can get away. As you found out last time, none of them kids like to take a bath, so after supper and before bed, I just let'em swim for a while out there in their kiddie pool. Oh, and put a squirt of shampoo in their hair, rub it in, and let them swim it out."

"Okay, honey," said Sally. She coughed, cleared her throat, and added, "You and Delbert just have fun and don't you worry one bit about my grandbabies."

"Oh, and make sure Tank has food and water," said Cassie.

"And don't fret about that no-good dog neither."

When Delbert and Cassie were ready to leave, they walked into the family room where Delbert said, "Okay kids, listen up. Mommy and me are goin' on a special trip. When we get back tomorrow afternoon, we're goin' to pick-up some ice-cream and a birthday cake from the market and throw a little birthday party for Mommy, but for now, jump up and give us a hug goodbye."

Darlene and Carly sprung up off the couch, ran over, gave their mom and dad hugs goodbye, gave their grandma a hug hello, and scrambled back on the couch. Joey, got up and sauntered somewhat sideways over to them, never taking his eyes off the TV, gave them a quick, stiff hug and strolled back to the couch, never taking his eyes off the TV.

Delbert and Cassie climbed into their minivan, but he jumped back out, went back into the trailer for his Styrofoam ice chest, and stuffed it in the van. They rode down the gravel driveway, drove through town past the *Lucky Burger* and the *Strike King*, and headed out to highway 33. Since the van's air conditioner barely worked, they rolled down the windows. Delbert cranked up the volume on the stereo. Both lit cigarettes.

A few miles down the road, Cassie reached over and turned down the music and over the rushing wind and road noise, she hollered, "Baby, I just want to remind you that Joey needs some new clothes and school supplies for when he starts the first grade in a couple of weeks."

Delbert took a last puff on his cigarette, flipped the butt out the window, and replied, "I got to rebuild a carburetor next weekend for cash, so we should be okay buyin' that stuff."

"Also," continued Cassie, "maybe we could go shoppin' soon for a swing-set for the kids. It'd sure be a big help when I'm baby-sittin'."

"Well, baby, start lookin' in the *Thrifty* ads for a used one."

Cassie inhaled the last of her cigarette, snuffed it out in the ashtray, and said, "Okay, baby, I'll get to lookin'."

"Hey, I wanted to tell you," shouted Delbert, "Mitch bought a paint sprayer to paint his house, so I've decided, that as soon as we can afford it, we're goin' to paint this ugly minivan."

"That would be real nice, Del."

After two hours of listening to Delbert's new *Kid Rock* CD and riding on curvy roads through dried-up, boring, brown hills, they arrived at the invigorating green coast just north of Santa Maria. They traveled the twenty miles up to Pismo Beach and drove to the pier parking lot where Delbert griped, "What the hell, I can't believe they're chargin' so much for parkin' now." They parked, paid, and strolled out onto the pier.

A cool, rejuvenating breeze blew away their financial and parental concerns as well as their memory of the hundred-plus heat back in Taft. They watched some surfers ride the waves and checked out a flopping fish a man caught at the end of the pier. After walking the pier to the end and back, they strolled over to the *Splash Café* for clam chowder in a bread bowl, and after lunch, they crossed the street to *Harry's Bar* to shoot pool and drink beers for the rest of the afternoon.

Sitting on a bar stool next to the pool table, Cassie took a drink from her cold bottle of *Bud-Lite*, and said, "Del, thank you baby, for bringin' me all the way to the beach for my birthday. I sure needed a few days away."

At the pool table, Delbert pointed his cue-stick at the corner pocket, bent down, lined up his cue stick with the cue ball, slammed the eight ball into the corner pocket, and said, "Just so you know, baby, comin' to the beach is only a part of my surprise. There's still more to come."

"Ohhh, Del, I can't wait. You ready to go now or should I rack'em up for another game?"

"Yeah, Cass, one more game and we'll head over to our motel."

As they played the last game, Delbert checked out his wife's bountiful butt in her tight shorts every time she bent over to take a shot. She won, they left *Harry's*, and they drove a few blocks to the motel.

The L-shaped, pinkish-brown, single-story motel was built in the 1950s and hadn't changed much. The place was only a few blocks from the beach, but without an ocean view. A swimming pool surrounded by plastic deck chairs and three palm trees sat in the middle of the parking lot. A neon sign out by the road showed a smiling seal above the words, *The Happy Seal Motor Court.*

Cassie sat in the minivan and smoked a cigarette while Delbert checked in. While he waited for his room key, he heard a loud TV and noticed the smell of curry wafting out the door of the owner's room behind the counter. He paid for the room, grabbed up his room key, and jumped back in the minivan. He backed up the vehicle to room number twelve next to a sign that read, *Please don't back in!* Both climbed out of the van and walked up to the room door. Delbert unlocked the door, shoved it open, and as Cassie stepped into the room, Delbert hollered, "Surprise! Happy birthday, baby doll!"

Cassie looked past the tattered orange drapes, the stained green carpet, and the low spot in the middle of the queen size bed with its nauseating green, orange, and brown bedspread. She was oblivious to the faded painting of a moored, sea-weathered tugboat with a seagull in the foreground perched on a pylon, nor did she see the artwork's ugly, driftwood-like frame. Her eyes missed the antiquated TV on the dresser, the TV's remote bolted down on the nightstand, the dingy lampshades, and the weird lamp hanging over two worn out chairs shoved under a small table with a cigarette burn. She didn't even see the tiny bathroom with the green sink, green toilet, and chipped, green shower tile. All she saw, sitting in the corner of the *Happy Seal* motel room number 12, for her birthday present, Delbert's surprise, was a heart-shaped hot tub for two.

"Oh my," she gasped, "Delbert, this is so wonderful! Thank you, baby! Thank you!"

"Well, Hun, you deserve it, so let's get this birthday party rockin' and rollin'."

Cassie turned on the tub faucets, while Delbert unloaded the suitcases and put them on the folding luggage stands inside the room. He unzipped his suitcase and said, "Here you go Cass, I 'membered to grab the kid's *Mr. Bubble* on the way out this mornin'."

Cassie smiled and right below a sign stapled to the wall that decreed *No Bubbles,* she dumped glubs of bubble bath into the rushing, cascading water.

Above the sound of the running bath water, Delbert hollered, "Cass, while you check out the TV and make sure it works, I'll jam across the street to the liquor store and pick us up a twelve-pack of *Bud.* Use that coupon by the phone and order us up a large pizza with the works and have it delivered."

When he returned from the store, he snatched his ice chest

out of the van, put the cans of beer inside it, and filled it up with ice at the motel's ice machine that had a sign taped to it that read, *No ice chests.*

He returned to his room and both stepped just outside the door for a smoke. They commented about how sunny, but nice and cool the weather was, flicked the cigarette butts into the flowerbed, and went back inside their room. While they watched the *Allstate 400 at The Brickyard* on *ESPN,* there was a knock on the door. Delbert paid for the pizza, tipped the delivery guy a buck, and shut and locked the door. He sat the pizza, paper plates, and packets of Parmesan cheese and dried chili peppers next to the ice chest on top of the small table that he scooted over beside the hot tub. He opened two cans of icy beer and placed a slice of pizza on each of two plates. He made sure the drapes were overlapping shut and he and Cassie peeled off their clothes. She tied her hair up with a scrungy, they climbed into the hot steamy tub, and slid beneath the bubbles, both moaning, "Ahhhh!" They ate hot, combination pizza, drank cold beer, watched the *Nascar* race, and soaked away their concerns of kids, jobs, and finances.

During a commercial break, Delbert turned to Cassie and asked, "Baby, you havin' fun?"

"Sure, Del, this is great! Thanks again for this nice birthday."

"So, are you happy?"

"Well, baby," she said, pausing to take a sip from her beer while she thought about it, "there's people who's got a lot more than we do—more money and fancier homes and cars, but what I think is, I've got a hard workin' man that can fix anything that runs on gas. We've got three smart and healthy kids. We've got a home that we can afford and a reliable minivan that's goin' to have new paint soon. We've been together six years without cheatin' on each other like Mitch and Doreen did and we only fight when both of us have drunk way too many beers. We can take a trip anytime 'cause we got my mama to baby-sit and to top it off, here we are, at the beach, sittin' butt-naked in a heart-shaped hot tub, drinkin' beer, eatin' pizza, and watchin' the races on cable TV. Yeah Delbert—I'm happy."

Delbert smiled, guzzled a few swallows of his beer, burped, and said, "Me too, baby."

After a couple of hours in the hot tub and after eatin all the pizza and drinkin' most of the beers and with a lot of under the bubbles touchy-feely, they climbed out of the tub. While Delbert dried off, standing there lanky and pale in only his mullet haircut and while the hot tub drained with a gurgling sound, Cassie stepped into the bathroom and shut the door.

After a few minutes of brushing out her long hair and putting on pink lip-gloss, skin lotion, and perfume, she opened the door and stood there, sexy and seductive, wearing his favorite, black, nasty-nighty exposing her firm breasts and sweeping hips.

"Oh, my world, Cass," muttered Delbert in a sort of trance, "you look, sooo hot!"

"Baby," she purred, "let's pretend it's your birthday too!"

DARKANCOLD

My name is Stephen Haylow. I'm a thirty-three-year-old regular guy trying to provide for my family. My wife, Sarah and I have been married for nine years and we own a modest three-bedroom home in Clovis, California. The demonic taunting occurred the day my wife and our three young sons, Jacob, 3, Joshua, 5, and Jeremy, 7, left for Southern, California to visit her parents. They were heading out for a week of summer vacation, but to my disappointment, I had to stay and work. I kissed my wife goodbye and implored her to drive safe, rubbed each of my rowdy boys on the head and told them to be good, and watched them all drive off in my wife's four-year-old, Ford minivan. I jumped into my even older VW Jetta and drove the five miles to my job at *Home Depot*.

At 5:30 that afternoon, after a busy day of helping customers and stocking shelves, I hung up my red apron and clocked out. As soon as I stepped outside the store, the dry 108° heat—typical for July in our San Joaquin Valley—knocked the breath out of me and punched me in the face. I strolled toward my car and with every step, the rubber soles of my tennis shoes stuck to the hot, tacky asphalt like stepping on spilled soda in a movie theatre. I jerked open my car door and adjusted the beach towel that protected me from the scalding leather seat and climbed inside the stifling sauna. The scorching steering wheel burned my hand and I yelped, "Hot! Sooo hot!" I started the car, revved up the engine, and cranked up the air conditioner. It blew out warm air taking awhile to cool. I grabbed the seatbelt, fastened it, and howled again when the searing metal buckle singed my hand. Beads of sweat trickled down my face and my soggy T-shirt and jeans stuck to my skin. I cooled off my blistering sunglasses in front of an air vent, put them on, and drove out of the store's parking lot toward home. I was excited to have the house all to myself, but sad that my wife and kids weren't home to greet me.

Halfway home, I felt a chill on my arms. Normally, the inside of the car cooled down just about the time I got home, but it was already freezing. I reached over and turned up the temperature knob but the raging vents persisted blasting out polar air. Strange—I could see my breath. Even stranger—the windows frosted up. I turned the temp-knob to the warmest red notch, the fan to high, and flipped on the rear-window defroster. Crazy—but the air blew colder. Even crazier—the windows iced up worse. I tried to wipe the windshield with my hand to see, but only smeared the frosty condensation. I switched on the windshield wipers. They worked fine but didn't help because the arctic storm was inside my car. My teeth chattered; I shivered. Alarmed, I tried to lower the electric windows to let in some summertime, but they wouldn't go down. I had the sniffles. Without warning, the fan speed increased as the wind-chill plummeted. I blinked my eyes, coughed, and rubbed my cold, numb arms with my hands. Snow flurries floated inside my car. Inconceivable. The radio clicked on, blaring a child's rendition of *Frosty the Snowman*. Irritating. Of course, its knob wouldn't turn it down or off. By now, ice crystals covered all the windows. I stopped at a traffic light, scratched the frost off my driver window and saw a carload of teens next to me. They made silly faces, pointed at me, and laughed until their eyes diverted to my backseat and all of their pimply faces contorted into terror. I shot a glance over my shoulder. Nothing was in my back seat except a mounting snowdrift. I reached over the steering wheel and rubbed the frost off the inside of the windshield. The traffic signal turned green and the car full of kids sped off. I slowly, cautiously drove off as well. Even though I was frightened, frozen, and snow-blind, I kept driving home, so I wouldn't have to pay for a tow truck. Just when I couldn't take the blizzard and *Frosty the Snowman* anymore, I rounded the corner onto my street. With my vision dangerously impaired, I slowed the car down to a crawl, searched for my house through fissures in the window frost, and crept into my driveway. While the automatic garage door opened, I shivered violently and moaned, "So cold! Sooo cold!" I saw something out of the corner of my eye and gawked in the rearview mirror. I gasped! I saw a man, no, a solid black, faceless shadow skulking in my backseat. I spun to see, but there was no one there. Creeped out, I punched the accelerator, lurched into the garage, and braked hard. The tires screeched on the smooth concrete floor and the car stopped an inch short of crashing into Jeremy's bedroom. I pushed the remote button and the garage door slipped shut behind me. The garage light snapped on and mysteriously off. I sat in the dark in subzero cold. My heart raced. I shuddered. I tried to shut off the car. It kept running. I tried to open the door. It remained locked. The worst dilemma—I sensed a presence in the car with me—a presence dark and cold.

Terrified, I screamed, "God, please help me!"

At once, the car's engine shut off and the air conditioner quit blowing; the doors unlocked and all the windows hummed down. I grabbed the icy door handle and tried to open the door; it remained frozen shut. I slammed my shoulder into it twice and it opened. Tumbling out of the car, I staggered over to the light switch and flipped it on. I peered at my car and to my astonishment, it appeared normal. No Christmas in July. While rubbing my chilled arms and wiping my runny nose, I marched into the house, sat at my desk, and made a note to call a mechanic. I called my wife and kids and felt relieved that they had made it safely to her folk's. I told Sarah about my car's devilish air conditioner. She too thought it strange. I chatted with the kids, who were having fun with grandma and grandpa. We said our 'I love yous' and 'good-byes' to each other and I felt better. For dinner, I heated up a family-size can of chicken-noodle soup and ate it all. I watched some mindless TV and then, still feeling chilled from my Siberian sleigh ride, I went into my master bathroom to take a long, hot shower.

While I stood under the steamy, pulsating showerhead, I thought about the bizarre occurrence in my car. I knew—at the core of my spirit, I knew—it was not simply a mechanical problem; it was a demon problem. I knew, because, I had stepped up at my church and volunteered to teach a teen Bible study and I knew, because I expected opposition to my spiritual growth, but never, had I anticipated another encounter with a demon.

I leaned my head against the tiled wall of the shower and as the hot water rained over me, I thought of Insomnos: a wily demon with scabrous skin, vomitous breath, and yellow hate-filled eyes. The beast reveled in murderous schemes and existed to proliferate confusion, fear, and agony on mankind.

Ten years had past since Insomnos had trespassed into my world, in the middle of the night, while I slept peacefully in my bed. At 12:06 a.m., the demon had leaned over me and whispered in my ear, "Twelve plus six, twelve plus six, addeth together; divideth by three, is six, six, six." Its tongue lingered with a lengthy hiss as it annunciated the x of each number six. I awoke with a start that night, feeling the creature's frigid breath on me. I couldn't see the beast, but I felt its presence and in my mind, I heard its raspy voice. Then, the creature, in a sawing voice of disdain, recited the rhyme for a second time, but louder, "Twelve plus six, twelve plus six, addeth together; divideth by three, is six, six, six." My heart raced as I had sat up in bed and planted my feet on the floor. For a third time, it taunted me, but this time, it shouted with seething hatred,

"Twelve plus six, twelve plus six, addeth together; divideth by three, is six, six, six!" I leapt out of bed, put on my robe and slippers, and went to the front room. The demon pursued me, loathing me, mocking me. I dropped to my knees, clasped my hands together, closed my eyes, and leaned on my lounge chair. I prayed, ignoring the demon's deafening static in my ears, and I beseeched God to reveal to me that which haunted me. Instead of an answer granted to me over time, in my world, through my human senses, my spirit was instantly whisked into the world of Insomnos—a realm void of light, that feasted on mankind's lies, thievery, and murder; that glutted on prejudice, pornography, and child abuse, and gorged on wars—civil wars, racial wars, religious wars—wars for land, wars for resources, and ironically, wars for peace. As our human iniquities fed the darkness—the darkness became darker. In this vast black emptiness, I had stood alone in a haven of light and encountered Insomnos. Face to face, we fought hand to hand—no weapons, except its hate against all that is good and my faith for all that is love. In the throes of the battle, I had cried out for help and God's glorious light cornered the demon, while the *Fire of Absolute Death* obliterated it from all that is, all that was, and all that will ever be.

Now, ten years later, another demon taunted me; however, this time, I was not swept into a vision to fight a grotesque demon in a dark otherworld. My spirit, my soul, and my body remained in this world—in the shower—naked.

I lifted my head and let the steamy water caress my face. I tried to forget my wintry toboggan ride, but I kept worrying about the grim shadowman in my back seat, when suddenly, ice cold water burst out of the showerhead. I yowled and jumped out of the frigid spray. I thought I must have used up all the hot water, so I stretched for the faucet, turned it off, and stepped out of the shower stall onto the linoleum floor. It felt like an ice rink. I grabbed my towel and started drying off. The towel was stiff and cold. The hot steam saturating the bathroom formed into a dense fog and the condensation on the mirror froze to a sparkling frost. I shivered. My teeth chattered. I grabbed the brass doorknob. The door wouldn't open. My hand stuck to the frozen metal knob, so I jerked it away and ripped off a bit of skin. I snatched up my wife's hair dryer and switched it on high only to have a snow squall blast out of it and hit me square in the face. Icicles hung off the showerhead and the toilet held a small frozen pond. The moisture on my body became ice crystals and my damp hair froze stiff.

In the reflection of the frosty mirror, I saw a dark figure lurking in the fog behind me. I spun around and it disappeared. Frightened, I trembled. The temperature plummeted, changing the bathroom into a hypothermic tomb. My shivering grew violent. My skin turned pale. My lips, tip of my nose and ear lobes ached. My fingers and toes became stiff and blue. I panicked and thrust my bare shoulder into the wooden door. I bounced off, slipped on the icy floor, and fell hard, bumping my head on the toilet. Lying there dazed, I looked up and saw the being looming over me. Things were bad—then, became worse. The lights over the toilet and sink blacked out. I crawled in the dark over to the vanity cabinet, raked out rolls of toilet paper, brushes, and cleansers and tried to burrow my way in, but I didn't fit. In the blinding darkness and the biting cold, I curled up into a fetal position, naked and shivering on the icy floor. My hands and feet were numb. I feared I would die. I thought of my loving wife and my little boys. They needed me and I'd be dead—frozen stiff. I sobbed and my tears froze. The bathroom grew darker and colder and I sensed the vile presence close to my face—so close, I felt each of its heaving, icy breaths. Terror stopped my sobs and I cried out, "G-G-God, help m-m-me! P-p-please help m-m-me!"

Instantly, the lights snapped on startling me. The showerhead dripped water again and the fog warmed to steam. I stood up, weak and shaken and easily opened the door. I muttered, "Thank you God, thank you." I grabbed a soft, dry towel, dried off every inch of my body, and dried my hair with the hair dryer. My body slowly gathered warmth and strength. My skin tingled and my extremities burned. I brushed my teeth and left the bathroom. Although it was midsummer, I put on my flannel pajamas and turned on the electric blanket. Exhausted, I turned off the bedroom light and crawled into my lonely, queen-size bed. I missed my wife and kids. The only light in the room was the red glow of my digital alarm clock and the light from a street lamp filtering through a narrow gap between the window curtains. The house was quiet except the bubbling aerator of a fish tank in my son, Josh's room. I fell asleep.

At 12:06 a.m., the bed shook. I heard my name, "Stephen!" called out in a deep, guttural voice like a warring enemy goading me out to battle. I jerked awake as the bed shook again, this time violently. I rolled over, sat up, and peered down at the foot of my bed. I yelled in horror and backed up against the headboard. A pitch-black, manlike creature stood at the base of my bed amidst a cold fog creeping just above the floor. I yanked the covers up around my neck. The inky image called my name again, but this time louder and with greater hostility. Ripples of terror rattled down my spine.

After a few seconds, my eyes adjusted to the dark and I saw the creature more clearly. The beast, the size and form of an average man, had no features; it was but a coal black silhouette of a man. I had read about how others had witnessed these dark, lurking shadows. They were not human, but fallen angels, existing so distant from the light of God's wisdom and the warmth of God's love that their defiant souls had absorbed the dark and the cold of their own abominations; however, even they, cast down beings from a world of endless night and shivering cold—have a soul. I was shocked though; demons normally remain hidden—but this one stood before me—in my world.

"Who are you?" I demanded. The demon didn't answer but laughed.

I heard crackling and peered into the night of my room. A frost slinked out of the fog and up the walls onto the dresser, the nightstands, and my desk. Even in my distress, I thought, oh nooo, that can't be good for my computer. First the fog and then the frost covered everything in the room. The temperature dropped below zero. I shivered. I heard the being laugh, a fiendish, airy laugh. The fog crept up and over my bed, freezing it into a queen-size ice cube. My electric blanket stopped warming. White sparkling crystals covered the room like a snow cavern.

In my iced terror, I yelled, stuttering, "W-w-who are you and w-w-what do you w-w-want?"

It didn't answer, but slinked around to the side of the bed, swirling fog in its wake. I tried to squirm away, but the glacial bedcovers trapped me.

It leaned in close and I grimaced. Face to face, I saw that it indeed had facial features—nearly invisible features, but they were there, lost in the black decay of frostbite and obscured in the gloom of its loathing. It had dim yellow eyes framed by a scowl of hate, a withered nose and shriveled ears, a deformed mouth from gnashing its teeth, and blackened, frostbitten skin.

"W-w-who are you," I stuttered, chilled to the bone, "and w-w-why are you here?"

It finally spoke and a chilly draft whorled around some of its uttered vowels. "My Priiince, nameth meee, Daaarkaaancooold." When it uttered its name, a gust of wind circulated about the room, swirling the fog, moving the drapes, and blowing a piece of frosty paper off my desk. The beast drew in a deep breath and said, "I bliiindth men in my daaarkness and keepth them alooone in my cooold."

"I'm not b-b-blind for I know the t-t-truth," I stammered, "and I'm n-n-not alone for God is with m-m-me."

"Your truuuth is a liiiie and your god is far awaaay."

"I s-s-stand on the rock of my f-f-faith and I believe God is always w-w-with me. Someday, I w-w-will be with Him in Heaven."

"Yooou will surely buuurnth in Hell."

"Listen d-d-demon," I growled, between my chattering teeth. "B-b-because of my human fears and w-w-weaknesses you have had your devilish f-f-fun with me, but I've experienced all of this b-b-before. Remember your b-b-buddy Insomnos—you know what happened t-t-to him."

"Yeees, the *Fiiire of Absooolute Death*. We foooought together in the great rebeeellion against yooour god. Insomnooos is nooo more."

"The same w-w-will happen to y-y-you."

"I feareth not your god. I desireth to seeth yooou. You are spoooken of in our legends of maaan—not as a heroo, but as an enemy. Our lord ruuuleth this earth and demandeth your wooorship. If yooou bow to our priiince, yooou shall possesseth godliiike powers."

"Your d-d-dark and your c-c-cold frightens me and your p-p-presence horrifies me, but you can not t-t-terrorize me into worshipping your p-p-prince of darkness. I love and worship m-m-my God, the Creator, the Light, the Word, and Who is m-m-my Salvation from all that is d-d-dark and c-c-cold."

"I shall destroyeth yooou and your faaamily too," it shrieked in anger.

The dark became darker, the cold became colder, and the frost masking the room crackled. I shivered violently and bellowed, "Y-y-you shall not! I-I-I will call upon m-m-my God and an a-a-angel will p-p-protect us!"

"I seeeth not an angel, nooor your god. It is daaark; it is cooold; and yooou are alooone."

"T-t-that is a l-l-lie!" I shouted in my quaking fury. "God, p-p-please, s-s-send an a-a-angel and s-s-slay this b-b-blasphemous b-b-beast."

Darkancold scoffed.

Instantly, there was a blinding flash. A cylindrical beam of light shined from ceiling to floor and at its center stood a radiant being clothed in a flowing white robe and wielding a golden sword. Though the being appeared human, its facial features were difficult to distinguish in the brilliant light. It stood taller than the tallest man, but contrary to popular belief—it did not have feathered wings. Upon the advent of the angel, the fog faded, the frost melted, and I felt a fiery hope within my soul that warmed my entire body. My teeth stopped chattering, my body quit shivering, and my terrified spirit ceased shuddering.

"Stephen," the angel spoke, calling out my name in a commanding, but passionate voice, "do not be afraid. My name is Rathaniel. Our Lord has sent me to protect you."

Darkancold departed from my bedside, slinked away from the mighty angel, and cowered in a corner of the room.

I kicked back the blankets, jumped out of bed, and stood behind the angel.

Darkancold hid its face from the angel's bright illumination and whimpered, "Pleeease do not slaaay meee with your *Sword of Eternal Death*! I wiiill retreeeat to my daaark and cooold."

"Demon, you know that eternal death is the punishment for trespassing into the world of man," boomed Rathaniel, "and you shall surely die!"

"I shall not!" snapped Darkancold and beginning at the corner where the demon recoiled, its black night and white frost spread chaotically across the room toward the angel and me.

Rathaniel raised his gleaming, gold sword; a sword defending the truth; a sword protecting God's beloved; a *Sword of Eternal Death*, and thrust it out before us. I blinked in its glare and imagined that it had been forged long ago of the same gold as the streets of Heaven.

Darkancold screamed a resounding war cry and a cyclonic wind whirled around the room. It shrieked again, charged, and sprung into the air at the angel.

As the demon soared, gnashing its teeth and flailing its arms, Rathaniel swung his shining sword and with a swoosh of divine light severed the head of Darkancold. The demon's cut off head and squirming body crashed to the floor at the angel's feet. The beast's lips trembled, its dull eyes rolled back in its head, and its torso instinctively twitched.

A frigid fog interlaced with a deafening discord of shrieks gushed out of the head and body of Darkancold. I heard the agonizing wails of abandoned babies and the cries of abused children; the moans of the sick and the laments of the dying. I heard hysterical pleas for help; shrieks of terror; shouts of anger; and screams of hate. I heard the thunderous sounds of war machines: rumbling tanks, roaring jets, and the throp of helicopters. I heard automatic gunfire, launching missiles, and exploding bombs. As I listened to the cacophony of human suffering, I dropped to my knees and sobbed.

All the wickedness that Darkancold had whispered into the minds of mankind; all the seeds of hate, lust, and folly that had sprouted in their hearts; all the lies that were cultivated; and all of its vileness that bore in us the bitter fruit of despicable corruption, horrid crimes, and bloody wars, intertwined with the chilly fog and swirled up and out of my bedroom, out of man's world, and into the ever-expanding nether world of darkness. As the fog and the clamorous chaos spewed out of Darkancold, its head and torso shriveled up like airless balloons. With a final bloodcurdling shriek, its frostbitten head and body disintegrated into a black powdery dust and whorled up into a blissless void.

In the blessed silence, I stopped weeping and stood up. Rathaniel turned to me and said, "Stephen, you and your family are safe. Fear not, for our God is always with you," and like switching off a huge flashlight, the beam of light and Rathaniel vanished. I quickly flipped on the bedroom light and saw that everything in my bedroom appeared normal—even my computer looked okay. I turned off the light, crawled back into bed, spoke a prayer of gratitude, and lay awake for a long while. I felt uneasy thinking about the dark and cold, but when I focused my thoughts on the mighty angel and God's protection, I fell fast asleep.

The next morning, as I drove to work, my car and its air conditioner worked fine, so I didn't called the mechanic. At the end of the week, my wife and boys returned home safely and I grinned at the sight of them.

After my horrific encounters with Insomnos and Darkancold, I pray, I will never face another demon. However, if I do, I believe that a powerful angel, wielding a gleaming, golden sword, is standing ready on the threshold of our world.

One-up

First of all, Clayton Rogers never thought that he would ever exceed his yearly sales quota and earn a trip to *Faballoy's* international conference held annually in Chicago. Second, he never thought that an insignificant distributor like himself from small town USA would ever one-up *Faballoy's* president of international sales and the host of the conference—Mr. Maxwell Shrewbury from Warwickshire, England.

Faballoy, a century-old, worldwide corporation specialized in carbide tools. Clayton, thirty-five years old, owned a small industrial company in Fresno, California. He'd been in business for five years, employing eight whining employees and been married for ten years with three screaming kids. He worked so long and hard that he hardly stopped to eat and since he grew up on a dairy in Tulare County, he looked like and talked like a lanky cowboy. *Faballoy* covered the cost of the three day conference—the hotel, meals, and the gala on Saturday night. Clayton scraped up the money to buy a roundtrip ticket from Fresno to O'Hare, along with a sport jacket, dress shirt, and tie to wear with his *Wranglers* and boots.

He arrived in Chicago on Friday, late afternoon, expecting the city to be windy and cold, but it was the middle of September, so it was warm and calm. He rode a hotel shuttle from the airport over to the historic *Drake Hotel* downtown, arriving just in time for the evening meet and greet. He met a few other distributors from around the country, but since he was beat from traveling, he hit the hay early. The next day, Saturday, the all-day conference was very informative. The attendees, about 100 in all, heard about the new products and learned how to sell them. That evening, after sitting in a chair all day, Clayton was ready to party. At 6:00, the gala kicked off.

Notorious Chicago gangsters of the Prohibition Era such as Al Capone and Bugsy Moran were the theme of the gala, so on entering the ballroom, the party goers were given plastic fedora hats and a handful of coupons for gambling. Roulette and black jack tables filled the room set-up like a 1920s speak-easy. A shiny black 1934 Ford four-door sedan sat in a corner of the room along with Tommy gun props for photos. A band played songs from the roaring twenties and thirties and all the servers dressed in period costumes. If you won at gambling you got to pick from an assortment of gifts. Due to the open bar, the attendees made a laughing stock of prohibition.

After gambling for an hour or so, there was a call for dinner, and all the attendees sat at tables with fancy white tablecloths, silky napkins, water and wineglass, knife, spoon, and two forks. Clayton sat at a table with a few married couples and a few men like himself who had attended the conference alone. To Clayton's surprise, Mr. Shrewbury—a silver haired man of about sixty with a horse face and laugh lines around his mischievous eyes—sat next to him to his right. The host introduced himself and sitting next to him, his wife Eppie—a buxom lady with a pixie face, flour-white skin, and long gray hair wrapped up in a bun. They all ate a scrumptious dinner amidst lively conversation. After dessert, while some drank more cocktails and others sipped coffee, Mr. Shrewbury, holding his glass of gin and tonic, peered around the table, and said in his hoity-toity British accent, "That was a most enjoyable dinner. Now, I have a story to tell."

All eyes at the table focused on the host as he took a sip of his gin and began.

"In London, early one morning, two bums still snockered from the night before, staggered up to the front gate of a nunnery. One man was tall; the other short. Both had disheveled hair, scraggy whiskers, and tattered clothes, and both reeked of cheap rum. They stumbled through the squeaky garden gate and stood in the courtyard among beds of vibrant flowers. The two of them peered up at a second-story window while the tall bum hollered in his cockney accent, 'Oh, Mother! Oh, Mother Superior!'

Mr. Shrewbury changed back and forth from speaking in his articulate British narrative to speaking in the gravelly voice of the tall bum.

Speaking in the narrative, "The shutters on the window remained shut, so the bum called out louder, 'Oh Mother! Oh Mother Superior!'"

All of diners at the host's table including Clayton stared, captivated, at their animated storyteller.

"The shutters swung open," Mr. Shrewbury said pretending to open make-believe shutters, "and Mother Superior, an elderly woman with heavenly compassion twinkling in her eyes, stood in the open window, gazing down on the two downtrodden men."

Mr. Shrewbury shifted to a high-pitched voice, mimicking the Queen of England for the voice of Mother Superior, "'How can I help you gentlemen today?'"

"Both men," he continued in his narrative voice, "out of deep respect for her, quickly attempted to comb their hair with their fingers and tried to yank down the creases on their clothes as the tall bum said, 'Wha' a beaut'iful day and wha' a lov'ly gard'en you 'ave Mother Superior.'

"Mother Superior replied, 'Why, thank you. It is a glooorious day and the bloooms are most cheery. So, how may I help you today?'

'Well, Mother Superior, my name is Witt and my chum 'ere,

'is name is Li'onel. We were jus' wonderin' if maybe you 'ave a lit'le nun 'ere 'bout this tall?'"

Mr. Shrewbury held out his hand demonstrating how Witt held out his hand about three feet above the ground.

"'Oh my,' said Mother Superior, 'Nooo, we do not have a nun who is that tiny here at the convent.'

'Are you sure Mother Superior?' said the short bum" who in Mr. Shrewbury's throaty baritone voice sounded like a cockney frog. 'Are you cert'in that you don't 'ave a wee, it'y-bit'y nun about this tall?'"

Mr. Shrewbury again held out his hand a yardstick above the floor. Everybody at the table, including Clayton sat enthralled by Mr. Shrewbury's lively portraiture of the characters and their exaggerated British accents. Each of the diners sported a broad smile anticipating the punch line of his joke.

"'I am most certain,' said Mother Superior,'" Mr. Shrewbury continued in his shrill voice of royalty, "'that we do not have a little nun here at our convent. For now, I must tend to my prayers and devotions. Please gentlemen, have a splendid day.'"

"She reached out and shut the shutters," Mr. Shrewbury narrated, "leaving the two bums standing in the garden. Both men rubbed their whiskers and then Witt turned to the squatty bum and muttered, 'See, I told you Li'onel. You've got to believe me. Last night, down by the wharf, after we drank all that rum ....'

'Yeah Witt,' Lionel croaked, 'tell me—what 'appened?'

'Well Li'onel—it wasn't a lit'le nun you made mad, passionate love to. Sorry ol'chap, ol'chum, but—you shagged a penguin!'"

Mr. Shrewbury burst out in hysterical laughter at his own favorite joke and pounded the table with his fist as attendees reveled along with their hoots and chuckles, making the joke seem a bit more funny than it actually was since it was their host who told it.

At the height of their merriment, Clayton said in his cow-town drawl, "I got a story to tell too!"

The entire table snapped silent and all eyes fell on Clayton as if Clayton as Bugsy Moran had just challenged Mr. Shrewbury as Al Capone to meet him for a massacre at the SMC Cartage Company garage on Saint Valentines Day. Mr. Shrewbury stared at him. His eyes narrowed with contempt and then opened wide with childlike twinkles. His desire to hear a good story was greater than his fear of being one-upped, so he said in his cockney Li'onel voice, "Let's 'ear it bloke!"

Clayton knew he ought not one-up the party host and president of sales, and he knew it was dangerous to follow such a parade of laughter, but he had drunk just enough seven and sevens to feel courageous. While his table partners were still wiping away their tears of laughter after hearing Mr. Shrewbury's joke, Clayton, in his country twang, started telling his.

"Up in Jackson—a small gold rush town in the Sierra Foothills and the seat of Amador County—a tall, noodlely man by the name of Delroy lost his job, due to lay-offs up at the saw mill. Searchin' the want ads, he noticed that the *Lost Dog Saloon* in rustic, downtown Jackson needed a bartender. Delroy, pushin' fifty, didn't drink much and mostly preferred readin' books on the techniques of fly-fishin', but since he needed a job and since he didn't have to know much about mixin' cocktails—'cause most the bar's patrons drank beer or whiskey—he called the owner and got the job.

On his first night of work, he pushed through the two swingin' doors into the small bar and felt like he had just stepped back into the California Gold Rush of the 1850s. Pine planks lined the floor, clapboard covered the walls, and wooden wagon wheels holdin' antiquated oil lamps hung from the ceilin'. The long cherry wood bar had lots of shiny brass trim and a brass footrest. In front of the bar sat tall wooden barstools with cast iron seats and behind the bar, bottles of liquor lined the shelves.

Worn photos of miners, mines, and minin' equipment along with gold pannin' tools hung on the walls. Country-western music played on an old dust covered jukebox. The elderly owner showed him around, trained him on the cash register, and left for the evenin'.

Within an hour, the house filled with locals and merriment. Things were goin' pretty smooth until an undersize man with an oversize mustache burst through the swingin' doors, yellin' hysterically, 'Big Bad Bob's comin'! Big Bad Bob's comin'! Run for your lives!' and bolted back out the swingin' doors."

Clayton hollered rather loud, playing the part of the yelling mustache-man, which captured the attention not only of the attendees at his table but of those at tables next to him. He took a gulp of his cocktail and then continued telling his story with greater confidence and charisma.

"Hearin' that Big Bad Bob was comin', people at the saloon dropped their cards and conversations and stormed out the front door, rushed out the back door, or like a panicky few, dove out the open windows. Outside, motors revved up and tires squealed as vehicles sped away. In less than ten seconds, the threat of Big Bad Bob had emptied the bar and the parkin' lot.

Delroy didn't know what to think or do. He didn't know how big and just how bad this Big Bad Bob was. The way people dashed out at just the mention of Big Bad Bob's name made him terrified. Nevertheless, he didn't want to abandon his job on the first night, so he hid behind the bar. Within seconds, he felt the wooden planks beneath his feet vibrate like a trembler while the booze bottles started vibratin' and clinkin' on the shelves. The wagon wheel lights overhead began shakin' and rainin' down dust. He heard a loud rumblin' sound outside that sounded like a cattle stampede. As the sound drew closer, it became louder, and as it grew louder, the walls of the saloon shook, and as the walls shook, antiques and framed pictures crashed to the floor. He covered his ears with his hands and snuck a glance over the top of the bar. By the time, the noise reached the front door, it sounded like a speedin' locomotive. Bam! Boom!"

The listeners at the table jumped a bit startled by Clayton yelling, 'Bam! Boom!' He took a deep breath and continued, "The front swingin' doors exploded off their hinges and flew across the room, crashin' into splinters! Delroy ducked, raised up slowly, and peeped over the bar again. He couldn't believe his eyes. A huge buffalo, as big as a Chevy Suburban charged into the saloon. The devilish beast had brown, almost black fur, two chipped horns (one longer than the other) and fiery red eyes of Hell."

Conference attendees within earshot gawked at Clayton, mesmerized by his rapid-fire, storytelling skill. He continued faster and louder.

"Strapped about the hairy behemoth's girth was a rawhide saddle and in the saddle rode a giant of a man. The man's savage, dark eyes bulged out of their sockets beneath black, bushy eyebrows while an unshorn beard and a bristly mustache hid most of the man's scarred face. From beneath a black, worn-out, cowboy hat, his long, shaggy hair hung to his shoulders and he clenched a smolderin' cigar in his stained teeth. On the right side of his thick leather belt, hung a holster with a pearl-handled pistol and strapped on his other side, a gleamin' Bowie knife. He rode the snortin' buffalo across the saloon as the wooden planks beneath its cloppin' hoofs bent from the sheer tonnage of its weight. It trampled into toothpicks the chairs and tables in its path. The wild man parked the furry mammoth in front of the bar, slid his scuffed, size fifteen boots out of the stirrups and climbed off the beast. The mountainous man, standin' just under seven feet tall, crashed down his massive fist on the bar splinterin' its wood."

Clayton slammed his fist down on the table startling the diners and splashing water from a few water glasses. He continued wild-eyed telling his tale.

"The giant bellowed in his boomin' voice, 'You! Hidin' behind the bar! Get me a whiskey! And make it fast!' Delroy jumped up, grabbed a bottle of *Jack Daniels* and with a tremblin' hand, poured the huge man a shot of whiskey. The menacin' hulk raked the shot glass off the bar and growled, 'Not a shot! Give me the bottle!'"

Acting out the part, Clayton swiped his hand across the table and nearly hit his glass of seven and seven. The pace of his storytelling sped up.

"Delroy sat the bottle down in front of the man and backed up, cowerin' against the shelves of liquor. The mountain-man snatched up the bottle with his huge rugged hand, jerked back his head, and chug-a-lugged. He guzzled half of the bottle, took a few pantin' breaths, and downed the rest. He slammed the empty bottle down so hard on the bar that it exploded into shards of glass, wiped his mouth and whiskers with the back of his hand, and turned to leave.

Delroy couldn't believe the thirsty menace was ready to leave so soon, so he asked timidly, 'Sir, before you go—would you—uh—like another bottle of whiskey?'"

All the attendees within earshot hung on Clayton's words anticipating the punchline of his story.

Throughout the telling of the joke, Clayton had been making eye contact with all of those at or near his table, but for the punchline, he locked eyes with Mr. Shrewbury and said, "The mountain-man sprung back on his buffalo, grabbed its reins, peered down at Delroy, and snapped in a deep voice that quaked with fear, 'I ain't got time! Big Bad Bob's comin!'"

There was a split second of silence as the punchline sunk in and then, the listeners exploded with laughter. Mr. Shrewbury nearly fell out of his chair as Mrs. Shrewbury chortled, exclaiming that she had to go to the lady's room.

Mr. Shrewbury burst out in his British voice, "Blimey, mate! That was smashing! You got me on that one! I'd love to see the look on that bartender's face when the real Big Bad Bob showed up! A toast for ...," he paused as he read Clayton's nametag, "for Clayton, for telling us a rollicking good story!"

Everyone at and near the table clinked glasses toasting Clayton.

For the rest of that evening, the next day, and at future conferences, whenever Clayton bumped into Mr. Shrewbury, the president of sales would point at Clayton, start laughing, and holler, "Big Bad Bob's comin'!"

THE KING'S WINEMAKER

The decrepit guard carried in one wobbling hand, a clay bowl spilling slop and in his other trembling hand, he fumbled with a sizeable skeleton key the length of his scrawny forearm. Throughout the centuries, jailers had grasped the wrought-iron key in their sweaty palms, rubbing a shiny spot on its bow while the notched end gleamed where it had repeatedly engaged the cylinder that unlocked the deadbolt which secured the heavy iron door. Upon opening the door and entering the cell, he quite expected to find the imprisoned man dead.

The guard, who was not really a guard, but a prisoner who, being an ailing man of little threat, was granted by the jail-master the odious privilege of toiling every day over a huge boiling vat of mush and maggots and serving it to the other prisoners instead of living his life-sentence rotting to death in his dismal chamber. Nevertheless, after twenty years of confinement in the dungeon beneath the stone castle, the aged guard had already mostly rotted. For certain, his latest pair of trousers were worn and only the stiff, soily stains kept the threads from fraying and exposing his malnourished nakedness. Barechested with a prominent ribcage and barefooted with long, dirty toenails, the only other thing that he wore besides his filthy pants was a sullied rope around his waist; a length of rope long enough to keep an emaciated man's pants above his bony hips, yet too short for a despairing man to hang himself. His limp, gray hair, damp from the steam of the bubbling slop and sweaty from the heat of the cooking fire, dangled to his shoulders. Pallid, sun deprived skin, stretched taut over his bony arms and legs. Black circles lurked under his glintless eyes cowering deep within their sockets and dark shadows of despair shifted about his rawboned face, and yet, upon this grimacing portrait of suffering, he flaunted a reminder of better days; days when he was a free man; days with his wife and four children; days of sunshine at his seaside estate; days of feasting on roasted pheasant and drinking fine wine; and days when people greeted him by his name—and what was this reminder that he flaunted of better days?—a full beard, perfectly trimmed, at one time black, but now silver and satiny, wearing it as a hairy badge of honor, as a fleecy declaration of innocence, and as a wooly symbol of survival. He kept his beard immaculate, snipping it with small scissors; a pair of scissors sharp enough to cut whiskers, yet too dull to kill a man.

The dim light of a smoking oil lamp hanging in the dark corridor, cast eerie, elongated shadows of an enormous rat scampering about the floor and of the feeble yet handsomely-bearded man, shaking pitifully, still trying to shove the key into the keyhole. Finally, he set the bowl of now cold slop down on the floor and using two hands, steadied himself, inserted the key, twisted it, and unlocked the deadbolt with a resounding clank. He gripped the door's iron handle with both hands, firmly planted his feet, and leaned his meager weight backward pulling the cumbersome door open; its screeching hinges echoing down the maze of corridors. He left the key in the keyhole, lit a sooty oil lamp just inside the cell, picked up the bowl of slop, stood at the doorway, and hollered in a voice ruined from decades of screaming hysterically in his own torment. "Slop! Come get your slop!" Usually, the caged man came and heeled, panting, begging like a hungry dog until the guard handed him the slimy fodder, however, not a sound arose from the gloom except the drumrolling toenails of scurrying rats. He called out again,

"Slop!" and listened, but heard no stirring of a man. Knowing that during the cold nights these imprisoned men frequently perished, not so much from the chill, but from abject despair, the guard mindfully entered the dismal cell.

The prison chamber, the height of two horses stacked, the width of three horses side by side, and the length of two horses nose to tail had been built long ago of irregular stones of various proportions abutted together with mortar. In one corner sat a wooden bucket of stale water with a thirsty rat balancing on the bucket's rim and in another corner sat a cast iron chamber pot.

A scrawny rat scampered under the guard's feet, causing the old man to stumble and spill a bit of slop, where upon, a pack of squeaking rodents converged on the splatter and licked it up. In the sooty, obscure light, he focused his eyes toward the middle of the stone floor and saw the imprisoned man lying silent, tightly curled up as if he suffered from a painful stomachache. The guard remembered when this condemned young man was once cheerful, robust, and full of passion, but now, deprived of the life he once cherished and bound by his horrible fate, the man appeared dead.

The guard set the bowl down on the floor next to the unmoving man, bent down, and checking for life, shook the man's shoulder. In a raspy voice, he asked, "You alive?" No answer. The guard shook him harder and asked again, "You alive?"

The prostrate man stirred and moaned a simple question, sounding more like a sick farm animal than a man. "Ammm I?"

"Yes, you're alive. I brought you slop. Now eat!" said the guard. "And don't break this bowl like you did the last one, making me punish you and you don't get to eat. You miss another meal and you'll surely die."

The man on the floor looked up with only enough strength

to move his eyes. He focused on the old guard and started to speak, but had to clear his dry throat.

The guard glared down at him and asked, "You got something to say?"

"Yes," he moaned.

"Well, what is it? Speak!"

The man below again cleared his throat, coughed, and finally groaned, "Niiice beeeard."

The ailing guard huffed, ignored the compliment, and since he had other prisoners to feed, he tramped away from the man on the floor, left the oil lamp burning—though he normally put it out—slammed the giant door, locked the lock, and took the oversized key. As he shuffled down the corridor and thought about his 'nice beard,' the etchings of anguish on his face shifted into a forgotten grin.

Down in the rat-infested chamber, the smoky oil lamp burned and in its faint glow, curled up on the floor next to his bowl of slop, lay the King's winemaker, Stefino Bestavino. He felt so weak that he could only stretch out his arm, lift his head, drag the bowl under his face, and plop it into the slop. After lapping it up like a starving mongrel and shoving the empty bowl away from him, he lay still for a moment. When he felt the surge of the meager nourishment, he crept on his belly over to the water bucket, shooed away the thirsty rat, raised up on his knees, cupped his hands, drank, and drank again. With wet hands, he washed his bearded face and swept back his long mane of dark hair. His chiseled face once tanned from tending the vines under the sun was now gaunt and pale from tending loneliness in the dark. His amber-brown eyes, the color of golden honey, had always stored glints of sunlight, now extinguished by the tears of shattered dreams, missed love, and a lost life. He still wore the same white ruffled shirt with open neck and billowy sleeves, now soiled, the same green velvet pants, now sheenless, and the same laced black boots, now scuffed, that he had worn when he had presented his latest vintage wine at the King's Harvest Feast. He breathed in deeply, slowly exhaled, bowed his head as beads of water trickled off his face and he prayed, "God, you are my only salvation from this pit of rats; this pit of despair; this pit where I will surely die. I am innocent. I did not poison the King. Please—set me free." He climbed to his feet and although he was tall, dashing, and only twenty-six, he shuffled bent and repulsive like the crickety guard over to the stone wall and placed his unsteady hand on a damp spot of mortar a foot thick at the crux between three stones. A spot he had relentlessly chipped away at for nearly a year, where, when he stood flat on his feet and pressed his ear to the wall, he could hear the faint sounds of life: children laughing, women chatting, men discussing, musicians playing, and oddly, baby birds cheeping. On his side of the wall there prevailed darkness, rats, hunger, and hopelessness, while outside the wall there bustled the village marketplace; a place bright and warm with sunshine, of music, poetry, and art, and for buying and selling vegetables, grains, milk, eggs, cheese, bread, chickens, pigs, goats, and goods of all kinds.

It has been said, that a man without passion is at death's door and a man without purpose is dead. Stefino loitered at the threshold of death and would have certainly died in his imprisonment if he had not transformed his zealous passion and purpose for making wine into an eagerness for digging; digging for liberty, for destiny, and for life; scratching, hoping to see a ray of light; picking, wanting for a breath of fresh air; and clawing, destroying every fingernail while muttering, imploring God for a way out.

Stefino held a decayed molar, which he had painstakingly wiggled loose with his thumb and index finger until he had yanked it out of his mouth. He gripped the tooth and scraped it against the moist mortar until its enamel wore away, and then knowing he would suffer the punishment of missing a feeding of slop, he smashed the clay bowl on the floor. Snatching up a jagged piece, he picked and scraped, removing one defiant grain of mortar after another as each grain became a tiny triumph in his quest to feel, hear, see, and smell the sweetness of life. Not knowing whether it was day or night, he slaved for many hours, driving himself on, ignoring his trembling weakness, but finally, overcome with exhaustion, he quit digging, concealed the bits of mortar in a rat hole in the wall, lay on the floor, cradled his head under his arms, and fell asleep.

He had a nightmarish dream of standing naked amidst a fierce storm raging with whipping winds and driving rain. Day became night as black clouds rolled overhead and with each flash of lightning, he saw that he stood alone in a barren land. Thunder clapped and he trembled. With no place to run and no place to hide, the tempest tore at his skin and he shivered. It beat him down and he dropped to his knees, pleading for the howling cruelty to end. Suddenly, the rain stopped, the wind ceased, and triumphant sunbeams punched through the angry clouds. He picked himself up off his knees and stood basking in glorious warmth; his bare feet sinking into the damp, rich soil of his vast vineyard. He peered out over the rolling hills and saw verdant leaves, wet and glistening in the sunlight. He saw ancient vines with clusters of plump, purple grapes, ripe for harvesting, crushing, and winemaking. Joy filled his soul and he raised his face toward the heavens and smiled and smiled and smiled—until he abruptly awoke in his dank cell.

His body felt stiff and cold from sleeping on the stone floor, however, his face felt a subtle warmth as he blinked his eyes to an unfamiliar brightness. He gazed up at the spot on the wall where he had toiled for so long and saw an answered prayer; a ray of hope; a beam of light the diameter of a feather's quill shining into the room. He laughed aloud, sprung to his feet, hobbled over to the stream of light, stuck his nose up to the small but magnificent hole and breathed the fresh air deep inside his nostrils. He smelled baked bread and the scent of flowers and he sighed. He closed one eye and placed his other eye to the hole and although the bright light caused his eye to tear, he peered out and saw up close the small downy heads and tiny beaks of two baby sparrows. He surmised that over many years, the sparrows had pecked at this gaping spot between the stones on the outside wall, removing the mortar and building a nest, now occupied by two little birds, thus, he saw light in half the time; truly, a blessing from Heaven. He peered between and past the cheeping heads and in the limited world of this little hole, he saw a young maiden selling bread and flowers; the loaves and bouquets stacked neatly in a wooden wheelbarrow. She stood five horse lengths away from the prison wall with her back to him; her golden hair gleaming with sunlight, streaming like a waterfall of glossy silk down to her waist. She wore modest clothes: a white long-sleeve chemise with unpretentious ruffles about her neck and wrists and a long, light-blue dress down to the sandals on her feet. A tiny, green bird with a ruby red throat, flew, zipping and hovering about her. It would alight on her shoulder until people approached and the thumb-size bird would again take flight. He had never seen a bird that could fly up, down, and backward and even hang in midair as if a puppeteer dangled it on a thread of yarn. He recognized nearly everyone who passed before his spying eye and desired to call out to Arturo, the inn keeper, Pippino, the pastry chef, Nico, the blacksmith, and Timido, the stable boy, but did not summon them to the wall, fearing that the jail-master would discover the blessed little hole and fill it with mortar, extinguishing the light, sealing off the fresh air, and muting the sounds of life.

For hours, Stefino listened, breathed, and stared from his cell of depravity at a world of abundance. When his legs grew tired, he sat on the floor, leaned against the opposite wall in front of the sunbeam, and closed his eyes. He listened to the chirping of baby birds and felt the warmth of the light comforting his body and soul. His tranquil mind embraced the light, wafted up its shimmering streamlet to the wall, escaped through the dazzling hole past the busy marketplace, away from the old castle, beyond the quaint village, and back to the coastal hills of his vineyard. His thoughts drifted back to a year ago when he toiled amongst the vines, harvested grapes, and made wine for a King; back before the Tallow brothers coveted the prestige of being the King's winemaker; before they tainted Stefino's wine, making the King gravely ill; and before an enraged and nauseous King Luna threw him in prison and forgot him.

Peaceful, happy, and lost in the memories of his former life, Stefino grinned. Suddenly, there was a loud clank followed by the shriek of door hinges. Stefino's day dreaming stopped, his eyes snapped open, and his smile vanished. He jumped to his feet, stumbled over to the beaming hole and trying to conceal it, leaned the back of his head against it.

"Slop! Come get your slop!" hollered the sickly guard.

"I broke my bowl," shouted Stefino, "I don't deserve slop today! Go away!"

The guard stepped into the cell and glared suspiciously, surprised to see Stefino standing against the wall and not dying on the floor. The glow of the light emanating from behind Stefino's head appeared as a heavenly halo.

"Am I seeing an angel," wondered the tattered guard aloud, rubbing his perfectly trimmed beard, "or might there be a hole in the wall?" He set the bowl of slop on the floor, ventured over to Stefino, and demanded, "Step away from the wall!"

"I cannot," stated Stefino, "this stone wall is holding me up."

The frail guard raised up his slumping shoulders and bent spine. Looking six inches taller and with a new surge of intent, he tried to shove Stefino aside. Stefino held his ground.

"Share the light," stated the exhausted guard, breathing heavily, "and I'll share the food."

Stefino's stomach growled at the mention of food as fatigue overtook him. Reluctantly, he took a step sideways and the beam of light kissed the guard right between his eyes, causing the old man to gasp and burst out laughing hysterically. He put his nostrils to the hole and sniffed, put his ear to the hole and listened, and put his eye to the hole and looked. He absorbed the light like a piece of stale bread dipped in milk and as the shadows of despair on his face vanished and as the tortured look gripping his jaw let go, the guard turned and faced Stefino. The old man's glowing face appeared like the face of a young lad full of wonderment who had just peered through a hole in a circus tent.

"It is a glorious sight!" exclaimed the astonished, old man, his eyes twinkling with awe. "You may keep this hole, but must share the light with me. Keep as well, the pieces of broken clay and use them to make this hole bigger. I will *not* tell the jail-master and I will reward you by bringing you a bigger bowl filled to the brim with slop, so that you can regain your strength for digging."

"Guard, by what name did they call you in the village?" asked Stefino.

"Ilario," muttered the guard. "They called me Ilario. Ilario Gallantano."

"Ilario—my name is Stefino. Stefino Bestavino. Thank you for your compassion."

Ilario didn't reply. He simply left Stefino's cell, locked the door, took the large key, and trudged down the corridor. He grinned, thinking of the bright beam of light, the breath of fresh air, and the glimpse of the bustling marketplace and he spoke his own name, "Ilario." He shuffled a few more steps and he spoke it again, "Ilario," and he drew in a deep breath and sung out his name, "Ilaaaaaariooooo," in a note louder and higher than the constrictive rasp in his throat; his name ringing out like a church bell, resonating throughout the dungeon.

Every day when Ilario brought Stefino his large bowl of slop, they took turns peering out the hole and when they weren't peering, they took turns chipping out the mortar, increasing the size of the beaming hole to a palm-sized window. The hole framed by the stones in the wall could not get any bigger, so they stopped toiling and just enjoyed watching the vibrant marketplace, the changes in weather, and the backside view of the young, golden-haired woman selling bread and flowers. Both men, eating more, basking in sunlight, and breathing fresh air, looked younger, felt healthier, and acted livelier every time they looked out at the purging world. Time passed and in the nest in the wall, the baby sparrows grew feathers and flew away.

One afternoon, for now Stefino knew the time of day, he peered out the hole as he did every day. Ilario brought him slop and while Stefino ate, Ilario peeped through the hole, listened to a string quartet somewhere out of his sight and moved his feet to their waltz. Ilario, smiling, humming the waltz, left to feed the other prisoners. Stefino watched the villagers pass by, hoping to see his elderly father, but never did. So his eyes followed the golden-haired maiden, watching her move about gracefully like a ballerina, selling her flowers and bread as her shiny hair danced wispy pirouettes in the breeze. He listened to her talking, laughing, and singing, her voice like the melodious strings of a harp, all the while, he was hoping, wishing, and praying that she would turn around.

Day after day, she did not turn around, until one sunlit day with seagulls squawking, children laughing, and a small band of musicians playing a pan flute, a lute, and a lyre, she turned around.

Unbeknownst to Stefino, below his view, in the soil directly beneath the hole on the outside of the prison wall, there grew a beautiful flower, a vivid, pink flower where bumblebees and butterflies gathered. The maiden's humming little bird took flight from her shoulder, zipped over to the wall like an arrow shot from a bow, and hovered right before Stefino's eyes. The tiny bird with its long, narrow beak and beady, black eyes, looked like a flying jewel; its head and body crested with green emeralds and its throat set with red rubies. Stefino silently chuckled with delight. The feathered little gem, unaware of Stefino hidden in the dim dungeon, floated to the left, to the right, backward, and dipped out of sight. The girl turned, searching for her little bird and she looked directly at Stefino, or so he thought, but actually, she peered just below the hole at her bird hovering, sipping the flower's nectar.

Stefino gasped at her beauty. He had fallen in love with her before she had ever turned around but now, viewing her front side, her lovely face and curvaceous figure stole his breath away, twisted his stomach, caused him to sweat, and made his green velvet pants feel tighter. She wore a sun-yellow dress tightly laced beneath her ample breasts; her creamy cleavage looking like two mourning doves perched above the laces. As she approached the stone wall, it seemed as though sunbeams chased her while the rest of the village fell under the shadow of a cloud. She stopped in front of Stefino at a distance where he could gaze at her from her waist up. She stood motionless like a young lady posing for an oil painting; her portrait framed by rugged stones and hanging on the wall of his cell.

She giggled, amused, and speaking with merriment, said, "So, Tobago, you found me another flower to sell. You may be a little bird, but you are such a big helper. Thank you."

Tobago must have drank his belly full because he reappeared, fluttering next to her. The bird zipped and zagged, twirled and danced about her as though it was happy to please her. She stepped forward close to the wall, bent down, picked the flower, and stood where now her lovely face filled Stefino's entire view. She swept back her lustrous hair, raised the bright pink flower to her nose, and sniffed of its scent. Stefino gawked at her angelic face gleaming in a host of twinkles like sunlight shimmering in cascading water and he sighed. He beheld her radiant skin, smooth without any creases of anguish and without any wrinkles of bitterness and his heart pounded. He gazed into her twinkling eyes, bluer and brighter than a cloudless sky on a summer day; eyes sparkling with wonderment, revealing her innocence, and his breath quickened. He fell under the spell of her enchanting smile; a smile parading perfect white teeth, rose petal lips, and charming dimples; a smile, so bubbling with happiness, so bejeweled with dazzling splendor, so bright, so blinding, he blinked as though he had peered directly into the sun. Indeed, a smile, so full of life, it could heal the sick; so full of love, it could stop a war; so joyous, it could make a somber face grin, an oppressed soul sing, and a troubled spirit rise up, defy darkness, denounce despair, and dare to soar high into a redeeming light; a light of hope, of faith, and of conviction that an innocent man—a man, like Stefino Bestavino, the King's winemaker—would soon be set free.

Stefino longed to embrace her, not from lust of her dazzling beauty, but spellbound by her twinkling grandeur. He stared silent with his heart pounding and watched her as Tobago alighted on her shoulder, however, as she turned to leave, his soul shriveled, his heart ached, his face contorted, his eyes teared, and the chilling reality of his captivity gripped him like a grave does a coffin and a coffin does a dead man. In desperation and panic, he placed his mouth to the hole and called out in a loud whisper, "Fair maiden, please do not fear me. I beg of you, please linger, if only for a moment longer."

The maiden, startled, whipped back around, her golden hair swirling with her and she demanded, "Who said that?"

"It is I," he spoke softly, "speaking to you from my prison cell and seeing you through this little hole in the prison wall."

She took a step back and peered at the hole in the mortar between the stones. She saw the sparse twigs of the abandoned bird's nest and beyond that, she saw the sunlight glinting off two eyes; eyes of desperation, weary and pleading. Tobago launched off her shoulder, hummed over to the hole, and peered inside. Frightened, he buzzed backwards, hiding behind her.

"I see you in your dungeon," she stated in a firm voice as her face fell under the same shadow that shaded the village and her smile with all its twinkles disappeared. "You are a criminal and locked away for the crimes you have committed. Upon sunrise, tomorrow morning, I will tell the jail-master of your breach in the prison wall and how you spy on and lust after young maidens."

"Please, sweet lady, hear me out," pleaded Stefino. "This hole between the stones is a blessing from Heaven and if it is taken from me, I shall never again see the light, never again breathe fresh air, never again listen to the sound of life, and never again gaze upon your beauty. Without it, I will surely die."

"Then, you shall surely die," she asserted. "You most likely deserve to die as punishment for your crime."

Tobago chirped a high pitch cheep which seemed to second her assertion.

"Please, I am innocent. I swear it on my father's name, my vineyard, and all, which is holy. Nevertheless, if you intend to tell the jail-master, I beg you, may I partake of your beauty for just a little while longer?"

"No, you may not lust after me in your depravity, besides, I have flowers and bread to sell." She turned to leave and snapped, "Come, Tobago."

Tobago buzzed a hummy huff and floated backward never taking his beady eyes off the hole.

The maiden walked away with her back to Stefino and ignored his hidden gaze all of the rest of the day. As the shadows of twilight lengthened and after she sold the last bouquet of flowers and the last loaf of bread, Tobago landed on her shoulder, she lifted up the handles of the empty wheelbarrow and pushed it out onto the cobblestone road. She took a few steps toward home, stopped, sat the wheelbarrow down, turned about, and stared, as if contemplating about the hole in the prison wall.

Stefino stared back, alert, anticipating, hoping she would return and talk with him, but she turned away and pushed the wheelbarrow out of his sight. The village marketplace emptied of people, animals, and goods, becoming quiet as the sun dropped behind the castle and eased below the horizon, blanketing with night all twinkles, glints, and glimmers.

Stefino sighed, stepped away from the hole, knelt down by his bucket of water and drank and drank again. He washed his face with his wet hands. The cool water felt refreshing and he spoke, "Lord of mercy, God of grace, please stop the jail-master from taking away my light of hope; my light of life; my light of joy; the light that You bestowed upon me—an innocent man. If the light is gone, I will die. Save the light. Save me."

He curled up on the floor and tried to sleep, but couldn't, knowing that at sunrise, without a miracle, he would lose his light, lose his hope, and lose his will to live.

When the first faint sunbeams of the new day peeked through the hole in the wall, he jumped to his feet, peered out, and waited for the maiden along with the jail-master to storm up to the castle wall, see the breach in the fortification, plug it up with new, solid, impenetrable mortar, and brutally whip Stefino, leaving him strafed and bleeding to die. Villagers began arriving and setting up their wares for sale. Seagulls cried out overhead. Chickens clucked in cages. Piglets snorted and squealed. The maiden had not arrived.

Stefino assumed, she must be telling Ugo, the jail-master right now about the hole in the prison wall and the brutal man must be clenching his snaggled teeth, gripping his cat-of-nine-tails, and stomping in his big boots toward the hole right now. Stefino trembled at the thought of angering Ugo: a freakish oaf whose small head, the size of a lad's, had not grown in proportion to his nearly seven-foot tall body. Suffering not only that malformation, his small face looked froggish with bulging, black watery eyes, drab olive-colored skin bubbling with warts, bumps, and lumps, and a rocky, hairless cranium. He wore a tent-size brown tunic with a wide leather belt, mammoth leather boots laced up to the shins of his hairy, bare legs, and coinciding with his amphibian angry face, his deep throaty voice croaked out cruel words. Most terrifying was that, the great pain he had suffered from all the ridicule during his childhood, he now rendered on the prisoners with his cat-o-nine-tails.

"No, no, no!" Stefino screamed, imagining the worst—but no, there she was, arriving alone with Tobago perched on her shoulder. Today, she wore a cream-colored chemise and a long forest-green dress with the same two plump doves perched above its laces. She pushed her wheelbarrow full of bouquets and loaves up to her selling spot, set it down, turned, and marched over to the hole in the prison wall. Tobago buzzed off in search of nectar. Tossing back her hair over her shoulders, she called out, "Oh, prisoner, are you in there, peeping out the hole in the prison wall?"

"Yes, I am. Good morning, fair maiden. I expected to see you along with an angry Ugo and after that—I expected a very bad day."

"I didn't tell Ugo, because I've been thinking. Every prisoner claims he is innocent, but the greater their guilt, the louder and the longer they cry out their innocence. But you stated your innocence only once and your voice was calm and full of faith and your eyes that I saw gleaming in the light of this hole, were pleading, void of rage, without threat, and I knew that you might indeed be telling the truth about your innocence. Since you cannot go anywhere and cannot hurt me and since I know your life relies on my mercy, I wanted to talk with you before I summoned Ugo."

"I am grateful for your mercy and your desire to converse."

"So who are you, this man locked behind this stone wall?"

"My name is Stefino Bestavino."

"I've heard of you. Many village girls, thinking you are handsome and wealthy, had their eyes on you for matrimony until the King threw you in prison. Also, I remember you own a vineyard and make wine. My father, the Captain of the *Brillante,* who has sailed around the world, knew good wine and out of all the wine that he had tasted, he said that you made the best."

"Captain of the *Brillante?* I recall meeting him once at the docks when I was shipping my wine to a prince in India. Nice fellow. I gave your father wine to drink during the long voyage. Your father is a highly regarded sailor, an incredible man, and a noble captain of one of the fastest and finest ships ever to sail across the sea. Please thank him for praising my wine."

"My father is lost at sea," she blurted out, her voice breaking in sorrow.

"I'm so sorry to hear that. And your mother, how is she surviving the loss?"

"Long ago, before my father vanished, my mother died from a cough and fever. I sell flowers and bread to support my younger twin sisters, Sara and Sella and my little brother, Angelo."

"I'm very sorry for your great loss. You are a wonderful daughter and a noble sister."

"Thank you. I do my best," she said composing herself. "So Stefino Bestavino, why are you in the King's prison?"

"I once was the King's Winemaker until the Tallow brothers poisoned my wine, thus ...."

"Oooh, I hate those Tallow brothers!" she snapped, stomping a foot. "They are ugly, smelly, and loathsome men if you could call them men. I'd rather attend the King's Ball with a mule than with one of them. Not a lady in the village will allow them near her."

"I agree. They are indeed repulsive and so is their wine. They are swine and their wine is swill. I found out about the brothers and their deeds against me through a guard, who is really a longtime prisoner, who spoke with another prisoner, who confessed his crimes to him in exchange for double helpings of slop. It was this other prisoner who helped the Tallow brothers frame ...."

"Oooh, those awful Tallow brothers," she interrupted again. "Every time I hear their name, I feel like beetles are crawling all over me and I want to scream. You would not believe what those disgusting men asked me."

"Try me. I would never under estimate their lewdness," said Stefino as he visualized the two crude brothers: Pisoffa, the older, taller, and skinnier of the two brothers who was not as hairy nor as smelly as squatty, big-boned Fugglio, but who was still hideous with his oily, black hair tied in a ponytail, his narrow, dark mustache slithering above his lusty sneer, and the bad habit of flicking his nasty tongue about his mouth to wet his dry, chapped lips. When he spoke, he always uttered his words in a harsh, condescending tone. In contrast, Fugglio acted passive, except when incited by his brother to be mean and then, he could be horribly mean. Ugly like his brother, but uglier, he had a black ledge of eyebrows, a broad nose, a pointy goatee, and he wore his black hair down to his shoulders in a medieval mullet with ridiculous square cut bangs. To add to his repulsiveness, he had a bad habit of fiddling with his ears. Fugglio had few original thoughts and mostly echoed what Pisoffa said. Though both were loathsome man-beasts, they both wore handsome tunics purchased with the sacks of money that they made as the King's winemakers. "I remember them well," continued Stefino "and I agree, they are very difficult to look at. I've heard tales that children wail at the sight of them."

"Children *and* the unlucky young ladies who they aspire to court. Both cry. A few weeks ago, it was the day after my twentieth birthday, I had just left the chapel, passed by the village fountain, and was walking home down Cobblestone Street when the Tallow brothers approached me, punching each other, wrestling to hold each other back, racing, trying to reach me first."

"And, my lady, what did the large, hairy rodents desire of you?"

"Well," she answered, "Pisoffa explained while Fugglio nodded his head in agreement that they had a proposition for me. They wanted to talk to me, because both of them adore me and they were tired of brawling over which brother should have me—like either one of them ever had a chance. So in their thick ape skulls, they decided to *both* ask me for my hand in marriage."

"Leaving it up to you of course to settle their dispute and their competition by choosing the least ugly, the less smelly, and the man who would cause you the slightest case of nausea."

"No, no, no, not choose between them one over the other, but to say *yes* or *no* to marry them both. I'd be one wife for two brothers as one husband."

"Marry them both! How dare they disrespect your honor."

"I know. How dare they. Disgusting! They told me that compared to my beauty each one of them measured but half a man, so if I married them both it would be like marrying a whole man. Albeit, an ugly, smelly, whole man."

"So, the buffoons would share you?"

"Yes. They made clear to me their preposterous plan. I would live at their chateau amongst the vines. During the day I would cook, clean, bake bread, and tend to a garden of fruits and vegetables. They would work the vineyard and make and sell the wine. I would sleep every other night in Pisoffa's bed and every other night in Fugglio's bed. The thought makes me ill. I fear what would happen to me if both were drunk and if both desired to have his way with me on the same night."

"A terrifying thought—what if you were with child? Whose child would it be?"

"Of course, if the child were beautiful, we would never know which brother was the father, but if the child was ugly, we could measure the degree of ugliness and determine if it was Pisoffa's or Fugglio's child. The kid would most likely pick up both of their bad habits, licking his lips like Pisoffa and twiddling with his ears like Fugglio; however, they wouldn't care who the true father would be. All that mattered to them was that the baby was of their lineage. Oh and they said, my little brother and sisters could live with us. How frightening! The thought of those innocent children around those burly men, eeew, it's all so sickening."

"Fear not; puke not, fair maiden, for you know that their proposition will never be. So as I was saying, a deranged man here in the prison by the name of Manzo Stellini who was arrested for streaking about the village naked told my friend Ilario ...."

"Ilario? Ilario Gallantano," she interrupted yet again. "My father knew him well. He owns the ships on which my father sailed. The shipping company supports Ilario's family to this day. Many years ago, my father told me that before I was born, the King, a young man at the time, had demanded free passage for all of his highborn friends to wherever their heart desired to sail. Ilario refused, embarrassing the King and the King threw him into prison. The King and his cohorts voyage for free anyway, yet the stubborn and pompous King will not release Ilario."

"Ilario is a good man and does not deserve his plight. Anyway, as I was saying, the Tallow brothers hired this exhibitionist Stellini to poison ...."

"Why did Stellini run about naked?" asked the young maiden with a screwy face.

"The times I saw him: a skinny, very hairy middle-aged man with bony buttocks, long flowing hair, and a big grin on his face, streaking through the village and past me, he looked like he was just having fun running naked in the sight of God and the villagers. Anyhow, being hired by the Tallow brothers, Stellini slipped into the King's wine cellar, secretly removed the bung from my barrel of wine; a vintage wine I had crafted especially for the King for the Harvest Feast and the lunatic poured ground hemlock into it. The thirsty, impatient King was the first to fill his crystal goblet with my wine and when he lifted the glass to toast me as his winemaker, I saw by the candlelight glowing beneath it, bits of debris floating in the wine. I knew that something was amiss, for my wine has such clarity that when one raises his glass to toast a friend, you can clearly see through the wine the face of whom you are toasting. Before I could stop the King, he guzzled the wine down his throat in his unappreciative, untasting way, and filled his glass again and gulped it down. For a moment, he smiled with delight and before I could pour wine to the rest of the dignitaries at his table, the King broke out in a drenching sweat, doubled up, and crashed in all of his three hundred pounds to the floor. For days, the King, deathly ill, spewed belly stew out both ends of his body. He nearly died, but lived, only to cast me into this dungeon."

"How horrible people can be. I believe you Stefino." She looked around, saw villagers gathering to buy and sell, and turned to leave, saying, "I must go now and sell my bread and flowers."

"Thank you, maiden," Stefino called out, "for not telling Ugo about my hole in the prison wall. Furthermore, I am grateful for our conversation today for I have been very lonely, but two quick questions before you go—no three."

She stopped, again drew close to the hole, and said, "Ask me."

"How is my father Orazio Bestavino?"

"I know who he is, but I have not seen him in the village for many months now."

Stefino felt anguish over his father and concern about his vineyard, but he moved on to his second question and asked, "What kind of bird is Tobago?"

"Tobago is a hummingbird and I named him after the island from which he came; the island of Tobago, near Trinidad in the Caribbean. My father, on returning from a sea voyage, brought him to me as a gift."

"He is a very amusing little bird. Lastly, lovely lady, what is your name?"

"My name is Melodina Miabello." She spun, hurried over to her wheelbarrow, and began selling flowers and bread. Tobago zipped over to her and alighted on her shoulder.

Stefino watched Melodina all day and every so often she would spin around, look at the prison wall, and smile. Stefino laughed with joy every time she did. Ilario brought him slop and while he ate, and as Ilario peered out the hole, Stefino told him of the young maiden's threat to summon the jail-master and of how she changed her mind, and of the proposition from the Tallow brothers, and of her hummingbird Tobago, and of her name, Melodina Miabello.

Ilario listened intently while peering out at a world filling him with joy and said, "She must be the daughter of Marco Miabello, the captain of the *Brillante*."

"Yes, her father was the captain of the *Brillante*," confirmed Stefino, "but he is lost at sea."

Ilario shook his head saddened at the loss of such a noble sailor and a good friend.

The two men stared out into the blissful sunlight every

day and over time, their sores vanished, their slumping spines stretched back to their regular height, and both men could be heard singing, their jubilant voices echoing throughout the dungeon.

One evening, after people left the marketplace, Melodina brought a piece of bread over to Stefino. She mashed it, stuffed it into the hole, and used a stick to shove it all the way through. Stefino grabbed it and gobbled it up all the while mumbling, groaning, how good it was.

An elegantly dressed man in his thirties, strolling home past the prison wall saw Melodina standing by the wall and talking to herself. He questioned her, speaking in a high-pitch, singsong, voice with a slight lisp, "Young lady—Melodina, is that you? What are you doing at the prison wall?"

She spun around and saw the man; a perky, feminine, fellow with cork-screw locks of chestnut-brown hair down to his shoulders, large green eyes glinting with gaiety, a petite, pointy nose, and big, fishy lips, standing on the road with his hands on his hips. She knew him. It was Giaboni, the village glass blower.

"Oh hello, Giaboni," she said, "I'm, uh, feeding hungry rats my left over bread."

"That is a disgusting thing to do," he spat. "Please, stop! You are making me terribly ill. Come now and I will walk you as far as my house where you can have a quick cup of tea and chat with my roommate Butano and me. "

"Okay, I'll be right there." She turned to the wall and whispered, "Stefino, I'll speak with you in the morning. Goodnight. Tobago come." The bird landed on her shoulder, she walked briskly over to Giaboni, and as she pushed her wheelbarrow down the road, Giaboni strolled, gaily swinging his hips alongside her.

Stefino, dreaming of, longing for, and falling in love with

Melodina, watched her every day. She visited him every morning and every evening. From the road, villagers might have seen the remnants of the vacated bird's nest in the cavity of the prison wall, but they never thought there happened to be a breach all the way through the wall. Most assumed that Melodina just wanted to rest in the shade of the castle wall, tired from baking nearly all night, picking flowers in the early morning, selling her goods all day, and taking care of her siblings all the rest of the time. If they did notice her talking, alone by the wall, they assumed she was simply speaking to her pet bird. So no one, except Giaboni that one time, questioned her or stopped her from dawdling by the prison wall. She snuck Stefino bread, vegetables, and fruits and he shared them with Ilario as both men regained their health.

Stefino and Melodina became cherished friends. They longed for the moments when they would talk about who they were and what made each sad, happy, angry, and afraid. They shared their sorrows of the past, their hardships of today, and their dreams of the future. She expressed her sorrow, missing her mother and father, and the happy memories growing up in the small cottage by the woods. He told her how his mother had died a few days after he was born and how he and his father had toiled together in their vineyard, becoming closer than any father and son. Both Melodina and Stefino spoke of being too busy with responsibilities to have ever fallen in love.

One day Melodina did not show up at the market place. Stefino worried that something had happened to her. He waited, never taking his eyes off his palm-size view. No Melodina. He peered, cranking his head about, trying to get a wider view of the marketplace. No Melodina. His eyes hurt from not blinking. No Melodina. His legs hurt from standing. No Melodina. Despair welled up inside him. Still, no Melodina. He mumbled repeatedly, "Where are you, my love?" Trapped, he could not search for her. If she was hurt, he could not help her. If the Tallow brothers so much laid a hand on her, he could not kill them. Frustrated, he pounded his fists against the stone wall.

In the late afternoon, at the height of his distress, he saw her, smiling, singing; her little bird, flying, humming, both coming down the cobblestone road. He dropped to his knees to rest his legs and to say a prayer, "My Lord, thank you for bringing my love to me safely."

She sauntered up to the prison wall and stood before the hole.

Stefino glared out at her and asked with obvious agitation, "Melodina, my love, where have you been?"

"I am very sorry, Stefino," she replied, "but when I tell you where I've ...."

He cut her off and snapped, "I have worried myself frantic. I am at your whim and ways. Please tell me if you cannot visit me or if you decide never to return. I have grown accustomed to seeing you."

"I am so sorry, Stefino, but when I tell you where I've been, it will relieve you of all of your distress. Last night, I decided not to bake bread nor pick flowers this morning. I walked out to your vineyard by the sea."

At the mention of his vineyard, his eyes sparkled in the sunlight.

"Your vines are healthy," she continued, "and the grapes are nearly ripe for harvesting, however, your father Orazio is ill. After toiling all spring and summer caring for the vineyard by himself, he does not have the strength to harvest the grapes and make the wine." She noticed Stefino's eyes drop and heard him sigh.

After a moment of silence, he said, "It will be the first time in over a hundred years since my great grandfather who planted the vineyard, who bequeathed it to my grandfather, who bequeathed it to my father who bequeathed it to me, that Bestavino wine will not be made."

"I told him that you are alive," she said, "and that you are well and it seemed to restore his vigor. We had a long visit. He is such a nice man. He told me that he had walked each day to the prison to see you, but Ugo had refused him. Your father is sick with worry for you."

Stefino growled, "That no-good, frog-faced Ugo!"

"I also walked to Ilario's estate not far from yours. My goodness, what a beautiful home on the cliffs overlooking the sea. The surf, the seagulls, the sand, all so wonderful. His wife, Valentina, is such a beautiful lady and his children are well. Please tell him that he has three grandchildren: a boy and two girls. All, very well behaved. Tell him, his wife misses him dearly. She has never remarried and is waiting for him until death parts them."

"I will tell Ilario. Thank you. My heart is overjoyed, but sad because Ilario and I are missing our family and our lives."

"Something else," she said, trying to cheer-up Stefino, "something special."

Stefino peered out and saw in her hand, a small chunk of something wrapped in a silk handkerchief. He smiled, anticipating his surprise.

She shoved it in the hole, pushed it through with a stick, and said, "Not long ago, a dear friend of my father's, an ancient sailor, stopped by the cottage to check on my siblings and me. From across the sea, he brought us this delight called *chocolate*. I want you to taste the last piece."

Stefino unwrapped it, held it in his hand, and although his urge was to devour it, he sniffed it and sighed. He bit off a chunk, let it melt in his mouth. It bathed his pallet with flavor and he moaned a deep, drawn-out, pleasure packed moan, "Mmmmmmm!" and burst out, "Thank you, thank you, Melodina! You are sweet! This is sweet! Ohhhh! Mmmmm!"

"Uhhh, Stefino, what's going on in there?" asked Melodina. "It's just candy."

"I knoooow," he groaned, "but it smells and tastes so gooood!"

The taste of the dark, bittersweet candy ignited a fiery passion in Stefino like a tiny flame touching dry kindling and he exclaimed nearly loud enough for villagers to hear him from the road. "This sweet morsel, it's feeding my passion, my desires, my lust, my love, and my craving for food, for wine, and to please you and make you quiver, Melodina."

"Oooh," she sighed, blushing with a slight tremble.

"Though I am imprisoned, I need to proclaim my passions. Please, my love, bring me pen, ink, and parchment!"

The next day, Melodina brought Stefino a quill-feather pen, a small pot of ink, and rolled up parchment and secretly, slipped them through the hole. Stefino grabbed them, knelt to his knees, laid the parchment on a flat stone on the floor, dipped the pen in the ink, and smiling like a child playing in a mud puddle, he wrote, pouring out his stormy passion like raindrops of words.

Every day, Melodina brought him more parchment and he would write by the light of the hole. At twilight, he would roll up the love letter and slip it back through the wall to Melodina. She in turn, would race home, feed her siblings, and once they were nestled in bed, she would sit by the fire, and while feeling the warmth and by its glow, she would read with great anticipation Stefino's passionate words; words of devotion, words of desire, words of intimacy; of touching, of secret places, of fantasies; words of whispers, words of heartbeats, words of breathlessness; of trembling, of sighs, of gentleness; words of reckless passion, words of true love, words of commitment; of ecstasy, of tenderness, of strength; words to make a woman cry just at the happy thought that there lived such a man who could still be manly, yet express such sublime passion for a woman.

Melodina could not keep her secret love letters all to herself. She gushed on and on with her best friends, Suzetta, a pretty girl with a dark complexion, bushy, coal-black hair, and brown eyes, and Cindarina, a refined young lady, fair-skinned with straw-colored hair and light-blue eyes. Suzetta was a handmaiden for the Queen and Cindarina was a seamstress for the village dressmaker. Melodina chattered without divulging the name of her secret man who freely expressed the passionate feelings of his heart and soul.

Suzetta and Cindarina read the arousing letters. They asked, pleaded, and pouted to compel her to divulge his identity, but Melodina feared if anyone knew, Ugo would find out and punish or maybe even execute Stefino for the breach in the prison wall. Therefore, the secret identity of her amorous admirer made the impassioned letters all the more mysterious, making the ladies all the more tremble, and causing the erogenous prattle to spread all the more quickly. The circulation of the letters started with Suzetta passing them on to other servants in the castle and with Cindarina passing them on to ladies coming into the dress shop. The letters oozing with passion traveled from one woman to the next as each woman read it, squirmed, sighed, passed it on, and became eager for the next. They kept track of the letters they had already read and of which ones they couldn't wait to read. It wasn't long before a raging fire of desire spread throughout the countryside like pillaging Vikings setting fires to thatched huts. The loud sighs and the throbbing heartbeats could be heard like the sea's pounding surf as young maidens, mature ladies, old women, and widows all wild with desire chased, cornered, and caught the men of their choice: shy men, bold men, poor men, and rich men; young men, old men, healthy men, and sick men; short, tall, fat, thin, homely, and handsome men, all men; all men except the Tallow brothers. No amount of passion, no matter how awe inspiring could arouse a woman's desire for one of them.

Stefino's father, Orazio, nearly fifty, was tanned from working the vineyard and the older version of his son with the same handsome face, golden eyes, and stature except his curly, dark hair was bordered with gray. During the worst of his sickly weariness, he met a widow named Amadora, the sister of his friend, Matteo, the cooper. She came to the Bestavino vineyard with her brother to deliver oak barrels. Orazio's eyes lit up when he had first seen her, a stout, middle-aged woman with a youthful face and child-like, sparkling blue eyes, wearing her beautiful brown hair in a colorfully, beaded braid. After the death of her husband, she was lost in despair for years and would not leave her house. Unbeknownst to Orazio, Amadora read Stefino's letters every day and it was his son's letters that had prompted her to leave her home and seek a friendship with Orazio, thus, bringing happiness to a sad, lonely widow, compelling her to nurse Orazio back to health with care and good cooking, hence, saving his life. It didn't take long and they too fell in love.

Ilario's wife, Valentina, a graceful woman with light-olive skin, a lovely face, blue-green eyes, and long black hair with strands of gray, searched and found Melodina in the marketplace and the two ladies met often at the prison wall, standing in the shade, talking to the incarcerated men. Valentina shared with Ilario all the details of the last twenty years and he cried with joy hearing about his children and grandchildren.

The stimulating letters circulated around the kingdom. Ladies, craving affection, intimacy, tenderness, and devotion nearly panted in the presence of a man. They used numerous weapons of woo: flirty winks, toothy smiles, alluring gazes, bewitching behavior, tantalizing perfumes, soaps, and shampoos, teasing and tempting, and cleavage, lots of cleavage. Married women kept their husbands close by and made sure they kept them gratified. Within months there were engagements, weddings, and with babies due soon—hasty marriages.

Queen Pia Luna, a short, rotund, middle-aged lady with globular breasts as big as casks of flour, as powdery white as the flour within, and as plushy soft as the cushions on her throne, walked in the courtyard garden at twilight. Dressed in an extremely tight red gown, with her compact buttocks concealed in her roundness, she looked like a big ripe tomato with shiny black shoes amidst the vibrant flowers and trimmed hedges. On her round doughy face, her rosy, pudgy cheeks appeared as cupcakes with cherry frosting and her puckered, petite, red lips looked as if as if she had just sucked on a slice of lemon. Her perfect dainty nose had a slight upturn as most Majesties do. She wore her long, red hair twirled up on top her head with a bejeweled hair comb and though her green eyes shined bright in the sunset, they reflected sorrow within her soul.

The Queen heard a soft whimper and peered over a hedge shorter than she, past a bed of roses pinker than her cheeks, and down a stone path to see one of her young handmaidens, Suzetta, sitting on a marble bench, reading a letter, and sniffing, pressing a handkerchief under her nose. The Queen approached her and Suzetta looked up; her dark brown eyes twinkling amidst tears running down her cheeks; her face framed by strands of long, dark hair sticking to her tears.

The Queen, speaking in her shrill voice like a violin being tuned, asked, "Why are you crying sweet Suzetta?"

Suzetta stood, curtsied before the Queen, and replied between sniffles, "I am so sorry, my Queen (sniff) for crying in your garden and I assure you (sniff) nothing of concern is wrong."

"Then, why are you crying dear girl?"

"It's just that (sniff) as I read this letter of love, I long for a man (sniff) who will desire me and shower me with such devotion and affection."

Suzetta's response touched the Queen's heart for she felt the same longing.

"Please, hand me the letter," commanded the Queen, "so I may read it and cry."

Suzetta gave her the letter and exclaimed, "A strong yet tender man wrote this letter for one lucky maiden (sniff), but it has touched the hearts of all maidens."

The Queen silently read the words written by Stefino; words of excruciating longing; words of restrained lust; words of burgeoning love, and her heart throbbed as her body tingled, awakening things asleep, opening things closed, and—poof!—a flickering flame ignited things extinguished, causing her to feel flushed from her wildly beating heart and from the steamy heat escaping from her heaving breasts. It had been a long, long time, since she had desired her husband, King Luna, but now, standing in the garden, reading the letters, she desired him in a squirmy, lusty, way.

She fanned her face and cleavage with the letters trying to cool down her caged carnal thoughts and after a moment said, "Suzetta, you are a very beautiful and shapely young girl; sweet, kind, and caring. You are without a doubt the best handmaiden I have ever had and I assure you, that someday, you will meet your own prince of passion. For now, help me get ready for bed; for tonight, I must be special for the King!"

Suzetta smiled and escorted the Queen to her bedchamber where they continued rambling on about the letters of love. She assisted the Queen who bathed in bubbles and perfume, dressed in a lacy, French nightgown, and released her fiery, red hair to flow around her face and frame her bulging breasts. At the request of the Queen, Suzetta summoned the court musicians, a string quartet that assembled with their instruments and sat on chairs in the corridor just outside the Queen's bedchamber. Lastly, Suzetta passed a note from the Queen to the King's servant who raced it to the King and then, Suzetta, leaving the prose of passion with the Queen, retired to her servant's quarters. Queen Luna, ready, willing, and hot with passion waited for her King.

King Cristoforo Luna in all his roly-poly royalty sat on his throne in the great hall of his court; a spacious, echoing chamber with a lofty ceiling and ornately framed paintings of all of his noble ancestors hanging on the walls. He wore his jeweled, gold crown tilting, nearly falling off the side of his head, nevertheless, it did not fall, tangled in his thick mane of golden, curly locks, spiraling back from his face, down to his shoulders, framing his childlike, forty-year-old face; a chubby face stretching out all wrinkles, creases, and smile lines; a round face with two chins, chubby cheeks, and hardly noticeable blonde eyebrows floating like clouds above gleaming, sky-blue eyes. His perfect, aristocratic nose had a slight upturn like the Queen's. He wore a green silk tunic, matching silk tights with a black leather belt donning a gold buckle, and about his shoulders, dangling to the floor, he donned a red velvet robe accented with gold trim. When he walked, his exceedingly bloated stomach bulged out drawing in his butt cheeks making them flat. He lounged in a high-back, red-velvet throne with gold plated armrests. The servants had removed the royal chair from the celebratory platform and had placed it in front of a long wooden table trimmed with polished brass. The table, as long as five horse lengths and piled with enough food to feed two large families had only one overweight king dining at it. The Queen did not join the King for dinner, choosing to remain in her bedchamber, preparing for a little erotic kneading of the dough with the King. The King had already drank a belly full of wine and ate his fill of bread, potatoes, turkey, pheasant, and duck, and now held in his pudgy hand a roasted leg of garlicky lamb. His chef, a short, bald, bird-faced man with squinting eyes and a protruding nose, opened the King a new cask of red wine with the name *Tallow Brothers* wood-burned into the small cask and quickly poured the wine into the greasy, silver goblet the King now held in his other hand. The King bit off a chunk of lamb and as he chewed, he drank wine from his goblet. He swallowed the bite of meat washed down by the wine and bellowed; his words echoing about the great hall, "This wine tastes like it smells—like a barnyard! No—like horse crap! It is not fit for a stableboy, nonetheless a King!" He raked the silver plate of lamb onto the floor and tossed the goblet at the chef who barely ducked it, but was showered with wine. The noise of the clanging plate and bouncing goblet reverberated about the chamber. Just as the King wiped his glistening jowls with the sleeve of his royal robe and opened his mouth to demand better wine, a servant asked permission to approach. The King granted him permission, so the young man stepped forward, bowed, and handed him the note from the Queen. The King read it and grinned; the sort of grin he presents when his pastry chef places before him a fluffy, flaky dessert dripping with honey. He scooted out of his throne, stood, belched, ripped a rear-roar, and staggered intoxicated up the spiral stone staircase to his Queen's bedchamber. Seeing the musicians, one of his eyebrows lifted with lustful surprise, knowing that when the quartet played outside the bedchamber door, he would have a night of amorous jousting with the Queen.

Queen Pia lay upon the pink, silky sheets of her feather bed; a kingly bed with four hefty pedestals and reinforcements solid enough to hold the amorous acrobatics of an abounding Queen and a portly King. She waited for the King, whom of lately, she despised for his gluttonous behavior, his drunken words, his lack of affection, lack of intimacy, and lack of pleasing her. As she waited, her burning passion began to fade, so she quickly scanned Stefino's letters of love and as she did, she again fidgeted at every word, rocking back and forth, feeling the fire ablaze beneath her gown. Just as she reached for her pleasuring, Parisian, peacock feather that she kept alongside her bed, the musicians struck up an overture and King Luna burst into her room. He slammed the door behind him, spun, and saw his tantalizing Queen propped up in bed amidst silky, pink pillows. In the flickering, glowing light of countless candles, he beheld her beauty, smelled her sweet scent, eyeballed her bountiful breasts, and gazed into her eyes begging him: *joust me; joust me long and hard*.

He licked his lips, seeing her as a sugary, glistening mound of French pastry; something to be devoured; something to bring him pleasure; something to satiate his voracious cravings. His eyes narrowed and he panted like a wolf spying a lost lamb and then, he grinned like a silly court jester, his eyes sparkling at the thought of such naughty merriment. He tossed his crown into a plushy chair, kicked off his boots, threw off his robe, yanked off his tunic, peeled off his tortured tights and standing there in only his rotund royalty and sovereign scepter, he leapt on the bed with timbers creaking, mattress squishing, and crawling across the bed like a crab fleeing the surf, he cupped a plump breast in each hand and plunged his smiling face into the valley of her cleavage.

"NO!" she snapped like a sprung violin string, shoving him away in concert with the last note of the concluded overture played by the musicians outside the door.

"No?" whimpered the stunned King sitting on his knees and peering at her with moist eyes reflecting hurt feelings. After a short moment of awkward silence, his wounded ego shifted over to his preeminent pride and in his regal, resonant voice, he decreed, "I am your King! You shall *not* deny me the fondling and suckling of your breasts."

"You are *not* only my King, Cristo," she retorted, "and I am *not* only your Queen, but you *are* my husband and I *am* your wife. With my family across the sea, with your family passed on, and with us childless after all of these twenty-five years of wedlock, all we have now is each other. Do you remember before we became, 'his Majesty and her Majesty', when we were best friends? Do you? We were simply, Cristo and Pia; two young lovers, albeit, a prince and a princess, having fun, making love with great passion, but now you stagger in here a glutton, seeing me as food on your table. You devour me like the roasted leg of lamb that you just ate for dinner and is still reeking on your breath. I do not feel like a lady nor do I feel special to you."

The King listened in his gorged stupor, slobbering, hiccupping, and belching and after wiping off his greasy chin with the back of his hand, he whined with all sincerity, "What must I do, my sweet Pia to win back your adoration? For in the place of it, I substitute a bounty of food and a barrel of wine, but all they do is make me fat."

"You can begin," she stated firmly, "with reading aloud to me this letter of passion from a mysterious man with a secret love for one of the sweet maidens in your kingdom."

She handed him the letter. He read the words silently for a moment, climbed off the bed, and pacing unsheathed next to the bed, he began to read the letter aloud. Unsure of himself, he began slow and garbled.

"*My precious darling,*

'*I cherish you*' *is upon every beat of my heart.* '*I treasure you*' *is upon every breath.* '*Only you; always you; forever you*' *rings like a church bell in my ears.* '*You are mine and I am yours*' *flows through my veins.*"

However, as the King read, the magical passion that Stefino felt for Melodina seeped into his soul, filled his heart, and he began to articulate the words, reading them with boldness.

"You stay in my soul, dwell in my dreams, and tarry in my thoughts, because sweetheart, you are special to me; special since my eyes first beheld your dazzling beauty, encountered your sweet nature, and heard your soothing voice; a voice that calms a wild man, frees a caged man, and gives hope to a despairing man. I would be lost to darkness; to despair; to loneliness if I could not gaze upon your splendor; a loveliness so heavenly, my spirit soars amongst the clouds, passes through sunbeams, and glides like a bird on a rising breeze. I long for you, no my love, I ache for you like a soldier returning home from war pines for his sweetheart; an ache that hastens my heartbeats, steals my breath away, and lures away my sleep with fantasies. You are my sunrise after a starless night; my rainbow after a tempest; and a cool, gentle breeze, kissing my cheek at twilight. When I gaze into your loving eyes, I see the reflection of a very happy man smiling back at me and it is I."

The Queen listened, squirming with delight as the musicians played with fervor and the King noticed her pleasure and as the words became his own, he read louder with booming confidence, spilling out his feelings, proclaiming his love for the Queen with uninhibited passion, unrestrained lust, and unbridled cockiness.

My soul is thirsty; is starving; is yearning for your affection. I will embrace you with all my strength as a man. Yet, I will be gentle too, starting at your toes wandering up to your nose, showering your body with tender kisses, caressing, teasing you with a long, silky feather, until with a hot gasp, you beg 'make love to me' and I will draw you in tight, face to face, kissing, feeling our hot breaths upon our cheeks, whispering in each other's ears, and when our bodies become as one, my only thought will be please her; please her; please her until her sighs become moans and her moans becomes gasps and her gasps rise to a panting climax of . . . . "

The Queen, tormented by desire could stand it no more. Stopping his recitation, she reached over, grabbed hold of his sword of wallop and dragged him into bed. He dropped the passionate prose on the floor, dove into her arms, and became lost in her soft-yet-firm peaks of pleasure. He raised his head, gasping for air and plunged his face deeper into her cleavage; deeper where he could hear her throbbing heart; heartbeats for him, not because he ruled a kingdom and she was Queen, but because she adored him. The King groaned as the Queen moaned pleasing each other. They made love as did lovers all across the kingdom and the accumulation of their own and all of their subject's lusty, hot breaths and scorching, body heat caused the temperature of the cool ocean air to rise and turn sultry.

Every night the King read a letter to the Queen and they made love like Stefino would if he ever laid his hands on Melodina. The Queen smiled which made the King smile and when the King smiled, everyone smiled. The kingdom blossomed with joy and burgeoned with love. The King and the Queen stopped overindulging with food and drink, strolled together often in the garden, and they slimmed down, feeling healthy and vigorous.

One evening as the King and Queen walked along the parapet wall on the roof of the castle, the King gazed out at the sunset, painting the village below in a golden hue. He peered out beyond the small farms and cottages to the cliffs overlooking the sea and glanced down the bluffs where his eyes beheld the Bestavino vineyard and his gaze rested on the rows of vines.

"My Queen," he remarked, "I am a very happy man. I have a beautiful wife who pleases every inch of me; I have happy subjects without a whisper of rebellion; I have all the food a belly could desire and I have a mysterious writer of love who furnishes me with passionate words to speak to my wife, inspiring her desire for me. I only wish I could partake again of the wonderful wines of Stefino Bestavino. Too bad, he tried to poison me. I never understood why. His family has always made wine for the Luna lineage of Kings. Although, I doubt his guilt, it was *his* wine that poisoned me, so unfortunately for my thirsty pallet, he and his passionate winemaking skills must rot in the dungeon below. Even so, in my magnanimous mercy, I have not had him executed because of the many nights over all of the generations that my father's father and my father, God rest their souls, and I enjoyed the luscious fruit of his family's vineyard."

Directly below where the King and Queen stood next to the parapet wall, down through the five stories of luxury and all the way down to a damp, dark dungeon cell, Stefino Bestavino continued writing letters by the diminishing twilight of the hole, expressing his great love and burning desire for Melodina, scribbling the words singing from his soul like a composer scratching out the notes of a great symphony.

Weeks passed and on a dark day threatening rain and with a chilly breeze whispering misfortune, Melodina stood at the prison wall with Tobago perched on her shoulder. She whispered to Stefino about her enchanting pleasure when reading his letters and how she desired him in all the same passionate ways in which he desired her.

Behind her, ten horse lengths away, the Tallow brothers had just finished buying a young pig to slaughter; the snorting, speckled, piglet now on a short rope held in the furry hand of Pisoffa. As both wretched brothers harassed Giaboni about his extravagant clothes, wiggle walk, and big glass blowing lips, and they tormented Butano, the village pants maker, about his flashy attire, spiked, blonde hair, schoolgirl face, and stout buttocks for modeling *Butano* pants, and right after Stefino passed his most impassioned of all love letters through the wall to Melodina and at the very instant that she pulled it through the hole and clasped it in her dainty hand, the Tallow brothers glanced over at the prison wall and saw her do it.

With the letter in her hand and a smile of anticipation of reading it on her face, the Tallow brothers immediately forgot ridiculing the gaily-dressed men and charged over to the prison wall, dragging the squealing piglet with them.

Tobago, frightened, took flight. The brothers swatted at the tiny bird, but it dodged their hairy hands and alighted on a branch amongst the pink blossoms of a plum tree; its tiny, ruby chest palpitating from fright. Melodina gasped and jumped back a step. Stefino realized that they were caught and his face contorted into that of a despairing man who would soon be beaten and alone in the dark.

"We saw you, Melodina!" Pisoffa yelled, pointing at the hole and drawing the attention of other villagers. "We saw you pulling a rolled piece of parchment from that hole in the prison wall!"

"Yeah, we sure did!" echoed Fugglio, reaming out his right ear with his index finger.

Pisoffa snatched the parchment from her hand, unrolled it, flicked his tongue around his chapped lips, and began silently reading it.

"Pleeeease, Pisoffa, give it back," pleaded Melodina, lunging for it.

Pisoffa blocked her grabbing hand and shoved her hard up against the stone wall.

"Leave her alone!" thundered Stefino.

A surly wind blew by beating up dry leaves in its path. The dark clouds rumbled off in the distance. The entire marketplace died; people stopped talking, birds stopped chirping, seagulls stopped squawking, dogs stopped barking, musicians stopped playing, and Pisoffa's piglet stopped squealing.

The brothers stared into the hole and saw glints of fury in the eyes of a man. Though the hidden man was imprisoned, though there was two of them and one of him, and though they never cowered away from any man, they both took a step back in fear.

As Melodina sobbed, the brothers took turns reading the letter aloud and they laughed at such sugary words of wimpy woo. Curious villagers gathered. Giaboni and Butano stepped up and with their hands on their tilted hips, they demanded in unison, "Stop it Pisoffa! Stop tormenting Melodina!"

Pisoffa laughed heartily, reached out, gripped Giaboni by his face and shoved the elegantly dressed man to the ground as Fugglio tripped Butano who in all of his adornment fell on top of Giaboni.

Stefino, frustrated, pounded his fists on the stone wall. He could do nothing, but lash out at them in angry words, sounding like a caged criminal.

"Please, Stefino," whimpered Melodina, "stay calm or things will only get worse."

"Stefino! Stefino Bestavino, is that you?" Pisoffa asked, chuckling with delight; his tongue moistening his upper lip.

"Yeah, Stefino Bestavino, is that you?" Fugglio repeated, scratching the hair in his right ear.

"Yes. It is I!" Stefino declared boldly. "The very man whom you framed by poisoning the King with my wine."

The brothers roared with laughter as the villagers murmured loudly at hearing his name, for they missed Stefino Bestavino's magnificent wine and knew him as a good man. Pisoffa continued reading aloud making a mockery out of every word, every feeling, and every proclamation of love that Stefino had expressed for Melodina. The crowd grew with more villagers. The clouds darkened. The wind whipped, slapping hats off men and bonnets off women. Seagulls screeched overhead. A dog barked somewhere. The piggy grunted and squealed.

Stefino endured the ridicule and as Pisoffa spoke the last word of the love letter, Stefino roared, "Now that you've had your fun, what will you three little pigs do now?"

"Well, Stefino," Pisoffa retorted, ignoring Stefino's insult, "we are going to fetch Ugo."

"Yeah, fetch Ugo," echoed Fugglio.

Melodina wailed uncontrollably while Giaboni and Butano, now standing, brushed the dirt off each other's buttocks. The crowd talked excitedly about now knowing the identity of the imprisoned man, the winemaker, and the mysterious writer of love as Stefino Bestavino.

The Tallow brothers charged off, dragging their squealing pig with them and within minutes returned with ugly, freakish, Ugo who galumphed up with a huge skeleton key dangling from a chain looped around his belt. He surmised the situation and croaked out an order sending for the stonemason. Within another few minutes, the stonemason, an older man, skinny yet sinewy and tanned from working under the sun, arrived with a bucket of wet mortar and a trowel.

Stefino peeped out the hole and saw Melodina sobbing, Giaboni and Butano hugging her, crying as well, the Tallow brothers grinning, Ugo scowling, the villagers grimacing, muttering, and whispering, and the stonemason looking serious, ready with wet mortar heaped on his trowel, and Stefino uttered, "Please, Ugo, before this hole is filled, may I speak?"

"Yes. Speak," grunted Ugo.

"Thank you. My name is Stefino Bestavino," he spoke courageously. "I want to again declare my innocence. I did not poison the King. The Tallow brothers, jealous of the prestige bestowed upon me as the King's winemaker, paid a man to place dried, ground hemlock into my wine; a man by the name of Manzo Stellini who as I speak, is in a cell down the dungeon corridor."

"Liar!" Pisoffa yelled.

"Liar!" Fugglio echoed.

Ugo yelled, "Shut up, all three of you!" and raked his hand across his throat as a signal to silence Stefino.

The stonemason, shaking, intimidated by Ugo, sloshed the mortar onto his trowel as Stefino screamed, "I want to proclaim my love for a very beautiful maiden; the recipient of all my love letters. Melodina, I love …."

The stonemason slapped the hole with wet mortar, sealing it and silencing Stefino.

Melodina wailed in concert with the sobbing of Giaboni and Butano, both dabbing each other's eyes with a silk handkerchief amidst the cruel laughter of the Tallow brothers, the noisy pig, barking dogs, screeching seagulls, and a horde of murmuring villagers.

After the stonemason finished plugging the hole with graceful strokes of experience, Ugo grabbed the timid man's arm and ordered, "Come with me!" They marched into the castle through a side door leading to the prison corridors straight to Stefino's cell. Ugo summoned Ilario.

Ilario, carrying bowls of slop, set them on the floor and fearing the worst, surmised that the little hole in the prison wall had been discovered. He followed Ugo swinging his cat-o-nine-tails and the stonemason carrying his bucket of mortar and trowel through the heavy iron door into Stefino's cell. In a corner at the back of his cell, Stefino stood awaiting his punishment. Ugo glared at Stefino. Stefino glared back at him while the stonemason quickly slurried up his trowel and by the dim light of the oil lamp, filled in the hole, and rushed out of the prison.

After a prolonged intense moment, the stare-down ended when Ugo blinked his eyes, looked at Ilario, and bellowed, "Guard, help me take this man to the *Chamber of Pain!*"

Ilario could not look into Stefino's eyes as he gripped him by an arm and Ugo gripped the other arm. They dragged Stefino out of the cell, down the maze of corridors to the *Chamber of Pain*: a bloodstained, stone-walled room with various devices and contraptions for imparting pain, hence breaking the body and spirit of a man.

"Guard, lock the shackles about his wrists!" commanded Ugo.

Ilario, never looking at Stefino's stoic face, lifted Stefino's wrists one at a time above his head and locked them in the shackles dangling from chains.

"Guard, remove the prisoner's shirt!" bellowed Ugo.

Ilario did so, looking away.

"Now shove him against the *Wall of Punishment!*" commanded Ugo.

Ilario hesitated, but did so.

"Now, back away from him," commanded Ugo, "so that my cat-o-nine tails may whip his flesh!"

Ilario did not move away, but remained standing next to Stefino. Stefino stared at the wall inches from his face. Ilario stared at the floor. A large rat scampered across his feet and vanished into a hole in the wall. The three men breathed heavily in the silence; Ugo anticipating, Stefino dreading, and Ilario contemplating.

"Guard, step away!" snarled Ugo.

Instead of stepping away from Stefino, Ilario sighed, reached over his own head, locked his own wrists in another set of shackles, and leaned against the wall with his bare back to the brawny jail-master.

Ugo's eyes opened wide with surprise, his mouth twisted into a sadistic grin, and his reptilian head jerked back with croaking laughter as his gigantic body shook with delight. He gripped the whip, flexed his biceps, and snapped the whip against the stone wall three times preparing himself to flog the two men. With each crack of the whip, Stefino and Ilario flinched as did other prisoners hearing the whip in the silence of their cells.

Stefino's eyes met Ilario's as if to ask *why?* and as if to say, save yourself old man, but Ilario just peered back in silence as if to answer, we are in this together and as if to say, I will not forsake you, my friend.

Both men stood against the *Wall of Punishment* with their eyes closed and breathing rhythmically, awaiting the imminent pain. As Ugo whipped their bare backs, both men cringed at the stinging pain, but neither man cried out. One lash to Stefino and one to Ilario. Another lash for each man and another and another and one more. After the fifth lash, both men dangled spiritless in their shackles. Ugo smiled at his power to inflict pain, not so much on Stefino and Ilario, but because whipping them became his retaliation to all those mean, faceless kids who made fun of him when he was a lad.

Ugo ordered guards to throw Stefino in a different cell than he had been in and pitch Ilario, who lost his status as a guard and the key to the cell doors, into his own cell. The heavy iron doors locked with resounding clanks. Both wounded men, lying strafed on the floor in their dark cells, heard Ugo's huge boots, departing, galumphing, and echoing down the dungeon corridor.

Outside the prison, the storm blew in with pounding rain. The crowd fled the marketplace, the Tallow brothers stomped home, the little piggy got slaughtered, Giaboni and Butano walked briskly under an umbrella, and Melodina with Tobago on her shoulder ran crying all the way home.

The next day, the storm had passed and a fog reeking of seaweed crept about the village. Stefino and Ilario lay groaning from their wounds in their stone cells. Melodina did not bake bread nor pick flowers, but ran to see Orazio and Valentina and told them the horrible news.

Ugo reported to King Luna who, pleased from a little morning merrymaking with the Queen, sat smiling on his throne in his entire royal attire. He granted his jail-master permission to approach. Ugo did, bowed, stood, and began speaking in his baritone voice to the King. "My glorious King, I've come before you today to report on an escape attempt yesterday by two criminals locked within our stalwart prison."

"An attempt to escape!" huffed the King. "So that is what the ruckus was all about in the marketplace outside the prison wall."

"Yes, my Lord. I thwarted their escape, arriving at the breach in the wall just as they were climbing through to freedom. They fought like roaring lions but with my bare hands and my brute strength, I stopped them, shoving them like meowing kittens back through the hole into prison."

A young and handsome court guard by the name of Enzo, who had witnessed the scene at the wall, heard Ugo lie to the King.

"Oh my!" gasped the King. "How dare they? Especially, when they know the punishment for escaping is a whipping followed by an arrow to the heart. Whip them!" he commanded hastily, "and summon two of the royal archers. One for each condemned man. Prepare the execution for tomorrow at noon. Place them against the wall where they attempted to escape. Let all the villagers come and see, so they will know—I am a King not to be reckoned with."

"Yes, your Majesty," replied Ugo gleefully, not telling the King that the men had already been whipped.

Ugo turned to leave but the King burst out, "Jail-master, stop!"

Ugo halted, winced as though he might be in trouble for lying, spun to face the King and casually asked with innocent eyes and a virtuous smile, "What is it, my King?"

"I am curious. Who are the men who will die tomorrow?"

"Their names, oh King, are Stefino Bestavino and Ilario Gallantano."

King Luna's face dropped and he sighed. He knew, deep down he knew that Stefino and Ilario were good men and deeper down, way down, almost forgotten, albeit still there, he knew that Stefino was most likely innocent and that Ilario had been sent to prison because of the King's own prideful immaturity. Both men had been spared execution because of his hesitancy over their questionable guilt. The King sighed once more at the thought of never again tasting the wines of Stefino Bestavino. Still prideful and fearful he would be viewed as a weak monarch, he waved with a flip-flap of his hand and Ugo spun, departed the King's court, and hastened to prepare for the execution and ready the archers. As per the King's orders, Ugo whipped Stefino and Ilario again, but only two lashes each as not to kill them before an arrow could pierce their hearts.

Ilario, barely breathing, near death, lay quiet in his cell. Stefino lay on his raw, stinging back on the stone floor and wept exceedingly loud, not from despair, not from pain, but from the thought of never again expressing his love for Melodina. His wailing could be heard by the prisoners throughout the prison corridors, up into the castle's opulence into the ears of the King and Queen, and outside to villagers in the market place. All winced and covered their ears with their hands. Even Ugo on the other side of the prison and the Tallow brothers on the edge of the village cringed at the sound of such resounding grief.

After a long while, Stefino stopped wailing, rolled onto his stomach, and crawled over to his pail of water. He climbed to his knees, cupped his hands, scooped up water, and drank and drank some more. He lifted the bucket above his head and dumped water down his burning back. Wet, dripping with water, tears, and blood, he prayed, "My Lord, I am innocent and so is Ilario. Please spare us from this injustice, but if it is our time; if there is a purpose; and if we are meant to die, then find true love for my love, Melodina, watch over my father and our vineyards, keep Ilario's wife, children, and grandchildren safe, and please forgive the cruelty of the Tallow brothers, Ugo, and the unmerciful King. Lastly, please welcome Ilario and I into eternity." He sat against the wall believing, waiting for God's miracle of deliverance from execution or salvation of spirit and soul.

Word of the next day's execution spread quickly throughout the kingdom. Of course, the flow of love letters had stopped and the villagers knew why; their amorous author, whipped and wounded, could no longer write and would soon die by an arrow to his passionate heart. Lovers across the kingdom yearned for a new love letter, whining like a drunken pirate for more rum, crying like a hungry baby for breast milk, or bawling like a starving farm animal for hay.

Execution day began with the sun hiding behind a blanket of sea fog, refusing to shine its gleaming rays of glory on such a travesty as executing two innocent men. As noon approached, the fog lurked back out to sea, seagulls soared overhead, and the court servants placed both royal thrones on a raised platform in full view of the execution. Villagers gathered, standing around the platform, sitting on walls, in trees, and on rooftops. Melodina, her little sisters and brother, Orazio and Amadora, Valentina and her children and grandchildren, Giaboni and Butano, and Cindarina, all stood at the front just behind where the archers would release their arrows. The Tallow brothers, drunk from guzzling their own bad wine, stood off to one side within one horse length, where they could jeer at the condemned men.

Thirty minutes before the execution, Ugo escorted Stefino and Ilario, both weak and staggering, into a holding cell where they could wash off, eat, and restore a bit of life and color back into them before it was taken away by an arrow. The King, feeling somewhat guilty for having them executed, sent both men a clean white shirt with ruffles about the neck, ruffles at the cuffs of the long, billowy sleeves, and ruffles down the shiny buttons to be worn with a pair of roomy, black pants and a cheap pair of black boots, a size to fit any regular man. He also sent them a soothing salve and bandages for their striped backs. Ilario pulled his small pair of scissors out of his soiled, threadbare pants pocket and trimmed his own and then Stefino's beard and hair to perfection. The fast friends encouraged one another, talking about bravery and honor. They planned to stare unflinching, unblinking, and unafraid, straight ahead at the sharp tip of the arrow and when the arrow pierced their hearts—they would bite their tongues and die without a gasp.

Up in the Queen's bedroom, four floors directly above the holding cell, Suzetta helped the Queen ready for her public appearance at the execution. Suzetta, gushing, told the Queen everything that she had heard: about Melodina Miabello, the lucky maiden who was the true recipient of the love and passion coming from the pen of Stefino Bestavino, and how he was framed by the Tallow brothers who coveted the prestige and money of being the King's winemaker, and how the brothers hired a man by the name of Stellini who poured dried, ground hemlock into the King's wine, and who is the same man now in prison for streaking naked throughout the village, and about how one of the youthful court guards, Enzo, her heart's desire, had told her that Ugo had lied to the King about the escape attempt, and that the hole was only big enough to pass through rolled parchment filled with words of passion; the very words of love which spread throughout the Kingdom and transformed the numb and boring relationship of the King and Queen into tingles and thrills.

The Queen gasped, shocked at the incredulous story, but nevertheless believed every word of it and summoned the royal guards.

At twelve-o-clock noon, the appointed time of execution, the trumpeters of the court blasted a fanfare for the King. The castle's huge magnificent doors swung open, the horn blowing ceased, and the court musicians played the King's anthem. The Queen, assisted by Suzetta, ran up to the King just as the doors opened. Out marched the King and the hurried Queen in all their majestic grandeur. The Queen kept trying to tell the King what Suzetta had told her, but he ignored her as he waved to his cheering subjects. The monarchs climbed the steps onto the platform, the King holding the Queen's hand, and they sat upon their royal thrones. Suzetta joined Melodina next to Cindarina and the three friends held hands for comfort. The Queen attempted again to tell the King all that she knew, but now, the trumpeters announcing the prisoner's walk of death, drowned out her words.

Stefino and Ilario, surrounded by guards and being prodded along by Ugo, stepped out of the castle and tramped over to the prison wall. Ugo shoved them, placing them directly in front of the small hole now sealed with mortar so that the King could not see the tiny size of it and know that Ugo had lied about his heroics and the escape attempt.

Stefino and Ilario saw the kingdom without the confines of a palm-sized hole. Awestruck, they peered up, squinting at a bright and spacious sky filled with fluffy white clouds and soaring birds. Trees, tickled by a sea breeze, dropped autumn leaves on lush, green grass growing along beds of vibrant flowers. Everywhere, there were villagers eager to watch them die.

Orazio bolted from the crowd and darted between the archers, attempting to embrace his son, but Ugo struck him down and the guards dragged him back to Amadora.

"Hey, lover boy," Pisoffa, licking his lips, taunted Stefino, "are you ready for one of the King's royal Cupids to shoot an arrow into your lovesick heart?"

"Yeah, Cupids," said Fugglio, poking his finger inside an ear and added picking his nose to his repertoire.

Stefino ignored the ugly brothers. He scanned the crowd and found Melodina. Their eyes met and her love and beauty calmed his soul.

Melodina, through tears of grief stared at Stefino and though he appeared rather thin, and hobbled a bit like a man beat with a cat-o-nine-tails, she thought he looked extremely handsome with his neatly cut hair and perfectly trimmed beard and her heart throbbed.

Valentina saw Ilario and thought how he looked so much older, but still her heart pined for him. Their sons and daughters cried with joy to see their father again and sobbed with grief that he would die so soon after their meager reuniting. Ilario waved to them as they pointed at him, exclaiming to their own little children, "There goes your grandfather, a wonderful man, however, when the arrows fly, you must hide your eyes."

Amidst the roar of the unruly crowd, Stefino shouted, "My King, who is wise and powerful and who has the discernment to grant mercy, may I speak from my heart before it is pierced with an arrow?"

The onlookers quieted. The King glanced at the face of his Queen. She nodded, with pleading eyes. He gazed into the tear filled eyes of Melodina and her friends. He stared into the distraught faces of all the family members of Stefino and Ilario. Ugo, Pisoffa, and Fugglio frowned, shaking their heads. The impassive archers waited patiently. The King turned and peered out at the villagers and they rang out, "Let him speak! Let him speak!" He sighed, granted Stefino permission to speak, and the crowd fell silent. Gulls called overhead, birds sung in the trees, and the surf could be heard crashing upon the shore.

Stefino said, "I am eternally grateful, my King." He gazed into Melodina's eyes, knelt to one knee, crossed his hands over his heart as if he had captured a butterfly upon his chest, thrust out his open hands as if he had just released the butterfly, and spoke, "Melodina, I promise my love for you will only die when I do, which unfortunately, well—will be in a few minutes." Melodina and Orazio wailed. So did Giaboni, Butano, Suzetta, and Cindarina. "When the arrow passes through my heart," he continued solemnly, "my heart will burst into praises of your beauty, your enchantment, your gracefulness, and I will feel no pain for my eyes will see only you. Do not see my spilt blood as blood, but see each drop as a declaration of my adoration for you. For many months, I have longed for you, lusted for you, and loved you. I dreamed of you being my wife and that you and I would be together, over all our days, making heavenly wine, raising beautiful children and grandchildren, and living a glorious life, every evening sipping wine out in our garden, gazing at the stars, and afterwards, retreating to the privacy of our bedchamber, where we would passionately kiss and where are bodies, longing for each other's naked embrace would ...."

As Stefino spoke, the King, the Queen, the archers, the guards, the musicians, and all the rest of the villagers recognized that his words were the same words of desire that they had read in the letters. They remembered his passion which had become their passion; a surging passion that had flowed through the village like a raging river after a season of drought. As he spoke of working the vineyards and his passion for making wine, they remembered his wonderful wine and they became thirsty for *it* rather than bloodthirsty for an execution.

Stefino finished speaking the words of his heart to Melodina and she yelled, "Stefino, my prince of passion, I love you and adore you with all of my heart!"

Everyone, including the Queen, began chanting, "Mercy! Mercy! Mercy!" One man in the crowd yelled above the chants, "Mercy for Stefino! Mercy for love and wine!"

The King turned and looked at his Queen and at his subjects chanting for him to show mercy to Stefino. He focused on the breach in the wall behind Stefino kneeling in front of it and saw that the patch of mortar was no bigger than his hand. There was no way a man could have escaped through it. Ugo had lied.

Ugo saw the King peering at the patched, small hole in the wall and afraid the King would stop the execution, he held up his hand for the crowd to quiet and in his low, throaty voice, shouted, "That is enough!"

Pisoffa grinned, licking his dry lips as Fugglio chuckled, repeatedly bending down his ear and letting it spring back.

King Luna looked confused, trying to decide whether to do something or not. Queen Luna scowled at Ugo. The unruly crowd simmered down.

Stefino stood and stepped back to stand next to Ilario.

Ugo bellowed, "We have assembled here alongside the prison wall to witness the execution of two men. Stefino Bestavino: sent to prison for treason and attempted murder for trying to poison the King with his wine. Ilario Gallantano: sent to prison for refusing the King passage on his seafaring ships. Both men were shown leniency by the King and not executed for their crimes, but now with their bold attempt to escape from the King's prison, they have been whipped and are now sentenced to death. Each will receive an arrow to the heart and then, who-so-ever wishes to claim their bodies may do so. Archers! Draw back your bows! And at my command, release your arrows into the heart of each man!"

The archers, dressed in green tunics and tights, simultaneously raised and drew back their bows. With stoic faces and glassy eyes of concentration, and with steady fingers holding the nock of the arrow at the corner of their mouths, they each aimed a gleaming arrowhead at the heart of each condemned man.

The King did not stop the execution for fear, that as King, he would lose credibility with his subjects. The Queen, wringing her hands, glanced over at the castle doors and saw, according to her earlier command, two royal guards dragging out a tall, bony, hairy man in a loin cloth. She glanced over at Ugo. His eyes gleamed, as he drew in a deep breath to give the archers their release order. The archers held their precise aim. She jumped to her feet and yelled, "Stop the execution!" startling one of the archers to release his arrow. It zipped between the heads of Stefino and Ilario and exploded into splinters on the stone wall behind them. Melodina screamed. So did Giaboni and Butano sounding very much like Melodina. The crowd gasped.

The King stood and bellowed, "Listen to the Queen! Stop the execution!" The other archer quickly lowered his bow and removed his arrow. The two guards hauled Stellini before the King and Queen and forced him to his knees. Stefino and Ilario stood behind him.

The Queen commanded the skinny, near naked man, "You must confess now Stellini and I assure you, at your own execution, you will not have to wear clothes."

Stellini smiled. Women gasped. Most of the men's eyebrows lifted, including the King's as he spoke concurring with the Queen.

Stellini quickly confessed before the King, the Queen, and the entire village about how the Tallow brothers had paid him to poison the wine to sicken the King, thus framing Stefino, so the brothers could be appointed the King's winemakers.

The Tallow brothers tried to slink away, but the guards seized them. Enzo, the young, royal guard from the King's court stepped forward and as Suzetta sighed with adoration, he told how he had heard Ugo lie to the King. The King already knew by the size of the hole that Ugo had indeed lied. More guards snatched Ugo. Beyond a doubt, the King knew that Stefino was innocent. The King stood, faced the crowd, and in a very popular move with his subjects, he shouted for all to hear, "I, King Luna, decree that Stefino Bestavino is innocent and shall be set free!"

The villagers cheered. All the flowing tears of Melodina, her girlfriends, Orazio and Amadora, Giaboni and Butano transformed without stopping from tears of grief to tears of joy.

Stefino stepped away from the wall and graciously bowed before the King. He glanced a solemn look at Melodina and cried out, "I am grateful for your mercy great King, however—I cannot accept it."

The eyes of the villagers darted about and their faces contorted in confusion. The King and Queen, Melodina, Stefino's family and friends, Ilario's family, and even Ilario had a screwy look of *huh?* The King asked Stefino, "Why?"

"I will only accept your mercy," stated Stefino boldly, "if you release another innocent man—Ilario Gallantano." Stefino glanced at Ilario as if to say, we are in this together and I will not forsake you my friend. Ilario, grateful, nodded and smiled as Stefino continued saying, "If not, I will take an arrow to the heart and you will never again taste my wine."

The King's pride welled up and after a brief moment of consideration while smacking his lips, reminiscing about Stefino's wine and as his wife gazed at him, pleading with her big green eyes, and as the crowd cheered, 'Mercy, Mercy, Mercy!' he sighed and proclaimed, "Ilario Gallantano, you too, shall go free!"

The crowd went wild, jumping up and down, whistling, clapping, hooting, and hollering their approval. The Queen leaned over and kissed the King on the cheek and the crowd cheered! Melodina raced past the archers and over to Stefino and she leapt into his arms nearly knocking the whipped and wounded man to the ground. They embraced, squeezing, hugging, and they kissed; a long, wet, tongue twiddling kiss like he had written about countless times and the crowd murmured, "Ooooh!" Ilario's wife, children, and grandchildren ran to their patriarch. With all of them weeping with gladness, they surrounded him, hugging him and the crowd sighed, "Aaah!" As Ilario sobbed with happiness and his family smothered him with love, he lifted up his tiny three-year-old granddaughter, Perla into his arms. The impish little girl kissed her grandfather on the cheek and again the crowd sighed, "Aaah." Many villagers wept tears of joy. Orazio limped over to his son and hugged both Stefino and Melodina. Amadora, Suzetta and Cindarina hugged them too and so did Giaboni and Butano. The villagers cheered, "Hooray!" The King's musicians struck up the King's favorite waltz, the King and Queen stepped down from their thrones and danced on the cobblestone street amidst their dancing subjects.

While the villagers danced, six of the King's beefy guards dragged away Ugo fighting and thrashing as more guards shoved along Pisoffa and Fugglio. Another guard hauled along at an arm's length, Stellini who had slipped off his loincloth and pranced naked in rhythm to the waltz. The armed guards tossed the four prisoners into the *Chamber of Pain,* slammed them up against the *Wall of Punishment,* secured their hands above their heads with shackles, and ripped off their tunics and shirts exposing their bare backs. Stellini hung naked from his shackles. Using Ugo's cat-o-nine-tails, the guards took turns whipping each man. By edict of the King, Ugo received five lashes for lying to the King, five more for being so damn mean, and five more for being so damn ugly. With each lash, Ugo groaned, croaking like a bullfrog. The King dismissed him as jail-master and banished him from the Kingdom forever. Stellini received five lashes to his bony body, howling like a dog with the sting of each lash. The guards dragged Stellini off unconscious and dropped him into a cell. Pisoffa and Fugglio received ten lashes each, both sobbing like infants the entire time. The guards cast the strafed brothers into the same cell that Stefino had suffered in over the past year. For a while, the hole, filled with the new mortar was a constant reminder of how they bullied their way into their dank, dark, cell, however, the King commanded the stonemason to remove the mortar from the hole so that villagers could stop at the wall at any time and taunt, tease, and poke fun at the Tallow brothers caged inside. Giaboni and Butano visited them often, lecturing and scolding them.

Immediately after Stefino and Ilario evaded execution, Stefino hobbled home to his chateau and vineyards with one arm around the shoulders of his father and his other arm wrapped around Melodina. Ilario's family surrounded Ilario as he marched out of the village on his own two feet and collapsed on the road. His children lifted him up and carried him the rest of the way home to their estate by the sea. Enveloped by their loving family and friends, both Stefino and Ilario quickly recovered their health, stature, and joy. Stefino and Orazio worked hard through harvest, crushing grapes and making wine. With the help of Ilario's family and many friends from the village, the Bestavinos restored their vineyard back to its heavenly splendor. Not long after the harvest, Orazio married Amadora in a small wedding held in their vineyard at sunset and they have waltzed ever since. Ilario again took the helm of *Gallantano Shipping Company*, rewarding substantially those loyal men and women who had kept the business afloat during all the many years of his absence. In addition, he commissioned a ship and crew to search again the latitude and longitude where Melodina's father was lost at sea.

On one sunny day tickled by a sea breeze, Stefino stood in his vineyard and as his feet sank into the cool, damp soil, he peered out over the rolling hills and perfect rows of vines. Feeling grateful to be home again, he gazed up toward Heaven. After thanking God for the miracles, he smiled, realizing—he was *not* dreaming; he still stood in his vineyard and after that day, he smiled every time he stood in the vineyard.

Thirty days after the King had expelled Ugo out of the kingdom and had slammed the Tallow brothers into a dungeon cell, the entire village showed up at the prison wall to watch the execution of the Tallow brothers and Stellini. The Bestavino's, the Gallatano's, and their family and friends did not attend the execution, but celebrated a bounteous harvest at the Bestavino estate, drinking wine and dancing in the sunshine.

At the execution in front of the hole in the prison wall, the crowd cheered, "Justice! Justice! Justice!" The King and Queen watched the execution from the top of the castle, leaning over the parapet wall, looking straight down. Both Pisoffa, pleading, licking his dry lips, and Fugglio, begging, fiddling with his ear took two arrows each to their hearts, one arrow for attempting to poison the King and a second arrow for making such damn poor wine.

No one claimed their bodies, so the village undertaker

cremated the brothers and cast their ashes into the sea. The King granted their vineyard to the Bestavino family as recompense for the Tallow brothers framing Stefino and for the time he suffered in prison, thus doubling the size of his vineyard. Immediately following the execution of Pisoffa and Fugglio, Stellini, with a stretching grin, took an arrow to his heart as he stood naked and hairy with all his notoriety dangling for all to see. The undertaker also cremated Stellini's unclad body and tossed his ashes into the sea.

After the grape stomping and barreling of the wine, and after restoring the Tallow brother's vineyard back to the glory it should have been, Stefino asked Melodina to marry him in a very romantic, long, drawn-out expression of his love, speaking of how he couldn't live without her, how he would make a good husband, how she would be happy at the vineyard, and how they would make wonderful, passionate love. After listening, smiling, twinkling, she placed a finger on his lips, stopping him in mid-sentence and replied, "I was ready to marry you after your first love letter. Yes, oh yes! I will marry you Stefino Bestavino!"

Months passed and the Bestavino vineyard turned amber, orange, red, and brown. The wind blew the dead leaves away, the nights grew cold, the days shortened, the morning frost covered the spindly bare vines, the fog reigned over most of the day, and when the glorious sun returned, bringing longer days and imparting its warmth, the vineyard again forgot the winter.

On the first day of spring; a day blazing with sunshine that unveiled the petals of varicolored flowers, unfurled budding green leaves, and inspired every tiny sprout to reach for the sky, the family and friends of Stefino and Melodina, as well as most of the villagers packed the King's cathedral to witness the union of the two lovers. King Luna officiated the ceremony, Ilario presided as Stefino's best man, Suzetta and Cindarina acted as Melodina's maids of honor, Melodina's twelve-year-old twin sisters, Sara and Sella served as bride's maids, her little brother, six-year-old Angelo helped as ring bearer, Ilario's granddaughter, Perla served as flower girl, and Tobago, hummed around just being cutesy. The King and Queen made certain that the nuptials would be of a royal distinction, commanding the servants to roll out the red carpet over the marble floor, hang gold ribbons from the ornate ceiling, polish up the wooden pews, clean the many stained glass windows, and fill the chamber with countless bouquets of flowers. On the altar made of walnut, sat a candelabra with three white candles and next to it, the book of Holy Scriptures; its pages trimmed in gold.

The wedding party filed in from a side door and stood at the back of the cathedral. Suzetta waved to Giaboni and Butano to begin and they sung a lovely duet in perfect harmony sounding like choir boys at the *Vatican*. The procession of bride's maids, Suzetta and Cindarina, the tiny flower girl, Perla, and the energetic, fidgeting ring bearer, Angelo, all dressed in fanciful clothes designed and sewn by Cindarina, strolled down the aisle in step with the music, lining up at the ceremonial stage. Five steps up and on the platform stood the King and Queen in front of their ornate thrones. Stefino, tanned, clean-shaven with perfectly cut hair stood on the middle step, grinning, dressed in a white ruffled shirt, velvet, navy-blue overcoat, courtly *Butano* trousers, and shiny black shoes with gold buckles. He watched the two huge entry doors, waiting for his bride, knowing that, that very night before the clock struck midnight he would consummate all of his love and all of his longing upon his cherished wife.

Amadora, who had been assisting Melodina, entered the cathedral from a side door, strolled over to the quartet and whispered into one of the musician's ears. After a silent three beat wave of the violinist's hand, the musicians struck up the wedding waltz and the colossal, castle doors swung open. The people stood, turned, and gazed at the opening doors. Light burst into the cathedral as though impatient from waiting outside and in its blinding brightness stood Melodina in her white satin wedding gown: a stunning, strapless dress adorned with intricate embroidery and seed pearls, full pick-up skirt, chapel train, and a corset style bodice that lifted her breasts like two snow-white bunnies snuggled in a satin basket. Beneath her lacy veil adorned with a crystal beaded edge, she wore her golden hair pinned in a fashionable up-style accented with a diamond-studded tiara. Around her neck dangling in her beautifully formed, yet modest cleavage, she wore a dazzling diamond pendant; both tiara and necklace loaned to her by the gracious Queen. Lastly, Melodina wore glittering high-heel slippers, so that she glimmered from head to toe. At the sight of her, the crowd murmured amidst whispers of, "She's so beautiful!" Cindarina smiled, pleased that the dress she had designed and sewed was so magnificent.

Melodina, in all her radiance, stepped into the cathedral and Stefino's heart pounded so hard that the King glanced down and saw the groom's corsage moving in and out on his lapel. Melodina stood silent for a moment as all eyes focused on her. A slight sea breeze rushed in as though late for the wedding and gently wafted her veil. She gazed up at Stefino and he saw her twinkling smile that sparkled through the veil and outshined the brilliance of the sunlight.

Ilario, with his perfectly trimmed, gray hair and beard, acting as Stefino's best man and also as Melodina's father, stepped up next to her and she placed her hand on his arm. The royal servants closed the doors behind them and Ilario escorted her down the aisle, promenading slowly and rhythmically down the red carpet to the steps leading up to Stefino. Tobago zipped around her a few times and alighted on the backrest of the King's throne.

The quartet stopped playing. The King cleared his throat and welcomed everyone to the wedding ceremony to witness the blessed union of two such wonderful people. In his Kingly, stentorian voice that echoed about the chamber, he asked, "Who giveth this woman to be wed to this man?"

Just as Ilario opened his mouth to say, "I do," the two huge doors swung open again. Everyone in the cathedral, distracted, turned to see who the royal guards had allowed to enter the wedding at such a tardy time. In sunlit glare and glory stood a silver-haired man, tanned and wrinkled yet handsome and distinguished, wearing the uniform of a ship's captain with his hat pinched under his arm. He stepped forward, the doors shut behind him, and he marched toward the ceremonial stage. Melodina's mouth dropped open, she let go of Ilario's arm, lifted up the train of her wedding gown, and rushed over to the man, leaping into his arms and the crowd moaned, "Oooh!" Sara, Sella, and little Angelo followed her, embracing the man too and the people murmured, "Aaah!" The stalwart sailor hugged them in return and the people mumbled, "He has returned from the dead."

Ilario smiled from ear to ear and stepped up to stand beside Stefino. Stefino smiled too, recognizing the man he had once met at the docks. The sea captain hollered with a mighty voice, the same voice he had used calling out orders to his men above the howling winds of a hurricane and boomed, "Yes, it is I, Captain Marco Miabello. I was lost at sea and washed up on an island inhabited by friendly natives. My loyal friend Ilario sent a ship and rescued me. On my return voyage, the sailors told me the story of Stefino Bestavino, about his love for my daughter, and her love for him. By God's grace and the friendship of my dear friend, Ilario, I am here reunited with my children and to witness the betrothal of my Melodina."

The people cheered as the quartet played while the sea captain escorted his daughter down the aisle to Stefino. Marco reached up and firmly shook Stefino's hand and then Ilario's hand. The father stood with his daughter and the King cried out again, "Who giveth away this woman to be wed to this man?"

"I do, Marco Miabello," he stated proudly and he opened his sea weathered hand, releasing the dainty hand of Melodina. She stepped up the few steps and stood next to Stefino, taking his hand as Marco sat down in a pew next to Orazio.

After lighting candles, reading of scriptures, exchanging vows and rings, and more songs sung by Giaboni and Butano, the King said, "Stefino you may kiss your bride!" and Stefino wrapped his arms around Melodina and kissed her with a steamy, passionate kiss that made all the maidens sigh while the Queen fanned her bulging breasts. The King, Marco, Orazio, Ilario, and the musicians merely lifted an eyebrow. Giaboni and Butano glanced at each other and grinned. Suzetta wished it was her and Enzo getting married. Cindarina dabbed her tears of joy with a handkerchief. The happy family smiled. Little Angelo and Perla blushed, covering their eyes with their hands.

The King pronounced Stefino and Melodina, 'Man and Wife' and the happy newlyweds walked arm in arm down the red carpet, out the huge castle doors, and into the sunlight where everyone congratulated them. Tobago buzzed around them a few times and hummed off to find nectar.

At the lively reception in the great hall next to the cathedral, the musicians played and the villagers danced. The royal servants served Stefino Bestavino's best wine. The bride and groom, the wedding party, and all the family sat at the King's table with the King and Queen. The King stood and held his glass in the air and called out, "A toast to the newlyweds!"

Stefino noticed the clarity of his winemaking skills and could actually see the King on the other side of his glass. He watched the King swirl, sniff, and sigh over the wine's wonderful bouquet. The thirsty, eager King drank a big mouthful, gasped, gripped his throat with his free hand, rolled his eyes back into his head, choked, drooled, dropped into his chair, and slammed his head down on the table.

The Queen gasped along with everyone else in the great hall. The royal guards dashed over to aid their poisoned King.

Stefino cried out, "No, no, no! Not again!"

Melodina's eyes filled with tears. Marco's face tensed. Orazio turned pale. Ilario shivered. Giaboni's lips quivered and Butano's buttocks puckered as the rest of the guest's mouths dropped open.

The King drew in a long breath and held it, held it, held it … and then, sprung up, bursting with hysterical laughter. It took a few seconds for everyone especially for Stefino and Melodina to realize the King was joking. Queen Luna nervously fanned her palpitating cleavage. Everyone else, still a bit nervous about the prank, laughed along with the King and naturally, Stefino's and Melodina's laughs were half-hearted.

King Luna, still chuckling, stood, lifted his glass of excellent, safe Bestavino wine and again began his toast, "A toast to the newlyweds, to Stefino and Melodina!" He gazed down at the two of them sitting to his right and said with sincerity, "May you both live long and continue making this fine wine for the King, may you have many healthy children to help you in the vineyards, and may you have an everlasting, burning passion for one another; the same burning passion that you, Stefino bestowed upon Melodina, your sweetheart, that spread to enliven my entire kingdom. To Melodina, a lovely and loving lady whose smile is sunshine, whose bouquets of flowers brighten our lives, and whose bread delights our stomachs. To Stefino, a winemaker of wonderful wine, an author of amore, and a poet of passion, to you my friend, I again bestow the prestige and the title as 'The King's Winemaker.'"

Available online and at your local bookseller.

Pirates and clipper ships are the setting for this seafaring story about the turbulent life of sailor Jonathan Bastell Meen. Born the son of a wealthy shipping magnate, Meen sails to exotic ports around the world. When he's not at sea, he lives in an opulent chateau, until evil deeds and catastrophic events rob him of all that he loves. Overcome with debilitating grief, savage jealousy, and rage, he leads a brash mutiny and becomes the captain of the brawny Mendocino. He sinks further into the atrocities of piracy, pillaging ships of the Pacific with his band of cutthroats, until a string of disasters and fateful consequences force him to fight for his own survival.

Available online and at your local bookseller.

Stop. Look over your shoulder. See the faces. Sure, there are a few happy people, rejoicing in their sunshine, but also, there are those hurting souls who are hiding behind their feigned smiles, lost in a fog of pain, woe, and confusion. They are the Faces in the Fog. Nineteen short stories: action, romance, sci-fi, drama, humor, horror, and suspense. Edgy, thrilling, and heartwarming ... this book has it all.

- Distraught skydiver contemplates suicide.
- Desperate sushi chef prepares toxic blowfish.
- Grotesque demon taunts godly man.
- Bees terrorize high school football players.
- Love blooms in an enchanted garden.
- Foreign correspondent interviews terrorist.
- Oilrig mechanic finds just a hand.
- All the cell phones ring at once.
- Dying mom makes last wish.
- Obese man discovers his destiny.
- Road rage erupts on clogged freeway.
- Son struggles with his father's death.
- Deaf-mute kid goes missing.
- Expiring old man establishes his life stamp.
- Hypercritical man loses eyesight … and other stories.